THE QUEEN OF THE TAMBOURINE

Jane Gardam

Chivers Press • Thorndike Press
Bath, Avon, England • Thorndike, Maine USA

This Large Print edition is published by Chivers Press, England, and by Thorndike Press, USA.

Published in 1996 in the U.K. by arrangement with Reed Consumer Books Ltd.

Published in 1996 in the U.S. by arrangement with St. Martin's Press, Inc.

U.K. Hardcover   ISBN 0–7451–4787–9 (Chivers Large Print)
U.K. Softcover   ISBN 0–7451–4795–X (Camden Large Print)
U.S. Softcover   ISBN 0–7862–0604–7 (General Series Edition)

The text of this Large Print edition is unabridged.
Other aspects of the book may vary from the original edition.

Set in 16 pt. New Times Roman.

Printed in Great Britain on acid-free paper.

British Library Cataloguing in Publication Data available

Library of Congress Cataloging-in-Publication Data

Gardam, Jane.
        The queen of the tambourine / Jane Gardam.
            p.   cm.
        ISBN 0–7862–0604–7 (lg. print : lsc)
        1. Mentally ill women—England—London—Fiction.   2. Social isolation—Fiction.   3. Large type books.   I. Title.
        [PR6057.A623Q84   1996]
        823'.914—dc20
                                                                                    95–43264

For
Rhododendria

For she's the Queen
Of the Tambourine
The Cymbals and the Bones.

Music Hall Song

Dear Joan,

I do hope I know you well enough to say this.

I think you ought to try to forget about your leg. I believe that it is something psychological, psychosomatic, and it is very hard on Charles. It is bringing both him and you into ridicule and spoiling your lives.

Do make a big try. Won't you? Forget about your bodily aches and pains. Life is a wonderful thing, Joan. I have discovered this great fact in my work with the Dying.

Your sincere friend,
Eliza (Peabody)

Feb 17th

Dear Joan,

I wrote you a quick little note last week and wonder if it went astray? I know that you and I have not known each other for very long and have been neighbours for a very few years, but somehow I feel I know you very closely. Perhaps it is because we first met in Church. I remember the sudden appearance of this new yet somehow rather familiar woman sitting in the side aisle, your glassy, slightly hostile look.

You seemed suddenly to have materialised there by some accident of the light. I remember that you did not kneel or bow your head. And when you were asked at the Church door whether you would like to join something or do the flowers, a look came into your eyes, and I have never seen you in Church again.

In my note I perhaps presumed on a friendship that was not quite as strong as I had imagined, and spoke perhaps peremptorily about your leg? Please forgive me if I have said too much, but I do hate to see Charles looking so low. A man whose wife has an undiagnosable leg at scarcely fifty is liable to be a 'figure of fun'.

Why not come over and see me? I'm busy with marmalade and have found a clever ruse for dealing with the pith that might interest you. It makes the marmalade wonderfully translucent.

Your sincere friend,
Eliza

March 6th

Dear Joan,

It is now more than a fortnight since I dropped you a little note about your leg and I know that you have that dog that eats letters and just

2

wondered if it and my second little message had gone astray? Nobody seems to have seen you lately, or even Charles, and the windows at thirty-four seem all to be shut. I asked Henry to go and investigate the lights when he went lamp-posting round the block last night with Toby, and he said there were definitely lights *there*, but they may I suppose have been only *phased* lights. Perhaps you have all gone unexpectedly away?

If you did not get my notes, they were just to say how sorry I am about your leg that never seems to get any better even after all the consultations you have had. I know the sadness when consultations come to nothing, through my work with the Dying. But, as I tell them, these things can be psychosomatic, even at the eleventh hour, and can sometimes easily be talked out either with a professional, often on the National Health—though I'm sure that Charles would never stint—or with somebody caring, like myself.

I would be more than ready to do this. Charles once said that at Oxford you were quite a *pretty* girl, and we all *hate* seeing you so sick—whether it is in mind or body.

Do answer this. Henry is taking it on the lamp-post run now.

Your affec friend,
Eliza

3

March 20th

Dear Joan,

I have just seen Charles going off down the hill to work and he is looking very haggard. I have tried to telephone you, but there is no reply. This makes me think that perhaps you are *ill*, and I am only too ready to do whatever I can, except on Tuesday, Wednesday and Friday mornings when I am busy with the Dying, and Wednesday afternoon which is Wives' Fellowship. No hope of seeing you *there*, as you once made very clear indeed!! In fact the second time we met you told me, with your splendid, incisive clarity, your views on the dear old 'Wives'. You would not listen when I told you that our friendly meetings are not *really* only for the wives of professional men, but for all of us without nine-to-five professions who believe that woman's ministry is in the *home*, in God and marriage and 'soldiering on'—which of course you do. Everyone has always said you are a terrific 'stayer'. Your garden is weedless and your dog so beautifully clean—as is your car. And you're a wonderful friend and neighbour, and, of course, mother, which is a mysterious area for me.

I have prayed about your leg, Joan, and hope that if you received my first note it did not

4

upset you. I'm afraid I'm very forthright. At the 'Wives' they say I'm 'fifth-right'—you see, there are some witty people there—and I do call a spade a spade. I do this even at The Hospice for the Dying. Be sure I shan't mind a bit, Joan, if you go for me for what I said. The patients often go for me. One of them said the other day, 'Any more spades and I'll send for Sister Phyllida.' But I can take anything, Joan, anything you like to say, for the love of Our Lord who endured all things for us.

And please understand that I don't rule out that your leg may be hurting. Psychosomatic illnesses are often painful. I know this only from hearsay, of course, never having had such an illness myself, in fact I have never had an illness in my life, but I pray that this may in no way harm my credibility (in the Jargon of the Age) or the affection I have always had for my sick friends, of whom, Joan, I count you one. Your absence these last weeks has really upset me. I think of it all the time. It has made me all the more eager and affectionately determined to help you.

Yours loving friend, E

PS Anne Robin told me yesterday that she saw you in the distance at the Army and Navy Stores the other day, so I know that at any rate you are *on your feet*. Henry has promised me that he will ring Charles at the Treasury today, as you have no answering-machine at thirty-four and there is no reply to any call or knock. We want you both to come here to dinner. Do come—and don't be upset by me. I have been wondering actually if you would like to come along and do some work with the Dying? I'm sure Mother Ambrosine would accept you, if perhaps you could disguise the leg-iron with trousers or a long skirt.

Or a drink one lunchtime? Or lunch at the Little Greek?

Affec, E

April 1st

Dear Joan,

I am sending this letter to the first of the addresses on the list you left for poor Charles to find on the hall table of thirty-four, it seems many weeks ago. We managed to contact Charles at last only yesterday—quite a month after you left him. I have lain awake all night, worrying and praying and asking forgiveness just in case my little note had anything to do with your disappearance. I can't believe that it could have done. It was only a gesture, tossed out in good faith from one friend to another. I am apt to write without reflection, believing in the Will of God.

It was very hard to discover anything from Charles when we finally got him over here and sat him down to dinner—with which he merely played. He has lost weight, is thinner than ever, and I am sure has been eating only frozen, and, so it appears, have the children. I did not say in my earlier notes, Joan, that Simon and Sarah have been going up and down the road looking scruffy in the extreme, not ethnic or bleached or oddly barbered, as would be natural, but *scruffy*. They come home from school eating things out of bags, in the Road, and carry cartons with straws sticking out. They throw the cartons in hedges.

Charles is frantic, Joan. At least, to be perfectly honest, he is clearly frantic *underneath*. He is, I know, not somebody who shows his feelings easily. Or even at all. Only you, Joan, can know what he must be going through: first there has been the ridicule of you with that leg, going up and down with Sainsbury plastic bags because you could no longer drive the car. Then there was the humiliation of your leaving him. And leaving him, I understand, *in* the car! And, as he has at length told us, leaving him with a pair of good shoes on your feet, and without the

7

leg-iron which he says he found lying in the bed. Like some totem. An evil joke. A malicious act.

Of course I am naturally prey to mixed feelings about all this, because my note has in one sense done great good. *You have flung away the leg-iron*, Joan. This—though I did not go into it in my notes—is what I have prayed you would be able to do. I spent several sessions in prayer on the subject in Church and around the house. What I cannot understand, however, is how Our Lord took my point perfectly about the psychosomatosis of the leg but allowed you in the method of abandoning the leg-iron to hurt—to the very quick—dear old Charles.

Poor, poor bewildered Charles. He tells us that you left the list of box-numbers and Consulate telephone numbers on the hall-table alongside my first note and that there was laid across them some sort of metaphor: an ear of corn. I can't think where you can possibly have found it at this time of year unless it was from the Gargerys' rabbits; or what it meant. No message, he said, of any other kind, not even a kiss or a goodbye.

Joan, I have to say this. I think that you are ill. I know that the whole business began when I wrote to say that you were not, but at 'Wives' today, when we were discussing it all, the general opinion is that you need HELP. After all, any woman must be sick who can

8

leave that wonderful house, those two energetic children, all Charles's money and dear, uncomplaining Charles himself. We have asked him to come and stay with us for a while and he has not actually refused. Is thinking about it. The children, he says, are quite capable of looking after themselves and never notice him, their A Levels being now so close. I can always run across with a quiche.

And that is another thing, Joan. The A Levels. How could you leave Simon and Sarah so close to their A Levels? One thing I, childless though I am, know is that then is the moment the young need a Mother's love. We live in competitive days.

I am trying *not* to be angry with you, Joan. I am trying to put what you have done in context and see it in proportion to the big, the serious act of life, which is Death. I have talked about it to one of my patients at The Hospice, or rather, I talked about it and he watched me, opening one eye. He listened wisely. The Dying have much to teach us, Joan, particularly not to ask too much of life—this life. Turkey, Afghanistan, Nepal, China—all this was done by *Victorian* women, Joan. There is no need for us to follow the intrepid trail again. It is the interior, spiritual trail that the new and liberated woman has to work at now, and there is no need to go to the East for that. There are splendid meditation classes to

9

be had in Woodlands Road. You are not seventeen, Joan.

I put all this to Mother Ambrosine, but you know how cynical the truly good can often sound. Mother Ambrosine said, 'You seem very taken up with this Joan and whatever it is she's up to, Eliza,' and that is true. I am. I just so wish, Joan, that I knew *why*. Why and how you could ever leave an attractive, loving man like Charles after all the tranquil years.

Affectionately, E

May 10th

Dear Joan,

I am now writing to the Consulate in Prague, which is number three on your list, and, if you are there, by now I do hope you are managing to see the sights a little and take photographs. I believe that there are lovely puppet-theatres in Prague and they would make a good talk for the 'Wives'. I wonder if you could possibly manage slides? I am writing *in faith*. I understand that Charles has had not one word from you and, when he comes to dinner, which is most evenings now, we all have a tacit agreement not to speak of you. I do speak to him about the children because they are almost present with us. We can hear the roar of their parties across the road, even while we are eating. He munches on. They continue far into the night.

I am worried about Sarah. I met her in the street the other day and congratulated her on being made a prefect and all she said was, 'Shitto, isn't it?' I always say to her, and to Simon when I see him, 'Any news?' but now Sarah only stares at me and poor Simon slopes off on that bike with the plastic radio on the handle-bars that bellows out Brahms.

I have to tell you everything about S and S, Joan, Prague or no Prague. It is your duty to know. I seriously think that Simon has been taking drugs. He has that bright look, and there is something about the shoulder-blades. Also—and I have mentioned this to Charles—I saw Sarah coming home very late the other night with a young man and she took him into the house with her. Certainly there was (after some time) music, and it was Mozart, but it was after one a.m.

Joan, it is the Mother's duty. How can you leave your children at this time in their lives? I shall write again to your next address on the same lines, though how long it will take to be delivered to Kurdistan I cannot think.

Charles is spending a great deal of time with Henry now and I think that Henry is helping him a little. As you know, since Henry became

11

a lay-reader he has had thoughts of entering the Church—after his retirement from the Foreign Service. As a beginning, he is learning counselling, and I believe that Charles reaps the benefit.

Charles is eating well now, I'm sure you'll be glad to know. He and Henry after dinner sit and talk a great deal to one another. They talk quietly and I sit at my tapestry.

Joan, I sometimes wonder if you went off like that in the hope of making Charles jealous? Let me tell you that, if so, it was a false hope. Watching him, as he sang in the Church choir last week his long, ascetic face, his great nose, his gentle glasses—I can assure you he will never look at another woman.

If he were the type for that—I may as well say it straight out, as I always do—if he were, as would be natural in a healthy man of his age, to turn elsewhere for comfort, he would surely turn to me. I do tend to captivate men because of my looks. This is not conceit but fact. I tend to get on with men very well. Henry used to say I had an unfair start—'Flat chest, long legs, black eyes, red hair.'

Initially at any rate I get on with them. When she presents me for the first time to the Dying, Mother Ambrosine says, 'Don't *talk* Eliza. Just let them look.' This is sometimes a sadness. My looks are something of a burden even now at fifty. They are something I have never been able to put to use. Henry used to say

12

that I should have been on the silent films or waving a hoop at the circus. This last is a quaint and imaginative thought.

Anyway, Joan, Charles does not look in my direction. I believe that there has been no other woman in his life but you. He lives for the day of your return, and your explanation.

He also knows, Joan, that you have not left him for another man—though I don't believe the thought would have occurred to him at all if I had not asked. He trusts you so. Anne Robin said that in the Army and Navy Stores you were buying only a *single* tent and sleeping-bag and making enquiries for only one defensive weapon. You were certainly travelling alone.

I shall continue to write, Joan, feeling as I do rather responsible for you. I know that one day soon you will remember the real life of every day, and dear Charles. If you do get to Kurdistan, I believe there are carpets. I hope you'll buy one. It would look lovely in the hall at thirty-four. It is a good idea, Henry and I always found in our years and years of travel, to bring something home for which the country is famous. This is a better memory than just to rely on what is in the head, or books that dwell on a general aura of romance. Don't for goodness sake drink the goats' milk. That is something I do know about.

Yrs, Eliza

Dear Joan,

I am sending this letter with the parcel you requested in your note, though, I may say, had the note not been in your handwriting, which I know from Christmas cards of yore, with 'picture of bearer' attached, I would not have allowed said bearer over my door-step. But I have not met a Kurd for many years.

I must say he's very good-looking. And very young. It is a pity he speaks so little English and that he arrived at an unfortunate moment. Charles, Simon and Sarah had all just walked in to tell us the great news that Sarah has won a place at St Hilda's at Oxford and Simon a musical award at Cambridge!! The young are odd now. When the Kurd walked in S and S were standing stolidly, Sarah pulling books out from the wall and dropping them on chairs, yawning, and Simon was twanging his braces. Charles had brought some champagne and Henry had just poured it. Naturally we offered some to the Kurd who downed a glass very quickly, took a flask of clear liquid from his pocket and dribbled it into glasses all round. He dribbled some out for the children too. Although they are of course strong teetotallers as a rule and Green as grass, they drank it and began to make arrangements with the Kurd for the rest of the evening, although I had hoped

14

that everyone would be staying for dinner here and I had a couple of frozen cauliflour-crumbles going round at that moment in the mike.

They went off down the street with the Kurd in the direction of the tube and I suppose London nightlife, making a great deal of noise. After dinner we watched the *News* and I said, 'Charles how can you be so calm after all that's happened?' Henry said, 'Charles is a calm man.' Then I said—I dare say it was the liquid from the flask—'But how can you be calm, Charles, with your wife en route for Himalayan territory in your Volvo, and this extraordinary man here to collect her jewellery?'

Charles looked very *down*, Joan, when I said this and he and Henry went across to the Church. After a while your friend—friend, Joan, your lover, I wasn't born yesterday—returned alone and behaved in a very obvious way, trying to push me upstairs towards a bedroom. Fortunately Henry and Charles reappeared about then and made him go to bed on the drawing-room sofa. In the morning he was still there, and immobile, with half the bottles from the drinks cupboard lying about him. We packed him off, still half-tight, at about three o'clock this afternoon, i.e. a few minutes ago, and he is head in hands on the front door-step as I finish this letter. Then he is leaving.

15

I said, 'Charles, you can't, you can't let him take her jewels. She is bleeding you dry—your car and so on.' Charles then said, 'She's chucked the car and bought a jeep'—just like that. So he must have been in touch with you and I think I might have been told before.

Anyway, I am feeling very miserable and shall end this letter,

Sincerely,
Eliza

❈❈❈

November 10th

Dear Joan,

Three months have passed and I am writing to Thailand in the hope that this is your next port of call. I dare say that you will have stayed some time in Kurdistan to await your jewellery. I was too sick for some time—sick at heart—to write about the end of that bizarre episode.

But perhaps now.

After finishing a letter to you, which I wonder if you will ever see, I walked out on to the door-step to hand over the packet to the Kurd. Charles had brought over from across the road the little Victorian lacquer box from your bedroom mantelpiece, leaving, no doubt,

16

a sad little gap among the pot-pourri bowls, the enamel-faced clock, the patch-box that says 'My love I'll treat with kisses sweet'. Oh, DO YOU NOT REMEMBER THESE, Joan? Poor old Charles!

I poured the jewels out into a sacking coffee-bag from Harrods, with a drawstring, and, as I did so, Charles and Henry as one man rose and left. They did not speak to the Kurd as they stepped over him, holding out their briefcases before them as they went, talking nonchalantly together. I said to the Kurd, who seems to have no name, 'I don't know how you intend to get these through the Customs I'm sure,' and he proved that he knew some English because he opened the emerald green dress he was wearing above his breeches to reveal his chest and hung the bag in among the hair. Then he kissed my hand and went away. Richard Baxter opposite put a shielding arm round Dulcie as they both came home from shopping.

Joan.

Joan—I'm not really, altogether, the fool I make myself out to be.

I ham myself up, don't I?

Joan, I'm frightened. I don't know why.

Joan, don't you think you should at least ring Charles from somewhere? He's such a good man.

Love, Eliza

Nov 20th?—I don't know

Dear Joan,

It is three in the morning and I am alone in the house because Henry and Charles have gone away on a Diocesan Weekend Theology Course. The lights are out at thirty-four.

Joan, I have to tell you something. I am in love with Charles. Please, please come back. I didn't want this to happen. I have nobody to consult, only the nuns and the Dying.

I don't want to be a husband-stealer.

Eliza

✳✳✳✳

Nov?, Saturday

Dear, dear Joan,

I am absolutely overcome by the wonderful present that has just arrived from Cambodia. I cannot imagine how you reached Angkor Wat and hope you are being careful. The situation there has never been stable in twenty or more years. I never got there. I always longed.

I have never in my life possessed anything so

beautiful as this glorious golden robe. I sit clutching it and stroking it. No word except *'from Joan'*—I do wish you had written a letter. I do so want to hear about the Kurd and if you got the earrings and pearls safely. I expect you sold them if you can buy such glamorous presents. Charles never mentions how he thinks you can be managing for money. Simon, when I once asked, said, 'No problem, she nicked the cutlery,' but I will not believe that.

Oh Joan, what a dress! I simply don't know when I shall wear it. I suggested to Henry that we might get tickets for Glyndebourne next year, just the three of us, but he and Charles stood staring at me as if I was mad. They are both growing more ascetic day by day. When they left for work this morning, I went across the road to find Sarah who is home for a few days, and there she was, all alone far down in the garden by the summer-house, out on the sitting-place playing her flute among the dahlias and late, late roses, all the bees still humming, winter forgotten to arrive.

The flute stopped in the middle of a bar. She said, 'Eliza!'

I said, 'Oh do go on, Sarah, it was lovely,' and she said, 'Not until I'm over the shock.' She walked all round me and said, 'She sent me one, too, but yours is better. Lucky old you. Where's Henry taking you to in that—the Churchmen's Society Ball?'

So I had to laugh that off.

Thank you very, very much, Joan, most sincerely and affectionately,

Eliza

December 25th

Dear Joan,

It is Christmas afternoon and I am writing at the far end of the drawing room looking out at the garden all covered in snow. The road is very quiet, most people being away with their families elsewhere, or walking off their Christmas dinner on the Common. I spent Christmas Eve with the Dying. They always make a big effort on Christmas Eve—the nuns, I mean. It's quite jolly. On Friday was Wives' Fellowship Christmas Party and I wore your dress. Unfortunately Henry couldn't take me as there was a party at work. Charles was attending a similar one, so I went alone as a 'help' and served at the Buffet. Lots of people complimented me on the dress and some—but not all—I told where it had come from. I did not tell the ones I feel will still be very upset by what you have done.

I came home alone and rather late, after the clearing up, and as the car wouldn't start I had to walk. Have I told you about my new car? It is one that Henry bought me on Charles's advice. Charles is not exactly a mechanically minded man, is he? Or rather, he has something of a mechanical mind but does not apply it to mechanical things. Also, he isn't a very talkative man, is he? Not that I'm used to talkative men. Henry over the years has grown more and more silent and, as this is going to be a very momentous letter, Joan, I shall be as outspoken as I was in the fatal note I sent you in the spring.

I think that the time has come to tell you that Henry is not really fitted out for marriage. This is not the reason why we have no children. That was an academic decision taken years ago. All the mechanical equipment is still there, perfectly normal, as far as I can tell of course. I haven't seen it for years and the only other I have seen, at least looked squarely in the face, so to speak, is on Michelangelo's David in Florence, which is of course marble and upsettingly larger than life. What I have come to face has nothing to do with all that sort of thing. Henry does not see women as of any particular interest. He is without curiosity. I said to him once, 'Women are governed by the moon,' and his face became taut with distaste. He said, 'I am afraid, Eliza, that you *want* the moon,' and I said, 'Well, in love, yes I do,' and he vigorously shook out *The Times*.

Soon after our honeymoon he stopped seeing me as something good to touch, Joan, even though in those days people turned in the street to look as I went by. When men sometimes sent me flowers—well, it was usually just duty, after an invitation to dinner—he would open the door on them and say, 'Eliza—flowers. Have you seen the dog's lead?'

After the first few months lying down together was very like being upon a Church tomb, knight and lady, hand in hand perhaps, but legs crossed, noses skyward. At some moment in any marriage surely, surely, one thinks of the other as a person apart? A woman should be her very self to her husband, interesting to him always even if only as the woman he once loved, chose, negotiated for, was scooped up by or at the very least considered to be adequate. Not Henry. I remember the two of us in our first house in St John's Wood in the early Sixties. It was scarcely lived in, we were on our travels so much, but I remember our being very happy then because of a delightful feeling of security and promise. It was working. It had not been just an Oxford romance, ending in the usual mess. It was a good time. But already I was no longer special.

Last year we had new beds. You remember—I know you do for it was when I first became interested in you. I saw you standing watching as they were being delivered. Then you quickly jumped in your car.

It is a solemn moment, Joan, when the first marriage bed is carried away. Farewell that battlefield, farewell those hills and dales. 'Farewell green fields and happy groves where nymphs have ta'en delight.' Henry was not precisely a nymph. I still feel—no felt—I could be.

Henry arranged the new beds at opposite ends of the room and said, 'Doesn't that look better? They might have been made to measure. Perfect fit.' And they did. And they were. But I cannot help feeling, Joan, that there was something blinkered in that statement.

I spoke to Henry about this. I told him, at about the same time I wrote you a silly letter saying that I was in love with Charles which I hope you never received. Not that it matters because I can imagine what you thought when/if you read it: 'Let's just wait.'

You are right. I now know so much more about what you must have been through these past years with Charles.

Well, after the beds, Henry started going to thousands of prayer-meetings all over London and the suburbs, even to North London. I noticed that he had gone off eggs. It was a joke between us. They were his schoolboy passion. His mother used to say, 'Lucky girl, you won't have to cook a thing, you can always feed him eggs.' This I thought a vaguely disgusting remark, but she was a vaguely disgusting

23

woman. Well, may God forgive me, for she's dead. Anyway, he went off them.

Then I perceived that he seemed to have gone off food altogether. He picked about. But he drank. How he drank. And how he kept on drinking. For a while. Then first the late-night whiskies went and then the wine. For some weeks he sat downstairs, drinking and then not drinking, after I had gone to bed, listening to his tapes. There was a particular *Requiem*—I can't remember which, but it wasn't Lloyd Webber. It surged through the house, a baleful and eternal sorrow. From number thirty-four came the jangled chords of Simon's and Sarah's cacophonous equivalents. The notes merged. They rose and sank, and the people of Rathbone Road listened. Sometimes Charles left number thirty-four and sat with Henry in the study, listening to the *Requiems*, too.

Then, after a while, it must have been about September, Henry stopped drinking. Altogether. For a long time he had been absent-minded about sex. It had always been very much now and then. A hit and miss, half-hearted business. One felt the strains of the *Requiem* sifting through his being. He flopped out like a flag on a windless day and after a while sex stopped altogether. I didn't like to say anything. I did once say on a sharp blue morning as I got out of bed, 'Remember Gascony?' but all he said, grey-faced, was, 'Eliza, we are old people now.'

At The Hospice the patients noticed that I was looking low. My favourite, Barry, said, 'You look as if you need a cuddle. You should be in here with me,' and lifted the sheet. He laughed because I blushed. He got it out of me—what was wrong. Well, not really. I didn't tell him all. He just said, 'Gone off the boil, has he, the Elder Statesman? Maybe,' he said, 'you have stopped liking him.'

Oh, Joan, that set me thinking. It set me weeping. Barry kept on handing me tissues from a box. I said, 'I don't know what's the matter with me,' and he said, 'I do, old cock. You haven't started yet.'

'Just not started,' he said, and shut his eyes. 'Life,' he said. 'Think it out. Don't ask so many questions and, Eliza, don't talk so much. Just get started living before I stop.'

Well, after going off sex, Henry went off me. Completely. That's the only way to describe it. He winced and looked away when I blew my nose. Shut his eyes in pain when I spoke on the telephone to my friends. Each evening I'd hear the click of the front door and from the kitchen or the top of the stairs I'd see him come padding into the house like a cat, put down his briefcase and look in the hall mirror. Very drearily, Joan. 'Ahem, ahem,' he would say.

At first he would grunt in my direction before sitting down in his study with the door shut behind him. One evening he came home carrying an electric kettle and an electric fire.

25

No word. Soon there was a little stove. A 'Baby Belling'. He began to sleep in the study after that.

I walked over to thirty-four, oh, three months ago, to talk to Charles about it. I rang the bell. No reply, so I walked round to the garden, looking through the windows. Everywhere shut up, Joan. Joan—if you could *see* your drawing room. Not that it is messy with Simon and Sarah both away most of the time there is no one to make a mess. Charles's life is passed in a crusade against mess. 'Pyjamas are put in the drawer marked pyjamas,' etc. Pressing my forehead to the kitchen window I saw that there are labels and memos everywhere, saying *'Dustbin Bags.'* *'More Weed-killer.'* And *'Dahlias in by Friday.'*

But the house is dead. Dead. All tidy and silent and dead. Thick with dust because Angela went months ago. She said it gave her the creeps and she kept seeing you about, pre-the leg-iron, laughing and calling as you ran down the stairs, long-legged out of the front door to the car. 'Ghosts,' she said. 'I'd say she's in the house somewhere, buried in the cellar,' but I made her apologise for that. I walked sadly back to your front door and humbly rang the bell again, and quite quickly this time Charles answered. At the open door he stood, solemn. He did not invite me in. I told him just a little about Henry, and he was no use at all. I said, 'I'm sorry to bring you my problems

26

when you have so many of your own.'

'My own?'

'Joan.'

'Bugger Joan,' he said.

I was sick, sick Joan, sick with the shock.

'*Bugger* Joan,' he said and shut the door in my face.

Well, the upshot is that, this Christmas afternoon, Henry has gone off to live with Charles.

They told me after Christmas dinner. Charles did the telling while Henry was upstairs getting his belongings together and when Henry came down Charles said, 'I've told her, Henry,' and Henry looked down at his shoes. Russell and Bromley. I'd not long ago gone all the way to Piccadilly to the repairer with them and back a month later to collect them. An hour's journey each way. He said, 'I'm sorry, Eliza. I'll write. Are you—you are all right, aren't you?'

'The less said at this stage the better,' said Charles easing him forward. 'I'll bring him back in the New Year to talk about arrangements.' And they went.

I watched them from the window—the front window on to the road, not this back window where I sit writing, looking out at the snowy garden, the branches of the tall trees ridged with snow and the birds' footmarks making pricky patterns on the lawn. Outside the front window all the snow is messed about and

27

brown, where people—Gillespies and Hardwicks and Gargerys and Oatses and Baxters and Robins—had gone off after breakfast for their Christmas dinners, most of them loading their cars with children. I thought how glad I was that Simon and Sarah had gone off skiing. With luck, all this will be over by the time they come back.

I mean—Joan! It's madness. I mean they're neither of them, you know, *pansies*. Homos. 'Gays' we have to say now. I never knew human beings less gay than Charles and Henry, in any way. Though of course one can never be sure. It's all a matter of genetic soup. But I mean, they're both so *cerebral*. What will the Treasury and H's people think? Perhaps it's just an old-fashioned thing like Holmes and Watson. They're both pretty Victorian after all. Why shouldn't two men live together? Two women can't live together now without everyone assuming they roll about in one bed. If Charles or Henry were widowed they are exactly the sort who would love to live in Albany. But side by side. There are men who sit dreaming of this as they watch their wives iron their shirts, plan their menus, answer their letters, never wondering 'and who would do all this then?' How do I know all this? I, impossible Eliza, Queen of the Suburban Realm? I know it.

I mean, Joan. Think of them side by side in a *bed* together. Or more than that!

They are cast in the mould of their fathers, Joan. Men of some power believing that somewhere there is a privileged, exclusive male world with butlers and old money, shooting parties you don't have to pay to attend, High Tables at which you sit for hours over the port and never need to speak of or to the working-class. D'you know something, Joanio? They're right. There is.

It is a world where you only know a very few people and they so like yourself there is no need of words, only the communication of familiar noises. That's why this sort of Englishman is still there, and so happy, still blinking in his London club, because whenever he sets eyes on the other blinking figures in their deep chairs he is looking in the glass. The size of those temples in Pall Mall, Joan! Kremlins. The women allowed in the servants' quarters of some of them have to eat apart, from a separate kitchen so dirty that the plate comes up with the table-mat when the waiter comes to take it away. Somewhere in these male clubs, beyond the political negotiations, the mumbling at the national *News*, there are ghosts—long-dead cricketers each with his great gold beard. And, somewhere in the heads of ruminative members is an adoring idle woman who means 'WOMAN', the help-meet, the set-piece, the accoutrement, looking like their mothers. They would all deny this, but it is true, and I only realised it today.

There are in both Charles and Henry vast plains of silence and inscrutability and secrecy which I have always accepted that I must not question. In Henry's job there are many things he has had to keep utterly to himself. It is his life apart from the job that I've just discovered enrages me: the traditional notion that his wife must accept that he should stand somewhat apart. Consciously apart. Not separate as we all are.

I suppose I've given him a hard time. I seem unable to get things right. I jump in while the heavenly host hangs back in terror. I do it at The Hospice. Often I've expected the sack from there and I expect that is why I don't have much to do with the very imminently Dying and rather more to do with the stacking of the dish-washers. Some of the Dying don't mind me, though. Barry says, 'D'you know what you are, Cock, you're a cure.' I'd not be surprised if Barry recovered, if you want to know—though it is a secret not usually admitted even to myself.

Joan, I do wonder where you are. I'd say that I wish that you would just walk in and we could talk, but if I'm totally truthful I don't want you to do that. Writing to you has distanced you from me, and I cannot remember even what you look like now. I dreamed of that Kurd the other night and awoke crying. I wonder just what he meant to you, how many others there have been and how far you went with them? Did you go off simply looking for men? Was it only middle-aged lust? Oh, I don't believe so. Was your flight menopausal? You always looked so bright and sensible, untroubled by the dark. Joan—instruct me.

It is getting dark in Rathbone Road now. Best thing for me to do is to get off to The Hospice in case Barry's gone, or something. It would be appropriate for the day. It would fit the Jobian spirit of things. But perhaps enough has happened for one Christmas afternoon.

If you could write—?

I'll post this in the letter-box by the Little Greek when I go out with the dogs, though it won't be collected for days, being Christmas-time. Joan, if you could write *now*, and tell me this and that. You'll be in Dacca soon, my own old landscape. Perhaps I could even come out and join you for a bit? I'd be very happy to do that. I don't feel awfully well these days.

I hope that you are having a happy Christmas.

Your friend, Eliza

❊❊❊❊

January?

Dear Joan,

The blackness of Christmas Day is now about a month ago and it is a very long space between letters. I have to ask myself, I suppose, just why it is that I continue to write. You were never really a friend. I knew from the moment I met you, and your irreproachable open face became wary, that you wanted to steer clear of my friendship. I sensed that in me you saw all that you must at almost any price avoid.

How I envied you as I stood sometimes—often—at the window. You were always so busy, tearing about in your little car, your front door ever open, your house always full of people. Young, easy-going people. Long lunches. Garden parties for charity. So well-organised, yet so informal. The way you would take the dog for a walk every day at precisely 2.45 and be back at 3.30. Your clothes always so right, your hair like a girl's. When you began to go grey you still looked young and sexy. And the way you laughed—laughed and called and waved as you jumped in the car six times a day and more. We all could hear your laugh all down Rathbone Road. We listened to your laugh—now it seems to me—uneasily.

Then I suppose I witnessed, one by one, all the stages of your disillusion, though I did not at once recognise that this is what they were. I tried to be friendly but always was met by the bright, over-enthusiastic glance that stands as a rampart. Then a sidelong, resentful and, if you don't mind my saying so, rather conceited glare. I did not like it, nor the way you began to lift part of your upper lip, so tired, so world-weary you had become. It was on the way to being a sneer. It was a sneer. I pitied the sneer and prayed for you.

I suppose I was only observing in you what was to be seen less dramatically in many women of our age in Rathbone Road: boredom, ennui, knowledge. The rich, middle-class, educated Englishwoman, tired at last by the rigours of mid-stream life, looking in the glass in the morning and seeing the face of a middle-aged woman look back. And unable to greet her.

The only one I can totally exclude from all this is Marjorie Gargery who is so fortunate in her tenacious absorption in her children's examination results. Having had a 'long family' Marjorie is safe for many years. Sam, if you remember, is still only five, and the four girls still at school. Hepzibah, being so clever, will supply Marjorie with interest and anguish through several post-graduate degrees, right up to the excitement of whether or not she will make Professor. Gladiola is a fecund child who will have many clever children and Marjorie can guide their progress with luck until her death. The great mysteries of puberty are to come for these girls yet of course. They may all go off examinations. I thought that Emma was looking distinctly odd the other day. She was mumbling about the National Front. And Grizel is getting very thick with her sports mistress.

There has been a loosening of behaviour in Rathbone Road since you left, Joan. I do not mean an excess of immorality. I mean that we talk to one another rather more. The result of your flight has been a divided Road. There are those who have become more reflective, others more showy. Anne Robin has taken to wearing a huge long rounded garment rather like an aubergine or a Sultana's maternity dress. It covers her whole body, which is not at all a bad thing. Others have become even more set in their old mould, especially the women over fifty, the Memsahibs, the 'Senior Wives'. I met two of these last week at an SW sherry party and the talk turned again to you. I said that you were very much missed and Lady Gant said she hoped that you were happy, she was sure, wherever you had gone, but somehow she doubted it and 'that is all I have to say'. I said to Anne Robin, 'So they have spoken,' and

Anne said 'Some of us have shown our teeth.' She stroked the front of her bell-shaped gown and said, 'There's a code we still don't break here.'

Why, Joan, do women bare their teeth at women who have moved off from their husbands? Lady G could not stand Charles. I'm sorry, but you probably know. Something about when he made a pass at her at a Gargery barbecue. Oh no—couldn't be. She'd have rather liked it.

I was very fond of Charles once, you know. Some months ago I thought I was in love with him and was in a panic about it. Part of it was excitement that the old stirrings were not dead, part horror that all might start up again. I wrote to you. A silly letter. Did I post it? Some I have, some I have not. None has been returned to me as none has been answered.

Living alone now, that is to say alone but for the two dogs, for Charles never suggested he take yours with him to Dolphin Square nor did Henry consider taking Toby, living alone I am having every opportunity to study not only the progress of my emotions but the nature of emotion itself. I have not done anything of the sort since my two short years at Oxford when I read some Moral Theory. I had thought it long long forgotten.

But a little must have stuck, for every morning now as I wake I find that I can slip easily into an analysis of my moral principles and my 'heart'. And with the fading out of sex these past three years I am able to observe and record myself and the emotions of those about me with a delighted clarity—even, I fear, with some conceit, for I know myself at certain moments to be both detached and wise, rather as if I were the only sober person at a drunken party.

Or at least that is what I was saying to myself, Joan, from September to Christmas Day and all through that dreadful black and white afternoon when the snowy lumps fell off the trees, splat, splut, fouling the humps of the grave-like flower beds. A nightmare afternoon. Once, I remember, I saw a black stone on the rockery begin to move. It came steadily forward over the whitened grass. It was the next-door tortoise, come up for air on a midwinter day. The day Charles and Henry went away together.

My detachment lasted through that afternoon even so, and all through my letter to you. The house was warm, the fire was bright, the dogs for once were both asleep, and there was enough food in the house for me not to have to shop for weeks. There would be no more shirts to wash and iron, no more darning of socks—dead black fish with holes for a face (I am the last woman in Europe with a darning needle), no more answering of invitations to things to which I am not invited, no more being secretary, keeper of diaries,

36

payer of bills, chatelaine.

Paying bills? I did just think somewhat about that. I will pray about it, I thought, and as soon as the banks are open again I will draw out everything from the joint account.

As I reached the end of my letter, and more or less asked you if I could come out to Dacca to join you there, I found that my eyes had turned to the wall beside the fireplace where hangs the portrait of Henry's ancestor, painted by the pupil of Gainsborough, and into my mind came the thought, 'twenty thousand pounds'. These were the words that Barry had uttered. He had asked me where I lived, about my house, how it is decorated, what is in it. When I got to the portrait he said, 'If it's the pupil of Gainsborough I've heard about, it's worth twenty thousand pounds. I could get you that from a man in Epsom.' There's gypsy blood in Barry—horses, cars, antiques.

I looked at the face. Just like Henry's. Narrow like a goat. I walked across to the picture, took it from the wall and peered at it to see if there was a signature. I turned it back to front and felt the splintery, cracked wood across the back. I turned it round again and tried to look into Henry's eyes. I made the discovery, Joan, that Peabody eyes are not the sort you can look into. Blackcurrants. I propped the picture on the desk and thought of Epsom.

The telephone rang. I was slow to answer.

Before I answered I turned the picture round. 'Hullo?'

'Thomas Hopkin.'

'No, it's Eliza Peabody.'

'I'm Tom Hopkin.'

'Oh, yes.'

'You don't know me.'

'That is so.'

'I'm down the road in a call-box. Just wondered if I might catch you.'

I decided, Joan, that this must be some sort of intricate private detective hired by Henry. Then I thought, what could there be to detect? Unless Henry has left me out of some paranoid and uncommunicated jealousy. Of what? Of whom? Barry is not even likely to have ever crossed Henry's mind and is dying of Aids. Barry, to Henry, would be an unknown entity. 'The Common Man.' He would say of course—and believe—that Jesus loves Barry, which would let him, Henry, out. And fancy, I thought, a private detective working on Christmas Day!

All my life I have felt events to be the result of my own sins. 'I have done nothing wrong,' I said aloud. 'It is Henry who has left me.'

Silence. I was about to put down the telephone when it occurred to me: This is not a private detective. It is a burglar. He is probably trying all the numbers in the street to find who is in and who is out. Christmas Day is the burglars' birthday. He has found that I am in,

38

and that I am alone.

'There are a great many people here,' I said, 'I am giving a party. I'm afraid I can't talk any more and I must feed my bull-terriers.'

'I only wanted to drop in some presents,' said Tom Hopkin. 'They are from Joan. I have just flown in. Would it be convenient?'

Well, Joan. Of course I said yes.

Then I realised what a very silly position I had landed myself in, solitary in the house. I wondered if I might in some way create the atmosphere of a jolly crowd, perhaps a sleepy, post-prandial murmur. I turned up the television very loud and also a cassette recorder and made it play a cheerful medley. The *Requiems* I laid aside. I shut the kitchen door so that the dogs could be heard but not seen.

Predictably, when the bell rang they both set up a furious barking and Tom Hopkin, when he stepped in, was met by a considerable impression of suburban Christmas life.

He stood on the mat, his arms full of parcels. Snowflakes stuck in splashes on his floppy hair and loose splats stuck to his big glasses. 'Tom Hopkin,' he said, 'British Council. Bangladesh, but that is not the bark of bull-terriers.' He went to the kitchen door and let them both leap at him. 'Jack Russell,' he said to Toby, 'shut up. Poodle, let go my leg.'

'I'm afraid he won't. He's not a bull-terrier but he has bull-terrier pretensions. Please keep the parcels from him. He eats paper. He's Joan's. I think he is one of her reasons for going to Bangladesh. Oh dear, we'll never get him back in his basket.' I had to shriek these words.

'Basket,' commanded this man, kicking out, and Toby went and hid under the kitchen table and your dog snarled uncertainly and slunk off and sat with his back to the audience under the stairs. 'I said BASKET,' roared your friend. Both dogs made for these with hung heads. They sat tense, with upward-rolling eyes, curious and yet accepting. Tom Hopkin shut the door on them and we walked into the sitting room while I watched the snow melting all over him and his glasses clear, like a robot weeping. Eyes that were not at peace.

'Could you,' he asked, 'turn a few things off?'

'Off?'

'The noise.'

I did. Television. Tape-deck.

'Radio?' he asked.

I did.

'Was that the party?'

'Well, yes. I thought you might be an intruder.'

'Ah.'

'You see, Joan has obviously changed. We don't know much about her now. The last friend who came, a Kurd, got very drunk. He wore a green dress.'

'Oh, Tacky,' he said.

'I've no idea. It's possible.'

'Good deal of hair?'

'Oh, well, yes,' I said and he said, 'How prettily you blush in the firelight. I do hate to ask, but is there anything to eat? I've not eaten since yesterday.'

'It's Christmas Day—nothing to eat?'

'I've been on a 'plane. I don't eat on 'planes. I fast. I sip water.'

'Do you—eat ordinary food? There's turkey and everything. And plum pudding and mince-pies.'

I went to the kitchen where the dogs gave me puzzled glances, but stayed put. I prepared a feast. I said, 'It will take a few minutes to warm up the plum-pudding,' and he came to the kitchen door and said, '*Plum* pudding. What a beautiful Victorian memory. Christmas was once every day. Gastronomically. You are an old-fashioned girl. D'you think, as it heats up, I might take a bath?'

He was sopped through, I now noticed. I could hardly say no. Indeed, before I could say anything he was off up the stairs and there was a roaring of taps.

I followed and said, 'Here's a towel,' and his bare arm came round the door for it. 'Hang on,' he said. 'Could you be sublime?' and passed out all his clothes. All of them. Socks. Y-fronts. Shoes. 'Could you just drape them round the stove?'

41

'And what will you wear?'

Silence.

'Would you like some of Henry's?'

'Would it be possible? A dressing-gown would do. Until mine are dry.'

'Yes. All right. Henry's dressing room's on the left,' and, downstairs, arranging brandy-butter in a fresh glass dish, I called up, 'Take anything. He has packed all he needs,' and poured myself a huge glass of wine, using the goblet vase which I usually put tall flowers in, and which stands on the kitchen sill. We had taken not one sip of wine at Christmas dinner. Henry and Charles had now and then lifted their glasses, wetted their top lips and dolefully dabbed at their mouths with sacramental slowness. I had drunk nothing.

I refilled the vase.

'On our knees would be nice,' said Tom Hopkin, your friend, suddenly appearing, and I spun round and shrieked, for he was wearing full evening dress. Black tie and rose-coloured smoking jacket and Henry's favourite evening shoes. His face was rose-coloured, too. His hair silky, blond and clean. 'What-ho,' he said twirling Henry's monocle on a chain. 'We don't do much of this in Bangladesh.'

I said, 'On our *knees*?' The curate's anxious face sprang to mind. 'Are you a parson?'

'A parson? I'm the British Council. I meant the supper. Could we have our supper on our knees?'

I waved the glass dish about.

'Supper,' he said. 'Here—out of the way—I'll finish it. Go and put a dress on. A nice one. Take a glass of wine with you,' and he topped up the vase.

So I went upstairs and changed into the gold dress and gulped down the wine and stood looking at myself. I burrowed around for lipstick and after I had put some on I took it off again. Lipstick is ageing. I poured scent on myself. Then I put up my hair.

Then I took it down.

Two trays of turkey. A new bottle open by the fire. Your friend observed me through Henry's eye-glass. 'She sent some earrings to go with that,' he said. 'Catch.'

I opened the earring parcel, Joan, and said, 'But they must weigh ten tons.' Then I screwed them in and found that they weighed feathers. I said, 'They're like the Fair on the Common. They're like tambourines. They tickle my shoulders,' and found that silence had fallen in the room and Henry's monocle shone with a steady gleam. 'Lucky earrings,' said he. 'Pouilly-fuissé? What shall we play on the tape-deck?'

'Most of them are *Requiems*. I don't think I want any music.'

'I certainly don't want *Requiems*. Are you quite comfortable?'

'Oh yes, very.'

'And I see that you were hungry.'

43

I looked down and saw that I'd eaten all my turkey, cold roast potatoes, bread-sauce, two kinds of stuffing and a green salad, my glass was empty and there didn't seem to be much pouilly-fuissé left in the bottle. I thought: Eliza take care, why was he asking if you were comfortable? And I tried to gather myself together to say something safe and hostess-like, such as: 'Well, I *am* glad you decided to telephone and how is Joan?' But all that came out was a sigh, and I lay back and wished.

'Why,' he asked, 'has that picture got its face to the wall?' He turned it round and said, 'Oh well, yes.'

'It's one of Henry's ancestors.'

'Poor fellow.'

'Henry is my husband.'

'Oh, I know about Henry.'

'Henry is—. Has Joan said much?'

'No. Not much. But one divines.'

'She never writes. At least, not to me. I write often.'

'Why do you write? Are you a relation?'

'Goodness, you are old-fashioned. It must be living with Indians. You must have been away a long time. Families here aren't important enough for letters any more. Not even friends write to each other much now.'

'Joan was your close friend then?'

'Well, she was hardly a friend at all. But she left a list of addresses—box-numbers.'

'Then why do you write? Sit there while I go

44

for the plum-pudding.'

I heard a great conversation going on in the kitchen and, when he returned with silver dishes and the bottle of Courvoisier that is kept in the drinks cupboard, its key, I swear, under the saucer in the study (your friends do drink a lot, Joan), both dogs trotted meekly at his heels.

'Very well,' he was saying to them, 'we shall see. It depends entirely on your behaviour the next half hour,' and he handed me plum-pudding and flourished a great white dinner napkin about. Then he sat down to his own plateful at the other side of the fire. The dogs gazed upon him. First one and then the other flopped down, arranged its front paws, laid its chin upon them and continued to gaze. My dog sighed.

'Much better,' said Tom Hopkin. 'Yes?'

'Yes, much better.'

'I like to see someone lick a spoon,' he said, 'I meant, have you found the answer yet to why you write so compulsively to Joan?'

I thought, Oh Lord, he thinks I'm a lesbian. He expects the usual throbbing steamy stuff. If I say no, he'll think I'm just not facing the new so-called natural world. Oh shitto, as Sarah would say.

'Looking at you and the blushing and so on I see that your interest in Joan is quite holy. Sex with you would not be paramount.'

I felt wretched.

'I haven't much interest in Joan in any way really, except for some reason I feel that I know her very well.' (I thought: What is it? He makes me tell the truth.) 'I told you—we were not even friends. If anything we were opposites. She reminds me of someone or something—I don't know. I think that I write because I feel a little responsible for her disappearance. I wrote her a letter telling her she was a hypochondriac and she should pull herself together. I prayed about it first. God often tells me what to do. Or He did.'

'Do you often advise people who are not your friends?'

I told him about working at The Hospice.

'You thought that you could help her in a medical capacity? Are you trained?'

I hung my head and said that it was mostly washing-up but that I do believe myself sometimes called to fling myself at a pen and sound off to people.

'Well, why are you so ashamed of it?'

He lay back in his chair. The fire sparked and crackled with a new log. The Courvoisier caught the light as it tipped here and there in his glass. His hair shone silky and young. I thought: this is the man I have looked for all my life.

'You are obviously an excellent woman,' he said, and I burst into tears.

'I am nothing of the sort. But I try.'

46

'What—try to be an excellent woman?'

'No. Of course not. You're cruel. Who could want that? Oh well—yes, I suppose so. I can't help it. I try to be good. It's the way I was brought up. I was too early for the self-fulfilment stuff, the "love thyself", the Germaine Greer feminism—too busy then, keeping Henry going. I know they all say I'm humourless and conceited and I talk too much and I'm self-righteous, but not even Lady Gant can say I don't try. To be good.'

'*Is* there someone called Lady Gant?' He smiled contentedly. 'And you try to *do* good?'

'Well, of course. Why not? I can't help it. It's what I was taught.'

'Well, *why ever* not. Another Courvoisier? Are you averse to getting sloshed? Tell me about Henry.' (A sharp glance at the portrait.) 'You said he'd left you.'

'I didn't. Did I say that? Nobody knows that. He only did it at lunchtime.'

'Today? At Christmas dinner? Well, big things do happen on Christmas Day—there are quite a lot of suicides. Did he do any washing-up?'

'*Henry*? Well, there wasn't much to wash-up. We none of us ate anything really. I knew something was brewing when he and Charles came in from Church. All of a sudden they just rose up and left. Before the pudding.'

'That does seem an inhuman act.'

I sipped the Courvoisier and wanted to weep

47

again; but, as I sat, I began to think, and having thought—the wine and brandy had not befuddled me, Joan, at all—as I thought, I realised that there were many things that might be said on Henry's behalf.

'There wasn't much for him to leave. It wasn't exactly a convivial Christmas. I never managed a child for him. Neither of us has parents. Scarcely a relation between us and all our friends make their own plans. Charles sat like a dead fish, his wife in Bangladesh and not even a Christmas card from her. I have really nothing to say to Henry now. I haven't had for years, although I do try always to keep a conversation going. I think that that may have been part of the trouble. I should have been enigmatic and silent. He is a very senior Civil Servant. My tongue tends to run away when we go to parties together and I haven't been seen about with him for ages. He is exactly the same seniority as Charles and they have become close friends. They are both interested only in their work and their religion.'

'What about love?'

'Love?'

'Do you and Henry love each other?'

'Love each other? Well. I don't—I don't think about it. I'm very interested in religion, too.'

'Go on.'

'Well, I suppose at our age, Henry's and mine, we should be trying to love God.'

'What, in the night?'

'Well, all the time. It's a Christian principle. I don't see why we shouldn't make that clear, like the Muslims do. And anyway, our beds are at opposite ends of the room. Henry says they look made-to-measure there.'

'And you think about God when you're in bed?'

'Yes. Sometimes.'

'And Henry minds? This is why you say there was little for him to leave behind?'

'Oh, Henry isn't in the bedroom at all now. He sleeps down in the study with a small stove.'

Tom Hopkin closed then opened his eyes. He looked at me.

'Eliza, Joan sent some sweets. Shall we open them?'

He sat near me on the sofa and we ate the sweets. Actually, Joan, they weren't very nice. They were so sweet they set my skin shuddering. I went cold-turkey. They wobbled all over and looked like pale, powdered flesh. 'Eastern delicacies,' Tom Hopkin said and I said, 'There are some chocolates. Barry gave them to me,' and we ate Barry's chocolates which were wonderful and two layers.

'Who's Barry?' he said on the third fondant whirl—he'd been down in the bottom layer for it. I thought seriously for an instant whether he was one I could tell. But no.

He put his arms round me then, and I felt the one along the back of my shoulders, resting

49

along the sofa, begin to strain further off into the distance as he pushed me sideways and down. I thought: I wish I could feel less analytical about this.

He heaved himself then with a cumbersome, lateral movement on top of me and I thought: What will be will be. Please God, I've never done it with anyone but Henry and I'm half a century old.

I waited.

'Got it,' he said and tweaked a book out of the bookcase beside the fireplace, brought it round the front of my neck and held it in both his hands before my face. He brought his cheek close to mine. 'Dryden,' he said, 'I'll read to you.'

After he'd finished the *whole* of *The Ode on St Cecilia's Day*, Joan, I didn't know where I was. I was upright, taut, fraught, watchful, frightened. And longing. Longing for the last verse. Longing for Hopkin. The book was so near our faces and he was whispering so musically in my right ear, his arms tight round me.

I thought, I am sitting alone in the house with a total stranger who has his arms very close to my jugular and is dressed in my husband's best clothes. He has drunk a bottle and a half of my husband's wine and three brandies. He is a madman. He is reading a most inappropriate poem. Soon I shall be raped.

'Wonderful,' he said and closed the book.

50

He let his face drop down into my collar-bone. The eye-glass made a clatter against your earrings. The tambourines shivered. He let the eye-glass drop.

When they find my body, I said to myself, some may be sorry; but I kissed Tom Hopkin first with my eyes open and then with my eyes closed. Then we rearranged ourselves and I kissed him again. Then I about-faced the eighteenth-century goat and slid backwards into Tom H's arms, then both of us rolled on to the floor. As he touched the ground he cried, 'Basket,' and both dogs obediently trotted to the kitchen. He left me, and went across to close the door, returned and joined me on the hearth-rug.

'Eliza?'

'Yes?'

'Is it possible to get a taxi?'

'A *taxi*?'

'I ought to get back to the flat.'

'What flat?'

'I have a flat in Warwick Gardens.'

'Warwick Gardens? But you were in tropical clothes. You'd just arrived.'

'No. I had dropped into the flat on the way from the airport. I'm rather absent-minded.'

I thought of all you hear and read and see about women taking the initiative now. There is a statutory phrase. 'You don't *have* to go.'

I tried it. He looked thoughtful.

I must have got it wrong. It still is the man

51

who has to say it. I thought things had improved. I thought all women did the decision-making now—Anne Robin, Marjorie Gargery, Lady Gant. I saw them all, acting according to the new fiction, the television serial, the cleansing rejuvenating feminist handout, each with her illicit man behind the fat, interlined curtains of each pleasant house, burglar-alarmed and window-locked and the chain up.

What men? What on earth do I know about it—about how any of them go on? I began to conjure up the men, Joan, who might bring a frisson to the lives of Robin, Gargery and Gant. The milkman for Robin, she is the soul of conventionality; the window-cleaner for Gargery, with his long sweeping arms to whisk her away. For Gant? What? Ha—a doctor. A young and terrified National Health doctor, flattened beneath the field of the cloth of gold. Rocking my head with joy, or hysteria, at her good fortune, I laughed and I laughed beneath the bony, delicious anatomy of this man who had come in from the cold and got himself into Henry's velvet jacket.

'Oh don't cry,' he said. 'Please don't cry. I've behaved very badly. I think it's probably jet-lag.' He sat up, wound away the eye-glass and put his glasses on. 'I was mad to go anywhere tonight. For me it's about four in the morning. My wife is much more sensible. She went to bed. I needed a bit of exercise so I brought round the parcels.' I sat on the rug and he padded away, to come back shortly in his own clothes.

'I've put Henry's things back. It's been very pleasant. Do thank him when he comes home—I'm sure he'll be back soon. I feel rather—well, rather bad you know. Good evening, dogs.'

I didn't see him out and it was nearly an hour after he left that I heaved myself up and put the chain on the front door. The dogs would have to do without a trip round the block tonight.

In the bathroom he'd left the most astonishing mess—soap on the floor, towels everywhere, puddles on the carpet. All Henry's clothes were flung about. I thought: Why does Joan send such terrible men? Are they to show me that there are some worse than my own? Is she telling me not to bother to follow her to freedom?

Joan, I think it would be a good idea for you to write and tell me what you're up to. Quickly. If I am to come and join you I have to sell the ancestor while Barry is still able to arrange it. A month already since Christmas.

I fell on my bed that Christmas night, Joan, in your dress and earrings and the bed began to spin. It spun me up and up and out of the window, and away and away. I looked down on the Road with its scuffed snow, its lighted tree in every window, its sleek motor cars turning calmly back into it again at intervals, families teeming out of them, carrying presents, calling to each other. Babies, parcels, bottles, toys, dogs, rugs, everyone home and dry. The highly successful, never hungry, Western-European family of man. The prize-winners.

Up and up I spun and over the horizon, then outward and outward and out of the world.

Towards heaven? There is nobody now to whom I can talk about heaven. Tonight I had thought that I might have found one. He had the voice for *St Cecilia's Day*. A heavenly voice. And heavenly hands. Well, perhaps it's because I am so caught up with heaven and suchlike that I am such a failure in this world. I should concentrate on one world at a time. But I wonder what God was about, putting me in this lonely situation?

I believe that I could suffer, Joan, I believe that I could even endure great misfortune, terrible grief in the hope of a glorious resurrection. But who can walk hand in hand with God when He seems to require of His servant Christmas night alone in Rathbone Road?

I am nevertheless your sincere, subdued neighbour, Eliza.

Happy New Year.

I slept on Boxing Day until lunchtime, Joan, and the dogs were frantic. I pushed them into the garden, then pulled on some clothes and took them for a walk on the Common. The sun had come out and so had the whole community, all wearing their Christmas clothes, the children with their bright new toys. The pond was frozen and people skated. The sky was coppery and gleaming above the snow. I walked into the woods for several miles, round the mere, in and out of the golf bunkers, round and sometimes over the snowy greens; up to the windmill, back down the grit track where horses galloped and people called to one another with plumes of breath coming from their mouths. I saw little clumps of folk I knew, but it is easy to avoid people on the Common. I waved sometimes as I veered away, once stood looking earnestly in the window of the antique-shop beside the riding-stables. The people passing—perhaps it was the low, orange sunshine that spread their shadows before them—looked much larger than they used to do when we first came to live here years ago; and so much better-dressed, so much louder, more self-confident, the children glossier, everyone rich. The dogs all shone with top-quality pet-food, leather leads and collars studded with silver like mediaeval bracelets. Only I unchanging in my immemorial grey

55

mohair and my old black boots. I went off home again to number forty-three, and slept again till morning.

Then I went to the bank and drew out all the money. We had twelve thousand pounds in the current account. Far too much, but Henry is hopeless with money and usually so am I. There was about thirty thousand on deposit, but they said I'd have to wait a day or two for that. The counter clerk was sleepy from Christmas, her neck all covered with love-bites and her bosoms sticking out of her white sweater. She pointed them here and there like a terrorist with a machine-gun as she whisked about spelling out my account on the screen, as if they and she had had a good time. A vulgar notion.

'Could I have it all out? In notes?'

She'd been yawning but stopped with a click. 'I'll have to get advice on that. I think you'll have to wait.' She slid round and down off the stool and whispered with a young man who looked up quickly from under his brows. He said, 'Oh, Mrs Peabody. That's all right,' and after a time the girl came back with a package. I signed for it and put it in a Sainsbury bag. I wondered if they would offer me an escort, but they didn't. Money isn't what it was. I left the bank and entered the Building Society next door to put the pack of money there in my own name. All the time I felt this was a mean and shabby thing that I was doing.

The man behind the counter said, 'Just a minute,' and went away to do some quiet talking and somebody else gave me a quick look, bobbing his head up from behind a partition. Could they, asked the first man, have some form of identification? I showed them my membership card for the Liberal Party, very old and grubby, almost collectable as an antique; a card for the University Women's Club—older and grubbier; one for the London Library saying 'valid until 1966', and a signed receipt from Harrods hairdressing which made them blanch though it was five years old. They nevertheless signed in the money and smiled pleasantly.

Then I went home and found Charles standing at the gate holding a bunch of Underground chrysanthemums, that's to say London Underground Railway chrysanthemums done up in a plastic cornet. They were a very crude pink and overblown. I asked if he had mislaid his key—he has had one for months—and I also looked nervously around his feet to see if his zip-bag was with him. It's his dirty-shirt bag. He and Henry have one each. He had not—and his shirt was not very white. He was looking, even for Charles, particularly grave.

'Might we have a short talk, Eliza?'

We went together to the sitting room where your dog—his dog—went for him, and I went off to make the coffee as he rolled up his trouser-leg to look at the damage. In the sitting room were the remains of the turkey and plumpudding, the Stilton cheese and a complex stilllife of empty glasses. The ancestor stood on the floor among cushions. The hearth-rug was in a twist and the fire was out. The curtains were drawn across and the room was lit only by the sun shining through the cracks, the saddest scenario. I hate drawn curtains. One of the long endurances of my marriage has been Henry's curtain-fetish. It came upon him slowly—at Oxford we'd lie together looking up at the moon, but these past three or four years he has reached the stage where he goes round each window every night as it grows dark, and sometimes rather before, smoothing and smoothing to eliminate chinks. In the bedroom he has insisted on a blind as well. In his dressing room he never draws up the blind until he is completely dressed, summer or winter. Since I have had my bedroom to myself I have taken all the curtains down. I mentioned them to The Hospice. 'Interlined Colefax and Fowler,' I said. All they said was, 'Eliza dear—first spades, then curtains. We have plenty of blinds here.'

However, after my adventures, Joan, with your friend on Christmas night, I had not touched the room in which we had spent such a glorious time. I had closed the door gently on it, as it might have been upon a shrine. Charles seemed uncomfortable there.

'Could you put a light on? I'm falling over things. *Hell*!' There was a crunching, flopping sound as the ancestor fell on its face. I heard him dragging back the curtains, and, as I arrived with the tray, he was holding his foot and looking with horror at the erstwhile Peabody.

'What's the portrait doing off the wall? Did it fall?'

'No. I'm thinking of selling it.'

'Eliza, it is Henry's? He's only been gone two days.'

'Everything's in our joint name.'

'But it's a family portrait. It's unmistakably a Peabody.'

'Yes. How is Henry?'

'Very troubled. Very unhappy I think, Eliza. If we might just sit down. I'd like to talk to you. It is going to be so difficult but I have promised Henry that I will try. You have been very good to me since Joan left. I don't believe there is another woman who would have taken on the shirts. I am doing this for you as much as for Henry.'

'Well, it wasn't so much the shirts. It's more the dog.'

'Oh, the dog. You know, I miss the dog.' (Joy broke over me like the sun over the winter Common.) 'I only wish that they allowed dogs at Dolphin Square.' (The sun went down.)

'Are you both at Dolphin Square?'

'Yes. We've borrowed old Felix's flat. It's a

59

very popular place you know.'

'Yes.'

'For people like ourselves. I miss the dear old Road of course. A secret society, isn't it—the closeness and kindness of English suburban life? Not the conventional press image at all. And Church of course. I miss St Saviour's. It's wonderful that you're able to keep an eye on the house—looking right across at it. You are so good, Eliza. Oh dear, Eliza, who would have predicted this last Christmas? Joan so jolly and all of us singing carols for the NSPCC.'

'Yes. Her leg hadn't started then.'

'It began last New Year's Eve—or thereabouts.'

He hung his bald head, your poor old husband, Joan, and I waited to see whether a tear might run down the great nose, but it didn't. 'I must stick to the point,' he said, and I looked at the nose again, concentrating on the tip. He began to stroke it and I thought of Gogol, Joan. I started to feel weak, laughter building up as it had on Christmas night when I had the visions of Anne and Gargery and Gant and co., rolling in their sitting rooms with the men of their choice.

I saw Charles look at me sharply.

'Laughing, Eliza?'

'I'm so sorry.'

'Henry has asked me to come and see if you'll give him a divorce. He says you have both been deeply unhappy for some years.

60

He'll see that you are properly kept, of course. He can allow ten thousand a year, after the house is sold.'

'And,' I asked, 'are you and he going to continue together?'

Charles looked wary. 'We are very much at one,' he said, 'though there are aspects ... Two men living together these days is still quite criminally suspect. It wouldn't be good for either of us professionally.'

'Does Henry say why he wants a divorce?'

'Well—oh, this is dreadful.' He clasped and unclasped his hands. 'Dreadful.'

We both examined the ashes in the grate.

'Can I get you a drink, Charles. Whisky?'

He sipped the whisky, then set it down on the gold and glass table and looked at it. Through the glass, on the floor, lay one of the joyous earrings of Christmas with its hook squashed in. I felt tears coming.

'Please be absolutely truthful, Charles. I've always tried to be truthful.'

'He says ... He's afraid ... He thinks that you are changed.'

'How?'

'Well, you have become strange.'

'Why?'

'Well, your obsessions.'

'Obsessions?'

'With everything. The Hospice. The Road. Joan, of course. The dog.'

'The *dog*? I'm obsessive about the *dog*?'

61

'And religion. And the way you're always analysing and observing—and lecturing. Talking of things outside your sphere. Politics, for instance. And talking so *much*.'

'*Politics*? But that's *him*.'

'At dinner parties. When people so much better-informed are present. You don't listen, you tell them. It is embarrassing for a man in Henry's position. The endless talking—do forgive me.'

'But I've always spoken out.'

'It's—I'm sorry, Eliza—it's the way you make a fool of yourself now. He says that you have crumbled. Nobody now would dream you had been to a university. Your prudence did not develop. Say what you like about equality of mind, *prudence* is usually a male attribute, especially in the Civil Service where of course there are still very few women, as we know. Making judgments is a female failing, justified by the dangerous word "instinct". Making judgments, Henry feels, has grown in you with time.'

'I have been married to Henry for thirty years. It's odd that he has just noticed all this. He has never hinted to me that I am imprudent and judgmental and a fool. How odd. It sounds very much as if he's scratting about for reasons.'

'Oh, he is a *kind* man, Eliza.'

'He has never been a kind man. You don't marry kindness, at least not at twenty.'

'That was a very long time ago.'

I said to him then: 'I understand Joan now to the ends of her fingernails, to the end of each hair, and I weep for her. Hurrah for her escape.' Looking at my own fingernails at this point, I noticed a strangeness in them.

'Joan?' he said. 'Joan?'

'What you are trying to tell me,' I said, 'is that Henry has found another woman.'

Charles looked amazed, 'No, no. Of course not.'

'Why not?'

'He's far too busy. And he's a religious man, Eliza.'

'Oh yes. I had forgotten that.'

*   *   *

After Charles had gone, I made a stab at clearing up the house. I fed the dogs and walked them, ate the leg of some bird, picked up the ancestor and put him in the car. I drove to The Hospice.

Just before I started, though, I went back indoors and found the earrings, unsquashed the one under the table entangled in the rug, and fixed them both in. They swung about. They should have been one more reminder of the humiliations of my visitation by your British Council friend, but they were not. They are any old Eastern things you probably picked up in some bazaar, dear Joan, so why do they

63

have talismanic properties? But they do. They lift my heart and free me—free me from Henry, Charles and the pronouncements I'm soon about to face from Rathbone Road. I tossed my head at Mother Ambrosine as I marched in to The Hospice carrying the baleful goat.

'Holy Mother of God, if it isn't Gypsy Rose Lee,' she said. 'And what's the picture? Is it for Barry? There's no room for a great thing like that.'

'How is he?'

'Remarkable. Remarkable. He's a lot better. It's a respite only, dear, of course, but so much better. I dare say because he's seen nothing of you the past few days. Wherever have you been, deserting us over Christmas?'

'There's been a lot going on.'

'There's been a lot going on here, too, especially a lot of washing-up. The washing-up has missed you—and we have missed you, child.'

'I've missed you, too,' I said, realising it was so. There is peace and strength in The Hospice. You catch it on the door-step. It smells of flowers, good food and polish. There's joy there as you walk in. And it was good to be called child.

Barry was sitting up in bed looking at the telly and didn't turn it off as I lumbered in. He raised a warning hand, then pointed a finger at my chair. I clumped down the picture, then myself and for a little while we both watched racing-cars go snarling round a track, now and then spinning off course and crashing into things. Once or twice black pyres of smoke rose up. Once or twice there was a flourish of fire-engines and people ran in rivulets like ants towards a juicy beetle and there was a surge and roar of excited applause and distress. The whine and scream of the race filled Barry's room and flowed into us both. He looked at me at last, pressed the button on his pillows and the whole jamboree vanished. 'Eliza, whatever's this?'

'It's a picture I brought for you to value.'

'No. This. You. The dangles. The Queen of the Tambourine.'

'They're a Christmas present.'

'They look more than that to me.'

'Why? Aren't they nice? I like them...' I wagged my head and the bells began to ring. 'They're imprudent, tawdry, foolish and out of character. Fun. Fun is hazy territory.'

'They're fun all right. They're the beginning of the day-break. They're the light at the end of the tunnel. You don't look like a Senior Civil Servant's wife. At last.'

'What does a Senior Civil Servant's wife look like?'

'Watchful. Neglected.'

'Henry's left me,' I said before he started to try to laugh. He is bones and bones, with bright eyes. His scant hair stands upright. Astonishingly today he was sitting upright,

65

too, though propped. Now there was almost space between him and his pillows, which I have never seen.

'Because of the earrings?'

'No. It seems that all these years he has thought me a fool.'

'Well, you are a fool, Eliza. D'you want a sweet?'

'Barry, hold my hand.'

'We're not allowed sex with the Staff.'

But he held it. His own felt a little warmer. The nails were less blue. He looked at mine. 'So pretty,' he said.

'How was Christmas? I'm sorry I couldn't get here.'

He was looking out of the window. It was snowing again. 'Get on the Common, did you? With the dogs? Loads of jolly?'

'Well only once. I had to. You can't be cruel to dogs.'

'Can't you?'

'You know I don't want them. I want to be here.'

'Then ditch them. And him. The time has come. Has he left you? Are you fantasising again? Eliza? I hope you're not changing into an ordinary woman. Eliza I want. Not just anybody. Don't start telling yourself stories and going daft.'

'That's what it seems I am. "Becoming strange," Henry says. And he says I make a fool of myself when I talk Politics.'

'Never met anyone who didn't, Cock. *Has* he left you?'

'He's gone to live with Charles in Dolphin Square.'

'Well! What think ye of Christ?'

'Barry, he wants a divorce.'

We both watched the snow. 'I'm sorry,' he said, 'I'm sorry, Cock. Unbelievable.'

'Why?'

'I don't see how anybody could possibly ever leave you.'

I said nothing in case I began to cry.

'I don't see why not,' I said in the end. 'All Charles said about me is true. I *am* a fool. I'm erratic. It seems I am unstable. I behave unpredictably, bossily, shallowly and my mind has no abiding place. I have insufficient to do after all the busy years, and an urge to do nothing. I look a freak—no interest in getting up in the morning. I haven't bought any clothes for years. I look like a voluntary worker, an agnostic, a Good Works freak, a municipal counsellor, a sick-visitor unpaid, and I do not care.'

'That's his fault.'

'It's not. I've plenty of money.'

'He doesn't see you.'

'How do you know?'

'I can always spot an invisible wife.'

'I've grown to like it—being invisible. You can see without being seen.'

'No. That is not true. You don't. You like to

67

behave like an avenging angel. Rushing with flaming swords, telling people truths—about their legs and that. You get burnt, but you get over it. That's you, Eliza. Be it. For God's sake, *be* it. What you really need, if you'll just be quiet, is love.'

'Who doesn't? And I *am* a fool.'

'Yes. Like I said. But a surface fool. Only on the surface. You *insist* on it, Cocky.'

After a bit I said, 'I rolled on the hearth-rug on Christmas night with a marvellous man.'

'There you are, see. Things are looking up.'

'No. He asked me if I would call him a taxi.'

Mother Ambrosine put her head round the door and said, 'If you could release her hand now, Barry dear, she has the dishwashers to stack.'

'Look at the picture,' I said. 'Tell me what it's worth. I'll look in for it when I go.'

*　　*　　*

But when I went back, the picture had been moved with its face to the wall, and I left it there. Barry had been laid down flat and seemed asleep.

'See you tomorrow,' I said.

In his sleep he sang, '*For she's the Queen of the Tambourine*.'

'Goodnight, Barry.'

'*The Cymbals and the Bones*.'

68

*   *   *

Well, I'd better get on with the rest of my thank-you letters now. Sarah and Simon sent me talcum-powder and soap. Charles gave me a card which contained another card inside it telling me that for a year I am a Friend of Redundant Churches. This means that I am authorised now to visit any decaying church in the United Kingdom, taking a friend with me free of charge. Henry gave me a pot plant—a transparent cyclamen, its flowers limp with thirst, its rubber-tube stalks bent down. When I watered it it gave up the ghost.

It is still quite snowy here and we had a white Christmas. I forget if I told you that. It seems a long time ago. I forget when I wrote last but think it must have been when your dress came.

Yrs, E.

4 February 1990

Dear Joan,

I have written you a great number of letters. I expect that they have been a burden—that is to say, if you have bothered to read them, for it is now about a year since you went off and I have had not one reply. As a matter of fact I have written many more letters than I have posted. I

69

am cautious now.

I gather that you are now staying in Dacca more or less permanently and I shall continue to write there. I have given up expecting answers and that, in a way, has made me freer. Many of the letters that weren't posted were not apposite. They would have told you nothing of interest or of use to you in your own situation, only mine: and since you do not seem to be able to take the slightest interest in that— well, why should you?—I use you now as diary only, as mirror image. I see you with bare feet on a shadowy verandah sipping lime-juice, skimming through my letters, thinking gratefully of all you have escaped. They can give you, I fear, little else. They are facts. They give neither of us even the solace of fiction.

Always, always you interest me, however, and still I can't see why. What is it about your flight that seems so inevitable, familiar, yet unfathomably mysterious? There is something pertinent to me about it, just out of sight. In shadow. What is the shadow? It is something much more serious than envy of you. It is certainly not a subterranean desire to be like you or become you, i.e. to be Charles's wife, oh my God, no! That nose alongside one on the pillow. Drooping over the cornflakes. Reared up before the shaving-mirror.

Sorry, Joan. I know I shouldn't laugh at someone else's husband even after she's left him. I couldn't laugh at all once, you know.

Before you packed off, I don't think I ever laughed. I don't suppose I'd laughed for—maybe ten years.

If, after all, that is what you have done—packed off. Nearly a year and nobody knows. Nobody knows a thing. Or perhaps some of them do and don't tell me. I get no news of you now, with Simon and Sarah flown and Charles submerged in Dolphin Square (I'm told they both swim up and down in that long green swimming bath every morning) and your friend Tom Hopkin quite disappeared. He is a short dream-memory, TH, and but for the earrings and the lymph-gland sweets I'd think him an hallucination.

I love the earrings still and so do Barry and the nuns. Barry says because of the earrings he wants to stick around and see what happens. He sings a song...

You know, I can't remember if I've told you all this before,

Eliza

Feb 12th

Dear Joan,

I'm sorry but this is one letter that has to be posted and which by some means or other you are to be forced to read and to answer. I shall put URGENT stickers on the envelope and I shall also telephone the Bangladesh Consulate to tell them that you are to be contacted at once. It is about Sarah.

It's all right. She is perfectly well, as I'll describe in a minute. No accident or sickness. Safe home from the skiing. You'd have heard if it had been something like that. The horrors always get through. This is a crisis of another kind. Here it is.

Yesterday Sarah rang me and asked if I would send her some things. Would I go across the road and collect them at once? Some shirts and sweaters. I went to number thirty-four and heard my feet clattering about. I climbed the sad staircase and up to Sarah's room and was just thinking that I should wash some of the clothes before I posted them, because they smelled of must, when the telephone rang. Not disconnected. You see how vague Charles has become. It was Sarah again and she asked if I was alone.

'Only ghosts.'

'I thought you mightn't be alone in your house. That's why I asked you to go to ours. It doesn't matter about the sweaters.'

'Is something wrong?'

'Oh no! Not a thing. Not the least thing.' Her voice, Joan, has changed. You know how she used to talk Birmingham/American—well, I suppose you know. Now it is a sort of clear, high, socially-OK voice of yesteryear, and

72

much much older than her years. It's rather like the Queen's. 'Oh, not a *bit*, Eliza. Just I'm rather...' Then the image shivered. The voice cracked. 'I just wondered if you might be coming to Oxford sometime.'

'I'd love to come to Oxford, Sarah. Thank you. I'd love to. I'll take you out to lunch.'

'No, not lunch. Could you come to where I'm living? To my room?'

'Well of course. I'll bring the lunch if you like.'

'No, no. That's all right. I'd just like to talk to you. I can't say more now. There's someone wanting the phone. Just behind me.'

'When shall I come? Next weekend?'

'I wondered' (careful cadences) 'if you could come today? This afternoon? There's a two-ish train.'

'I can't come today, Sarah, I have to be at The Hospice.'

'It's terribly important. Could you change it?'

'Well, I *could*. Sarah. Couldn't your father...?'

'Are you joking?' she said in Birmingham, then 'Oh, Eliza' (Her Maj.) 'please come!'

'Could you meet me at the station?'

'Well, I'm not actually able to leave my room at present. Could you get a taxi? You know Oxford. I'll give you my address.'

So I rang Mother Ambrosine who said that she could cope and Barry was beginning a

73

tapestry and had the football. I arrived in Oxford in the early afternoon and went bowling through the streets looking at all the orderly and competent young, clean and tidy, and all the girls with washed hair—full circle again to the time when I was one of them, though I never looked so fierce and sure. And, in my second year, of course I left them.

Sarah's lodgings seemed to be some sort of religious house, presumably found for her by Charles. Did you know this? I hadn't realised that Sarah is devout. From all the BVMs in the vestibule niches I thought it must be Catholic, but when at last I opened the door—nobody paying any attention to the bell—there were photographs of Greek- or Russian-Orthodox priests all the way up the stairs glaring from inside their beards. Two or three godly-looking, willowy people—small-headed men with fluting voices and bony women with good profiles and woollen stockings—were standing together in the hall. They looked through me but stopped talking. One man blew his nose. There was a hint of incense. On a board there were lists of Divine Service in the Chapel, a very great many. It looked like a religion that knew what it was up to.

I smiled but nobody spoke. I went up to the top floor and knocked on Sarah's door.

'*Hullo!*' said the Queen. She looks beautiful, Joan; bronzed from the skiing, and Charles must be giving her a very good allowance to judge from her pink silk suit. Her face is like an advertisement, lipstick shining, and the *exact* pink; hair well-cut, fingernails that never saw a sink.

'*Darling* Eliza!'

Her eyelashes are all turned up, two semi-circles dyed black. They reminded me of my long-forgotten terrible cousin in Harrogate the day she left school in 1954. Her hands were covered in enormous rings. There was a crucifix on the wall and various pictures of saints. Otherwise it was almost bare. A plastic bucket stood about, 'For the leak in the roof,' said Sarah. 'This top floor is pretty scruffy. Excuse me one sec.,' and she left the room. I wandered about.

'Coffee?' she said, coming back with some.

'Oh, yes please.'

'Excuse me.' Out she went again. This time she came back carrying a milk-jug, but it was empty. 'Isn't it a lovely day?' she said. 'So glad you could come.'

We drank our coffee or at least I drank mine and she looked hard at hers and put it down. She said, 'Half a sec.,' and carried hers from the room, returning without it. We sat for a while looking at a picture of St Ursula surrounded by her eleven thousand virgins.

'You said it was urgent, Sarah?'

'Yes,' she said. 'I'm going to have a baby.'

* * *

75

I'm sorry, Joan. I'm telling it exactly as it happened. Without doubt you'll get a formal notification from Charles in the end, but this I want you to hear precisely as it unwound. That is as it should be.

I said, 'Sarah! It's only your second term.'

She said, 'I know. I'm silly.'

'You are more than silly. You are utterly irresponsible and wrong. All your music! All those years!'

'Oh, the music's still there.'

'Yes, but *you* can't be. You can't stay at Oxford. Oh—you lunatic child.'

'I'm not. It isn't going to make any difference.'

'Sarah, are you by any chance thinking I'll organise...?'

'No, of course not.'

'I expect everyone will advise it. They will be advising it now.'

'Nobody knows yet.'

'They will. And I'm sorry. I can have nothing to do with abortions.'

'Good Lord, neither can I,' she said and we both sat looking at the eleven thousand virgins standing in clumps like a herbaceous border, all singing. Singing flowers. Eleven thousand mouths held open in neat ovals, effortlessly on top C. Easy lives.

'Oh Sarah. Why did you send for me? I know nothing about this. I never had a child. I've never looked after one.'

76

'I know, but you should have done, Eliza. You'd have loved it. You'd have loved a child.'

'What are you saying?'

'Well, I—we—we were just wondering if by any chance you felt that you could look after it for us? You and Henry. Just at first, for a year or two.'

'Are you mad? Do you think you'd be allowed to hand over a baby to a—to an acquaintance of your mother living in south London and you in Oxford—a woman who wouldn't have the first idea what to do with it?'

'You would. I know you would. You could do anything. You are so successful, always. Look how the dog settled in, and Daddy.'

'Sarah!'

'Well, it was the first thing I thought of. I know that it would be all right. I thought of you at once. Instinctively.'

'Sarah, apart from anything else, Henry isn't living with me any more.'

'Where's he gone now?'

'He—well, he's living with your father as a matter of fact. In Dolphin Square. He's left me.'

'What—for Daddy?'

'No. Nothing like that.'

'We must thank God,' she said, looking at St Ursula's ecstatic face, 'for small mercies. Or maybe not. Might have been the very thing.'

'Eliza,' she said. We had been sitting silent. All we could hear was the January wind

77

battering the dormer window and a holy sound drifting up from some other virginal choir in the chapel below. 'Eliza—excuse me.'

When she came back she said, 'It's bad at present. I looked it up in a book in Blackwell's and it says it will be better after the third month.'

'Sarah, the child's father...'

'Yes. We're going to tea with him. That is, if you don't mind. I said you'd come.'

'But it's an intimate matter. It's a thing for your parents. Your own father...'

'Look Eliza, *be* sensible.' (Brum again.) 'And Ma's in Bangladesh having experiences.'

'She must come home.' (Yes, Joan.)

'I think she won't. She's ill you know. Gone potty. Flipped. We can't get near her. It's a year now.'

I should like to be able to tell you now, Joan, that at this point Sarah began to cry. She did not. She crossed her silky legs, took an old-world powder compact out of her pocket and looked this way and that, searching her face for signs of weakness. Again she reminded me of my dreadful cousin, Annie Cartwright, thirty years ago and I cannot say why, but thinking this, the room became suddenly cold. I found that I was shaking. It was a relief when Sarah did something equally unsophisticated but true to her own self. She took a small white handkerchief from her pocket and began to suck the end of it.

'Oh, all right, Sarah. All right. Of course I'll come. When are we to go?'

'Half-past three. We're late. Tea is three forty-five until four-thirty.'

'I suppose it's a college. We never had tea when I was an undergraduate, except a bun or a tray we pushed along. Won't it be very public?'

'No, it's a college but it's very quiet. We'll be in the Fellows' drawing room. He's a Professor.'

'Sarah—he must be ninety!'

'You're out of date Eliza,' said the Queen, collecting a handbag and, great heaven, gloves. 'There are some *frightfully* young ones now. Reg is barely fifty.'

'Reg?' I said. Somehow Reg did not sound like a Professor. Had she been duped, I wondered? Had I misheard? Was it the college janitor? Porter? Approaching the porter through the great gates of a college, announcing ourselves to him through the glass of his little office, it seemed unlikely. A delightful man. He smiled with avuncular pleasure on seeing Sarah who seemed to be familiar to him. He said that Professor Hookaneye was expecting us and that he would ring through.

'Hookaneye?'

'Yes,' said the Queen. 'They come from Tewkesbury.'

'I honestly don't see that where the

79

Hookaneyes come from…'

'Oh golly,' she said, and disappeared behind a golden buttress.

Beyond her, over the greensward, I beheld a very slender man as tall as Henry, six foot four at least. He towered above us, suspended in the air as on a magician's string. His long head looked like a Leicestershire sheep.

Well, Joan, first I suppose I should reassure you in one department. He is perfectly respectable. He is I think probably the most respectable man I've ever met. He was wearing a pale grey double-breasted suit, dark blue tie and highly polished shoes. He walked carefully, his head a little dipped. He had thick grey hair like a helmet. Every possible bit of him was covered up. I never saw a man who showed so little skin—unless perhaps a member of the IRA or Klu Klux Klan and I've never actually seen either of these. The idea of Professor Hookaneye's nakedness was awesome. A holy mystery.

'I'm sorry to say,' said he, 'that we must go first to my rooms. The other member of our tea-party is late.'

'Other member?'

'Yes. We're only allowed one guest per Fellow, so I have had to call in a colleague for the godmother.'

I looked round for the godmother and then glared at Sarah.

'I'd be *quite* happy to miss tea,' I said, 'and

80

talk here.'

We had arranged ourselves on his Grecian sofa. I wondered if this was where the seduction had taken place and looked intently at the Professor who had put his finger-tips together as though in prayer. This seemed hopeful. We sat. The gold buildings shone in through the window. The room was a miracle of order. A tome stood upon a lectern. It appeared to be written in Sanskrit. I thought the Professor's eyes had taken on a peculiar look when I said, 'talk'.

I said, 'I should like to talk to you *at length.* The sooner this is over the better.'

He said vaguely, rather cross I thought, 'But I think you would like to have the experience of seeing us all at tea?' He gave me a nervous— and I have to say it—sweet though bewildered smile. 'Don't you think your godmother would like that, Sarah? Sarah has often visited me here by herself, Mrs Peabody. Haven't you, Sarah?'

'Yes, I'm *quite sure she has,*' I said, looking at him very straight. 'Of course I should be honoured to go down to tea, but *would it be private enough*? I think that there will be much to say. With Sarah's mother in Bangladesh and Charles not readily available. Charles is her father...'

'Oh, I know Joan and Charles,' he said with ease.

'I am then even more surprised.' My

81

blackest stare I could see was giving him pause. He seemed in deep thought now, watching me carefully. I examined my fingernails and found them interesting. They had a hazy green line beneath each rim, pale, marine and eerie.

Then he swung himself off his wing chair and said, 'Oh, you know, Sarah—shall we risk it, hey? Go down to tea without the other chaperon?' and led us off through many a twist and turn along pattering marble passages and into a chamber where figures sat about in the shadows like uneasy thoughts, either alone or in well-behaved little groups, eating and sipping and now and then glinting at each other. There was a very cruel silence as Professor Hookaneye paced by with the two of us. I almost felt sorry for him, and tried to make myself invisible so that Sarah could look like the sole, permitted guest, but as I was wearing my old green trousers, zip-jacket and the earrings—I had had no time to change if I was to catch the train that Sarah had commanded—this was not easy. Sarah was certainly not invisible in her sharp pink silk and Fifties Harrogate jewellery (wherever had she found it?) and gleaming legs. She was like a flamingo in a poultry house.

There was a vast round mahogany table with plates of thin bread and butter, slab cake, Marmite and honey. We had to help ourselves. Reg brought us cups of faint tea and led us to a far corner so that, he said, we might observe.

I observed. All those skulls full of brains. Some of the finest brains in the world. I could almost see the brains. The heads seemed lit from within so that each white spongey mass shone in the semi-darkness like a miner's lamp or a gigantic glow-worm. An internal halo.

Halo, by God, I thought, examining Professor Hookaneye who was lying back stirring his tea with benignity. What if I were now to say loud and clear, 'Professor Hookaneye, what do you propose to do about Sarah? Were you really serious in suggesting that I should adopt your child?' I thought of what had happened to Sarah in his ascetic den, her young life spoiled, her future in sad collapse, all her care-free flute-playing in the roses done. I debated whether to pick up my slice of bread and honey and slap it on his face.

But he talked quietly and precisely on, giving us a friendly and delightful rundown on the great men before us. 'I thought you might like to see the Chapel and our dining room,' he said to me ('Go with him,' mouthed the Queen) and we processed from the room followed by glances that said, 'Two guests! *Two* guests!'

And poor Sarah at the entrance to the dining room fled again. Reg Hookaneye said, 'She doesn't seem quite the thing. Overworking'— and I was speechless. But he and I wandered on until we came to a room where after dinner each evening dessert is taken. We stood looking at silver candlesticks and a fruit bowl like a Van der Meer and a great flagon of port set ready. So beautiful.

'It is a privilege to be part of it,' he said—what a dear humble man he sounds. I said, 'Since we are alone, Professor Hookaneye, I should like to sit down for a while and have this business out with you.'

'Oh, we can't sit here,' he said, 'I can't possibly let you sit down here.'

'Nevertheless we have to talk some time about Sarah's baby.'

'Sarah's *what*?'

Then he turned so white that the colour seemed to drain even out of his suit. He seized the back of a throne, pulled it away from the table and collapsed on it. He stared at me.

'But you knew why I had come?'

'You ... She said only that she wanted to bring her godmother to tea.'

'Professor Hookaneye—do you mean you didn't know? About your own child?'

He stared on and on. Then he laid his head down beside the grapes. I heard voices outside, one Sarah's and the other a pleasant voice that seemed familiar. 'Sorry I was late for tea, Reg. Unforgivable. I was in the Codrington. Good heavens—Eliza Peabody!' It was Tom Hopkin, very bright, his glasses flashing with good-nature.

'I think,' he said, 'Good Lord, Dr Hookaneye has fainted. Here, I'll take his head. Somebody get hold of his feet.'

84

'I will,' said Sarah, tottering up.

'No, no, I will,' I said, 'Sarah mustn't lift anything heavy.' And then I thought, Well perhaps she should.

In the end she and I took a long thin leg each and Tom the narrow shoulders and we carried Dr Hookaneye out of the room and on to the quadrangle to lie him down on the pale stones near a drain. No one was about. We paused.

And then Joan, a very horrible and extraordinary thing happened. Hookaneye disintegrated. The lanky, beautifully finished, excellently dressed body of Dr Hookaneye shimmered and vibrated and melted and liquified and began to twirl itself down into the mediaeval drainage so that in no time at all only the toe of a shoe showed there—polished black, like the top of a little lost cricket ball. Dr Hookaneye, Joan, was gone.

I raised my eyes to the others and beheld Tom Hopkin leading Sarah away. She appeared to be weeping. Her head was near his shoulder and his arm was round her. I looked back at the drain and blop, blop, bleep, gurgle, now the toe juddered, shuddered, reverberated and all in one movement was gone. The drain was full of Reg. Pray that the college tonight is not troubled by cloud-burst. I ran to Sarah.

'I'll see to her,' said Tom.

'I must find her Tutor.'

'I shall find her Tutor. You must go. Go home, Mrs Peabody. Have a long rest. You don't seem yourself.'

'You called me Mrs Peabody!'

'Do go, Eliza, I'll ring.'

'I shall have to tell Joan. I shall tell her everything.'

They stood staring. Tom then stepped across from Sarah and kissed me on the cheek. He lifted a finger to my face, traced a line affectionately along the edge of it. 'Eliza, Eliza,' he said.

'You'll miss your train,' said Sarah. She looked rosy, invigorated. She was not being sick.

'I'll find you a taxi,' said Tom.

'You are obsessed by taxis.'

'I must take Sarah home.'

'Will you report...?' I looked back at the drain.

'What?'

'Well, the disappearance of Dr Hookaneye.'

'Oh, he's always doing it,' said Tom. 'Don't worry. He'll be right as rain in the morning.'

'As rain! As right as rain?'

'Don't *worry* so, dear Eliza,' they said together, like two nurses.

'I think I'd like to walk to the station.'

And saying goodbye to the delightful porter (had he seen? was he used to it, too?) I set off through Oxford with feverishly beating heart, coming at last to the gates of my old college.

And there I quite forgot about the station but turned automatically in through the gates and enquired for my own old Tutor who I knew still occupies her old rooms. I knocked on the door and found her as always perched on the window-seat, pen in hand. Through the window, behind her, willows swung their ropes about, studded with buds. I could see young women walking in twos and threes, calling and laughing, their hair flipped by the wind. Alert, light on their feet, feeling the spring.

'Eliza—but how nice. Do sit.'

I sat with her and for a time did not speak.

'You have caught me between tutorials. Dear Eliza—why didn't you write? We might have arranged for a talk. It must be four years.'

'I had to come up all of a sudden. To a sort of—godchild.'

'Not your child, alas.'

'No.'

'Are you still sad about that?'

'Not today. Not now. I know now that I couldn't have coped.'

'Your godchild is in trouble?'

'She is in some—I think she is in the power of some evil energy. Some malign force. It attacked me, too. Something very queer. As if we were wearing other people's glasses. Her lover...'

But in the quiet room I knew so well, with the parchment-covered cocoa-tin of coloured spills in the grate, the nice noisy gas fire, the white bookcases all over the walls, the blue Pissarro oil-sketch between the windows and the silver cigarette-box on the table beside a pile of essays—the smell of books, ink, flowers, peace—I said no more. Let me give thanks for this unchanging place.

'Cigarette, Eliza?'

Whoever now offers cigarettes? But who knows, should I accept, that some long and scaly thing may begin to surge and swell and spill out of the box, flow over the table, down and across the old Persian rug at my feet, reaching me only to wind itself, wind itself...

'Something is wrong, Eliza.'

'No. Not at all. Just rather a strange afternoon. I don't understand the young any more.'

'Has this girl a mother?'

'Oh yes. She's run off. To the East.'

'How very antique. And she has left you in charge?'

'Yes. No. Well, not in so many words.'

'Has she a father?'

'Yes.'

'Then leave it to him. They have to make their own beds in college now, literally and figuratively. And lie on them. And suffer if they find that they are full of coals.'

'Oh, she's been lying in beds all right—but then so did we. She looks so lost. So unhappy. I must go now, Dr Pye. Goodbye.'

'Come back soon. Write to me.'

'I never write letters.'

I was gone, and in the windy street I looked for some cloak to put round myself, with which to wrap the same body and bones that had walked this road to the station thirty years ago—the same arrangement of chemicals, water and fat that had been in flaming love with Henry. A body that had given up Oxford for him, all its self for him, in a public renunciation ceremony in Merton Chapel.

Oxford to Paddington. In the train I write you this letter in an exercise book bought on the station. Envelope too. I close my eyes. I try not to think. I write on.

Fields and cows. Streets then hedges. In the hedges, new blood-red shoots and white worms, the straw-stalks of last year's flowers. Here for a season, then goodnight. This the end of my day, Joan, is the beginning of a new age for you. Your first grandchild is coming. Someone is eyeing you out there in Bangladesh, an invisible eye nobody has seen and that up to now has only seen the dark. It will find you. When you are dead he will talk about you. 'My grandmother went crazy and disappeared to Bangladesh and nobody ever saw her again.' You and Sarah will never be on your own again though. You will take equal shares in this new human being. There is no father, for Dr Hookaneye is down the drain.

89

He is washed up, and I shall post this at Paddington.

Sincerely yours,
Eliza

❧❧❧

Very dark the house is, very thick it smells (poor dogs). The phone is ringing.

'Hullo?'

'Oh, Eliza.'

(La, it is the Queen!)

'Eliza, I'm so terribly sorry.'

'Don't apologise, Sarah, you are right off-course apologising to me.'

'We wondered—Mr Hopkin and I—we wondered if . . . Are you all right? Eliza?'

'Quite all right. Just a little puzzled. No—not all right.'

'Eliza, I should have been clearer. I think you misheard. Professor Hookaneye is my *godfather.*'

'But that is even more appalling.'

'He has nothing to do with the baby. I said we were going to have tea with my *godfather.* Not the baby's father. The father's just a guy at Merton. I don't like the father much. I wouldn't dream of involving him. I thought you and Uncle Reg might just—you know—give advice. Are you there? The father's a first-year too. But when I say father—Eliza?'

'I'm sorry, Sarah I must ring off at once.'

90

'Why?'

'I wrote to your mother. On the train. I posted it at Paddington.'

'Oh my glory,' cried neither the Queen nor the Brum-Bronx but Sarah's heart's blood, 'Great heaven!'

'I'll send a telex. A fax. A "disregard" message.'

'But, listen, Eliza, don't go yet...'

But I did, which will soon, pray God, explain much to you, I flew to the post-office which was of course by now closed.

Fax. How does one send a fax? You need an office. Henry's office. I stepped into the phone-box on the High Street and realised it was eight o'clock in the evening. All would be shut. I'd have to ring Dolphin Square. What if I got Charles? A risk to be taken.

'Hullo? Oh, hullo Henry, this is Eliza.'

A sticky silence.

'Henry. It's not about us. Or the dogs. It's urgent. I have to send a fax to Joan.'

'Oh, Eliza, please.'

'It's very short. Will you get it done somehow? Get it to Bangladesh? Find the Embassy number—you must know how. Sarah's in trouble. She's not in quite such trouble as I thought she was, but she's still in fearful trouble.'

'Eliza,' little nervous cough, 'Eliza dear, take hold for a moment.'

'Let me just dictate—oh, Henry, please.'

'Since we are at last speaking, Eliza, could we perhaps mention for a moment the current account?'

'Oh yes. Have it back. I can manage. It was hysteria. But please could you send this fax?'

'Yes. My dear. Hem, hem—of course. Also, Eliza, why won't you answer my letters? About the portrait? Somebody wrote from Epsom offering to buy it. I'm rather perturbed.'

'Tell him it's not for sale. Your wife is unauthorised to sell it. Anything, but just ... To Joan: "Terrible mistake Hookaneye godfather not father disregard letter written in train Oxford to Paddington have made muddle. Writing again Eliza." All right?'

'All right of course. Hold on. "Hookaneye godfather". Is it some code? I don't understand...'

I rang off and reeled into the road and watched the cars roll by. Then I turned homeward, the long way round, through quiet side-streets, walking slowly, looking first over one garden hedge and then another. Hard polished knobs of spring bulbs were showing, one small lawn an embroidery of crocuses. Now and then there passed me by the home-coming men of the parish in their crumpled London suits. Their briefcases for the stint of the evening's work looked heavy, their mouths taut, eyes in a glaze of desire for the double Gordon's. Some said, 'Oh, *hullo*, Eliza,' and made as if to stop (I've not been about much

92

recently) but I smiled and drifted on until I came to the doors of St Saviour's.

Our Church stays open quite late. We risk our treasures. Anyway, there's always someone inside. Tonight the organ roared. Someone practising. A shadow or two lurked about the pews and a light clatter was coming from the vestry. I knelt in a pew and waited for God.

He was not at home.

When in doubt, pray. By rote, if nothing else is possible. Traditional instruction. Until you grow calm and the line clears.

Our Father which art in Heaven whatever have I been doing in Oxford? Thy will be done in earth as it is in Heaven help Sarah what a terrible mess she's in and I'm sure I don't know what to do about it and forgive us our trespasses sounds very like youth and silliness but after all not *that* inexperienced think of all those boys at school, and Mozart at one a.m. She must know something of men by now Thy kingdom come Thy will be done and maybe it is as well we don't know whose this child may be Shakespeare's was a shot-gun wedding there is always some sort of pattern perhaps? In earth there are so many mysteries as is not in Heaven and when it comes down to it why should I *not* look after Sarah's child? I might be allowed. I have nothing else in my life except The Hospice. I must fight for my sanity my kingdom, and Thy power and Thy glory for ever and ever, Amen.

I looked up to see the Curate looking down on me. I made the sign of the Cross and got off my knees.

'Sorry, Eliza. Thought you were free.'

'Oh yes. I'm free. I'm perfectly free.' I waited for him to say, 'How are you? I've often called but you've never been in. Can I help you in any way? I've heard about it all.' That's what the Vicar would say, but we never see him—the parish is too big and he's worn out. The Vicar and his wife are marvellous they tell me, but miles away across the Parish. The Curate said nothing.

Looking at his sharp face I thought, I ought to try him. There must be something in his head except parish difficulties. After all it takes six years to become a priest—long as a vet. He must have learned something about sick souls since the first flush of his vocation. Even though his sermons are all about his summer holidays.

'Could I talk to you, Nick?'

'Of course. You could. You could.'

The organist pulled down the front of the organ and clicked off the switches and clattered out of the south door, calling goodnight. The pew-dusters seemed to have departed. The Curate and I were alone in the last of the day, the single, clear-glass window near us still bluish. the big Cross on the altar shrouded in black gauze for Lent. 'It's getting dark in here,' he said. 'Can't see my watch. I'm off to a meeting. Late already, I expect. Oh dear. Get in touch.'

I thought, Sit down here and now. *Look* at me. In this pew in front of me. Turn your head sideways and bow it a little. Kindly. Christ listened. He really *thought* about women. The woman taken in adultery. He doodled with His finger in the dust. (Wonder what he wrote? 'Let her be.') Christ listened quietly. I said, 'I suppose I couldn't talk to you *now*? You see I'm frightened. I saw someone disintegrate today.'

'I'd forgotten you work at The Hospice. Yes, the first sight of death is a shock.'

'It wasn't a death, I don't think. It was at Oxford.'

'Oh, there's a lot of disintegration there. Look, Eliza—I'm so sorry but I have to go. There's a Finance Committee.'

'Yes, all right.'

And it happened again. I was looking at the pointed, worried little face, the busy black eyes flicking away through an invisible appointments-book and found that I was looking through skin into bone and beyond the bone into the squashy pillow of the brain. Through the contour map of the face and out again through the bristly back of the neck to the carving on the lectern behind him. 'I'm seeing through you,' I thought and even, I suppose, said, for he replied, peering down at his watch, 'Seeing through me are you Eliza? Oh dear—sorry about that.'

Soon—I waited for it to happen again—he will liquify and flow away. He will become nothing beneath the cloth. He will become water. Water under the bridge. Water running away down through the iron mesh and the aisle's heating pipes and his shabby cassock will be left lying, and his shoes, that I see are a pair of boy's shabby trainers looking out from below the hem, will be lying alongside.

As I looked, rather tenderly, at the trainers the Curate began to solidify again, to hold his shape. When I dared look again at the face, I saw its poor little mouth, sharp little teeth bared in a Pastoral smile. 'I don't want to take up your time selfishly,' said I, 'but—I'm so sorry; I've not asked before—but I must talk *now*.'

'The trouble is, Eliza, that it isn't *my* time. My time is not my own, especially today. It's been a frightful day. I've had three committees already. There are simply not enough of us.'

'You should let us help you.'

'Us?'

'Women.'

'Oh well—you all do marvellously, but come on, Eliza, full participation is something you and I really *would* have to talk about.'

'Well, could we?'

'I'm really frightfully sorry...' and he was gone with a flick and a flourish of skirts.

* * *

96

When I reached the bottom of Rathbone Road two streets away I climbed the hill to our flat bit at the top—the top of the top, the peak of the peak—and my feet were dragging like weights. The Gargerys were in their front garden preparing for summer with paper sacks of fertiliser and shining garden implements. 'Come and have a drink,' they called. 'We never see you now.' She took off her gardening gloves and shook them, and he laid aside his half-moon edging-tool. They came quickly to the gate. They looked at me curiously. 'Come and celebrate. Don't go home alone. Sam has got into Mrs Rigby's.'

'But he's hardly five.'

'Oh *yes*!' They laughed and he put his arm around her. 'There's an entrance exam and a year's waiting list for Mrs Rigby now.'

She said, 'She won't take them unless they can read, you know.'

He said, 'And the Basics.'

She said, 'She likes them to be able to sing in tune.'

He said, 'Feet on the ladder. Do come in.'

I said, 'It's been a long day. Give Sam a kiss from me,' and I felt their troubled eyes at my back. Good Gargerys. So perfect. It will take them half an hour to clean the forks and trowels. They will clean them, still in their gardening gloves, their hands and nails all pure within.

'I've been ringing and ringing since last

time,' cried The Queen as I stepped into the house and picked up a frantic telephone. 'Where did you go to? Eliza? Are you there? I didn't finish. You went tearing off before I finished. I wasn't telling you only that Uncle Hookaneye was my *godfather*, I was telling you that it is *all right*.'

'All right?'

'Yes. Something has set me right. I must have relaxed or something after tea, when Uncle Hookaneye had to leave us. I think it was you, Eliza. You were so marvellous, coming all this way. And I did truly mean it—I *would* have trusted you to take my baby.'

'You mean there's been some development? With the father?'

'No, Eliza. I mean it is *all right*. I wasn't going to have a baby after all. It was a phantom pregnancy. Like a dog.'

So that I can now sign myself your undeniable friend,

E. P.

March 10th

Well—here I am again.

I thought, Joan, the next morning that I might clean the house, beginning with the kitchen. You remember that I told you—that is, if it was a posted letter—that Angela long since left you, left number thirty-four? Well, she has now decided to leave me at number forty-three. After twenty years, Joan. She was with me long, long before you came upon the scene. We have been through great events together, Angela and I, and I have told myself for years how truly loyal she is. Never a word when Henry began to live in the study. She never even commented when she had to clear up all the spilt soup and tins and bits of bacon round the Baby Belling. She didn't object when we had to take in your dog. Very oddly, she used to say, 'What dog? I don't see another dog,' even though your dog hated her from the first and let her know it.

Angela's never been a talker, of course, and by no means is she cheery. Slap, bang, crash, and you know she has arrived. Sniff, slam, sigh, and the monologue about the rareness of buses from Fulham gathers momentum for the morning. We both, if you remember, were upset when she suddenly yelled at us that we were paying a bus-fare two years out of date (though she's way over sixty and travels on them free) and there was always the business of the manner in which she received presents: the stiff and brief nod and then the stories of the good fortune of her friends who have employers so very grateful for almost no work at all.

I can't say I've ever really *liked* Angela. She is one of those who by her presence makes a claim for gratitude. 'So good of you to come on such a wet day, Angela. Of course I'll run you home.' Making conversation in the traffic-jam on Putney High Street while she sits with a safety-pin mouth.

I suppose, Joan, Angela really couldn't stand us, when you come to think about it. And from our point of view it is a great strain to have someone in the house three mornings a week whose pleasure is to register dislike, even though you call it her eccentricity. But I did love the once-beautiful bloom on the bath, the cleanliness of the kitchen floor and the dazzle of the door-knocker. One day I came home and she had shampooed the dog. She had hosed down his basket in the garden and laundered all his rugs. Toby lay under the table, quivering. I said, 'How kind of you, Angela. What a washing-line of rugs! I'm surprised you didn't hang the dog up too,' and she said, 'Hang it I'd like.'

Henry and I always thought her brusque but true. Underneath the venom, a gold heart that loved us.

A month—oh maybe more, maybe several months ago—I came down one morning and she was clashing and bashing as usual at the sink and I was yawning. I said, 'Ah, Angela, hullo, let's have some coffee,' and she spun

100

round with the mop in her hand and her eyes alight with hate. She screamed, 'No. I've had enough. It's the end of the line. It's the end of my time.'

'Oh, but Angela, what—?'

'Four buses passed me. Up at five to clean seven offices and staircases. Grandchildren measles and here's filth, and you in bed and that fag hanging out of you. And them earrings.'

'Angela!'

'And him gone poor soul. Driven to that Belling. Then driven even away from that Belling. Gone I'm not told where nor yet explained to. It's him I've worked for all these years if you want to know, God help him in his high position and nobody to look after him and him so polite and serious-minded, never various. I'd work for him yet, but you no more. I'm finished here.'

'Did you say all this across the Road when you left them? Is this a repeat performance of thirty-four when that family split up?'

'You're talking your rubbish again. I'm leaving.'

'Oh Angela—twenty years.'

'You was a different woman twenty years ago.'

'Would you like Henry's address? I'm sure he'd like some help at Dolphin Square though it's rather far from Fulham. They both would.'

'*Both*,' she said. 'So that's the way it is. I

101

can't say I'm surprised,' and the door exploded on her for the last time.

And so, Joan, today, after a poor night's sleep, I come down to my unloved kitchen—fag and earrings—sit at the table, behold the dogs and think, Shampoo today would not be amiss, but sit on.

Make coffee, long-armed. Behold dresser covered in marigold plates from my mother's country childhood. Behold grime on plates. Sit on.

Look at Aga cooker, reflect on nativity of trickles down its front, the grease and gravy on the once-so-shining domes. Sit on.

Again, long-armed, open kitchen door for dogs to go out. Dogs stretch and walk stiff-legged to smell the day. Watch dogs scratch, roll, rub down their ears, sigh, pee hugely, and return to their basket.

Think of Oxford. Think of Sarah, now presumably addressing herself to her work.

Think of the eleven thousand virgins.

Think of love.

Think of Henry stepping towards me over Magdalen Bridge. Think of me at twenty blushing as he approaches. Tongue-tied with longing, but such chaste kisses.

Think of wedding in Merton Chapel, Henry morning-dress, very sage for his few years, and me in a cream silk suit—raw silk, not at all shiny. Henry with First Class Honours in Natural Sciences and a small motor-car with a

102

lid and little windows of what looked like horn, as in a mediaeval castle. And the two of us belting across France—Henry going quite fast!—looking at real mediaeval castles en route. Staying at cheap inns. A stone stair overhung with creeper leading to an upper barn-like room with stone walls and old beams and a bed like a galleon.

Through the shutters in the morning, dazzling slits of sunlight. Cock-crow. People calling in the fields. The *petit déjeuner*. Coffee in bowls. Sitting to drink it on the window-seat, the sun already hot. Outside the rolling vineyards going to the horizon, rows of charcoal stumps, red earth, promise. Henry's beautiful hands, Joan.

The front door bell rang and after a while I answered and it was Anne Robin. I lit another cigarette.

Could she come in?

'Gosh, Eliza,' she said. 'I say. I haven't been here for ages. How lovely.' (Surveying chaos.)

'Milk? I'm afraid it's only instant.'

'Is it de-caff? Oh gosh, sorry, but it's this silly health thing.'

I found the de-caff. 'Sugar?'

'Oh, crikey, no. Eliza—oh, hullo Toby. We don't see you about much in the road now, do we? Eliza, how are *you*? We don't see you either.'

She has the most polished cheeks. Do you remember? Clear eyes. The whites are blue as a baby's. And clean, clean fingernails. And toenails I'm sure. Broad white edges filed into broad half-moons. I droop. Standing. Over my coffee cup. Her hair looks just washed, beautifully cut and each particular hair doth stand like a golden wire. With the solicitor husband and his international practice, the five healthy children all now at boarding-school and scarcely needing her, with her own effulgent bounce and so much money she doesn't know what to do with it, she now writes fiction. Her little study is all done out in William Morris wall-paper, sixty pounds a roll. Her word-processor stands on her George III writing-desk near a vase of flowers à la Vita Sackville-West. She is always being interviewed on television as the fully mature woman with the perfect life. She is asked her views on Margaret Drabble and Proust, at least she was until she confused the two. Then she came whizzing down the ladder somewhat and was nearly out of the game for good. She never speaks of that!

Beside the word-processor and the flowers is a photograph of husband George when young without the gin-hammocks. I remember now that it was you who said—the only unkind thing I remember of you: why does everybody dislike George?—that it must be some sort of trick photography, one of those things done on the pier by sticking your face through a hole in a cardboard figure. Anyway, there's George in gold and white braid, like *Lives of a Bengal Lancer*. Before he took the old yo-ho.

'How's George?'

'Oh goodness, *George*. He's *fine*. I suppose. Of course I hardly see him. When he's home I'm away on one of my promotional tours, and vice versa. He's in Hong Kong at present. Isn't it sad the way none of us sees much of our husbands now? In the Road I mean. We've all done so well. Got so rich. And my dear, the next generation will be richer still, they work even harder. It's the penalty, isn't it? It's a hard one.'

'It's good that you have your work,' I said, not jumping.

'Oh—my *salvation*! My children's books. Well, that's what people call them.'

'Oh, but I'm sure they're not.'

'I'm not a bit ashamed of it you know if they *are*.' Her cheeks had begun to glow.

'Of course not. I didn't mean that at all?'

'Mean what? After all, there's Mrs Molesworth.'

We looked into our de-caffs and thought of Mrs Molesworth and I found that tears were trembling in my eyes and were about to splash out, tears of longing. Longing for a white-stockinged, pig-tailed world. Bat and ball. Lemonade. Days ages and ages long, and people laughing. Anne was examining my filthy kitchen.

'I've just heard,' she said, 'that you've lost

105

Angela.'

'Yes. Long ago. She first left Joan, then me.'

Anne Robin looked serious, 'D'you want someone else? I'm sure mine would give you an hour or two.'

'Oh, no thanks. There's nothing to do now, really, since Henry left. I might as well clean up after myself.'

'*About* that...'

'Yes?'

'Oh well, nothing. I just wondered if there's anything one could do?'

'About Henry? No, I shouldn't think so. He's gone off with Charles, you know. He wants a divorce.'

'So it is true? Nobody quite knows.'

'Well, I don't quite know myself.'

'I mean, we wondered if you'd like to talk about it? In the Road? You've always been so good whenever anything went wrong. The nice notes you used to send. And the advice you used to give. "Counselling" it's called now. So natural and unprofessional...'

'I wrote a note too many. I wrote a note to Joan.'

'Ah,' she said. 'Now *Joan*.' She looked at me nervously.

'Do you ever feel you have written a word too many, Anne?'

'Too many? Well, mine are just tiny books you know. Not didactic in any way. Just *fun* books. No, I don't think I've written too many.

Nothing like as many as Enid Blyton did. I have the same difficulty as she did you know, they just *flow* out of me. I just use the same plot again and again and nobody notices. I wish I got more reviews though. I say, you won't tell anyone all this, will you, Eliza?'

'I'm sure that children are very pleased you write so much. I expect they love you.'

'Yes. Well, no. Well I'm not sure. You know the awful thing is, Eliza, I'm not sure that children read my books at all. I'm just known in the Children's Book World and creative writing classes. But—you won't tell a soul this, will you Eliza?—it seems so conceited for someone like me to push in among the wonderful people like Salman Rushdie and Beckett and Lancaster Forbes and so on, but actually I've had an adult novel accepted. Under an assumed name.'

'I'm so glad.'

'You see, I always thought of myself as an adult writer even when I was a child. I mean, no child would ever want to be only a *children*'s writer, would it? And look at Blake. There's nothing more childish than Blake, is there? I don't see much difference myself between adults and children, do you?'

'Yes, I do.'

'Oh. Really? I didn't know you ever thought about such things, Eliza, I mean not having had any children.'

I watched the dark face of the de-caff.

'My trouble is that I had so many children and kept them around for so long. None of them went away to school till they were ten you know. When they were at home I think I began to think like a child. They seemed older than me. I *am* a bit childish.' (Oh my dear Anne, you have been listening at doors.) 'And I've rather had to grit my teeth in the adult novel to do the—you know, the sexual bits. The girl who advised me on it—you know, my Editor, she's very young and utterly contemporary and hungry-looking, d'you know her hands shook all the time with nerves, a nice girl—well, she asked me to put in a masturbation scene.'

'Whatever for?'

'She said that these days it's expected.'

Mrs Molesworth hastily left the room and, 'I'm sorry, Anne,' said I, 'I'm hopeless at this sort of conversation. I don't read that sort of thing.'

'*Don't* you? But, you know, we mustn't be prudish. We ought to reflect the real world.'

'But masturbation isn't the real world, Anne. It's just fantasising.'

'It can be quite nice in itself,' said Anne, and then turned puce.

'What I do like about you,' I said, very quick, sharp, fast before she fainted with shame, 'is the way you tell stories. That tale you told about Joan buying the tent and the gun in the Army and Navy Stores...'

'That wasn't Joan,' she said, 'I'd never call

anyone *Joan*. There's no one called Joan under the age of fifty. There's absolutely *no one* called Joan in my books.'

'Not a book,' I said. 'It was Joan—our Joan. You were telling me about Joan. At number thirty-four.'

She leaned forward and looked carefully in my ash-tray and at my heap of stubs. Then at her chalky half-moons. 'Eliza...'

'Yes?'

'We're so worried. In the Road. We've been talking. We've been having meetings about you.'

I looked at her.

'Eliza, I suggested and they—well, some of them—agreed that you must get a job. Get something to do.'

I said, 'Ah.'

*　　*　　*

For, you see, it happens, Joan, that Anne and her friends do not know that before any of them came to live here, soon after I had stopped travelling abroad with Henry, I did have a job, of a kind, for a short time. I took it out of shame for my idleness and with reluctance, for I was marched into it by Lady Gant.

In those days Lady Gant sat on many committees about the town, having in attendance an unpaid shadowy creature called

109

Bella. Bella Bentley. She was always smiling. You can still see Bella about, still in her Sixties mini-skirts and bouffant hair, though she's all of fifty. Sometimes she wears little suits with brooches. She lived in those days somewhere down by the railway in a bed-sit and did a clerking job in London, though I think it must have been part-time because almost every afternoon she could be found at Gant's standing in the hall smiling at mountains of old clothes for jumble sales, or in the sitting room wading through toppling piles of papers and accounts, or in the kitchen making passes with her hands above elderly sandwiches and heavy jam-sponges awaiting transport to fêtes. Gant floated about giving orders. It was before she got this tumour on her head—did I mention that?

One day Gant asked if she could come and see me. 'For luncheon,' she said. 'Nothing elaborate,' and in she swept with Bella behind her, Bella smiling, the legs beneath the mini-skirt grown rather stringy. Gant wore her usual look of outrage, the face of a portentous mushroom. As they took off their coats Gant passed a finger over the hall table and examined it for dust. She was not aware of doing it, any more than she knew that when she picked up her fork for the cheese soufflé (packet; still learning to cook after diplomatic immunity—still am) she polished it with her napkin. Bella not only noticed but noticed me

110

noticing and out of loyalty picked up her own fork and dabbed at it; whereupon Gant cried out, 'Whatever are you doing, Bella?'

'Now, what we are here for, Bella and I,' she said, 'is to see if we can persuade you to work at The Shires. I know you've recently been out of sorts. The best thing in the world for you would be to get really busy. We don't ask much of the Secretaryship of The Shires. Minutes, accounts, liaison with the State sector now and then, that sort of thing. It's a friendly little committee. What I call a listening committee. And of course there is the rota of drivers to be drawn up. The drivers who take the babies into London for adoption. You would be called upon to do some of this. Most rewarding.'

I said that there was nobody in the whole country who could be less qualified to do this work than I. It was impossible.

'That attitude, Eliza, has often proved the foundation of a useful, dedicated life. Bella, don't keep all the butter to yourself. After all—what on earth are you doing with yourself now that you are back in England? Cleaning this great house all day?'

I said that I lived a private life and did not care about team work of any kind.

'You know The Shires of course?'

I did. I did.

The Shires, dear Joan, is gone now but not long gone—just before you arrived here. It was a home for unmarried mothers that stood for

111

nearly a century in the middle of the Common. It was founded by three mysterious sisters in Derbyshire, called Shire, who had most startlingly for Derbyshire left all their wealth to unmarried pregnant girls unpopular with their families. It was a fine solid house with encouraging views and healthy air. There was a kitchen of scrubbed tables and a dormitory of reliable iron bedsteads, a hall and stairs uncarpeted and vast. There was opportunity therefore for exercise, for the girls did the housework at the early stage of pregnancy and helped with the cooking towards the end. When their time came they were driven to the local maternity hospital where they stayed for up to two weeks and were then driven back to the home with the baby who was usually all set up with an adopting family longing to have him or her, but there was no compulsion to give the child up other than a briefing once or twice a week during the period in residence explaining the enormous advantages the girls were withholding from the child if they did not. There were only two rules at The Shires. These were that no mother was allowed to breast-feed and no mother who fell a second time was allowed to come back.

The girls were well prepared before and after the birth of the child for the day when they were to give it up. They were encouraged to dress themselves and the baby in their best clothes. It was obligatory that every mother should hand the child over herself. It was, they were told, vital. The baby would be taken into the arms of a motherly official dressed convincingly in blue and starch, at an address in Belgravia. This woman would whisk the child kindly away into an adjacent room where its new family would be waiting. Usually two or three mothers would be done together, for company afterwards. After the hand-over they were driven by one of us on the committee to the nearest local transport, their luggage of the last months lifted out and with a hand-out of money, depending on their circumstances, they were waved off. 'Most of them,' said Gant, 'are very grateful. Many of them are quite well-educated with an Anglican background. The sort who want to spare their parents' reputation. They go home as if it has been a long holiday—oh, it's as old as time. A few send Christmas cards to us for a year or so but on the whole we hope to lose track of them. We respect their privacy.'

'It sounds rather exclusive.'

'Not at all. We take all classes. There's a small means-test, but anyone can apply. Of course we try to encourage attendance at the eleven o'clock service.'

They did indeed. For over half a century there had been two rows of balloon-like women seated at the back of St Saviour's. What the first ones had been like one can only imagine, but the present-day ones were extremely talkative and ate a lot of sweets in noisy wrappings. Once or twice there was a crisis—even once the clanging of an ambulance bell. The girls now were in no way shy of the congregation, met their kind nods and smiles with interested looks. The congregation for its part held mixed views on the girls, and some of the sidesmen were nervous of those with swollen ankles who had to be helped up the altar steps to Communion. Sometimes there was a suspicion of threat and truculence in the air. But the girls liked St Saviour's on the whole, and at coffee after the service sat at their ease in the parish room, stroking their domed fronts. Almost everyone except Lady Gant thought that the girls should be allowed to sit scattered about the Church, not confined to the Magdalene pews, and at coffee time they often said so. The girls seemed to have no opinion on this matter and Lady Gant never wavered in her conviction that it was all much safer near the door. 'In a body,' she said, 'with Matron and Bella in charge, and if possible the Chaplain.'

Now the Chaplain to The Shires, oh Johanna, was a man called Father Garsington and he lived above the girls in a private apartment at the top of the house. From the beginning, and for obvious reasons, it had been stipulated that the Chaplain should be a married man.

Father Garsington had been appointed so

long ago, however, that his wife, who did not go about, had been forgotten. Those who tried to recall her remembered only a refined sort of woman in very old silk dresses—she had been in touch with that very good dress-agency, run by that Duchess, for clergy wives. There had been a perpetual string of seed-pearls round her neck and above them the shiny, unlined face of a girl. Her eyes were innocent, her hair in slides as it had been since school. She had met Father Garsington at Cambridge and Cambridge had been and still was her golden time. Nothing had happened to her since. Father Garsington had come back from the War very dickie—'Oh, very dickie indeed,' Gant said. Both Garsingtons kept to The Shires and to each other.

As the years passed, the fallen girls had grown noisier and the Chaplain's flat quieter and towards the end of the establishment's life, when the girls were getting hard to find and rebellious about carrying up the Garsingtons' trays of lunch and supper, the Chaplain and his wife became like two old owls living almost invisibly in the rafters. Father Garsington, a gentle man, carried up the food-trays uncomplainingly, prayed often, walked each afternoon on the Common, but was seldom otherwise seen. On a board in the hall was a time-scarred notice saying that the Chaplain was available for counselling, but few girls availed themselves of this opportunity.

Once, a Jamaican beauty, six feet high with teeth like a Bechstein, who could have eaten six Father Garsingtons every day for snacks, gave him a bottle of rum for Christmas. 'And a kiss,' she said, and put her arms around him, her cheek against his, and rocked him in his chair. She laughed and laughed and danced and clapped and he said, brick red, 'Now then, now then Rosie.'

'Rosie has given us some rum,' he told his wife, 'and a new scarf for you.' Mrs Garsington took the scarf and smoothed it on the counterpane, saying that it was rather bright. The rum, she said, would do him no good whatsoever, with his breathing, and would come in nicely for the bottle-stall at the next fête. Father Garsington, however, put the bottle in one of his Wellington boots in The Shires' coal shed and had a good tot every night when he was seeing to the cat.

When Rosie left The Shires with her curly-headed prune—who had his mother's eyes of liquid black light—Father Garsington stood about at the gates. Rosie was not going off to Belgravia in a car. She was keeping her baby and had gone striding off with him, breast-feeding as she went, to the bus-stop on Common Side. When she'd disappeared, the Chaplain didn't hurry in but watched the trees on the Common—a rainy day with the wind blowing cold drops at him. Mrs Garsington stood in her high window, looking down. One

116

of the girls told me this, when I was waiting to give Gant a lift home. The girl thought I was a new inmate. I felt so proud.

My turn to drive the Belgravia trail—I took the job of course; did I say that? no need: you remember Gant—my turn did not come for several months. I attended the monthly Progress Meetings, tried to do the Home's accounts, and attacked the secretarial work without the least knowledge of it. There was a Government Social Worker co-opted on to the committee now, 'by Law, unfortunately,' said Gant. She was an Englishwoman called Mrs Djinn. 'One of the Old School,' said Gant, 'nothing feminist or aggressive. We insisted. We've managed perfectly well for nearly a century without interference by the State.'

Mrs Djinn was indeed no feminist. She was old and tired and cynical and on the point of retirement. She wore hand-knitted mustard-coloured cardigans with sleeves made huge by handkerchieves as she was subject to a perpetual cold. Her eyes had seen everything and expected nothing and the reports she wrote on the girls drained them of all life. The act that had brought them to her notice held for her neither mystery nor the slightest interest. The sex-act for Mrs Djinn was after the nature of a viral infection that might result in nasty flu, something not yet eradicated from the human species. The urges of the body were but fallow, stony fields for Mrs Djinn, and her face was that of a desolate wooden idol. Yet, one day after one of the Monthly Meetings, there called for her at Gant's house a lean brown dreamy-eyed Indian son.

And another surprise—I hope you're enjoying this little perambulation, Joanissima carissima—another surprise. One night, during the five months when I was working for The Shires, I walked miles and miles from home. Henry was abroad. He was in Washington, now I come to think of it. It was a damp evening, rainy and blowy, and I walked fast down the hill, over the railway and into the little streets. I passed the black stump of the paper-works, the tin block of the motor-tyre company, the greyhound track walls like the sides of a ship—white light and a sea roaring within. I got to Mitcham—miles and miles from home. It is our horizon, up in the Road. I walked the deadly Mitcham pavements in the rain thinking of the miles of lavender fields that would once have been under my feet. When The Shires was built the Chaplain's wife in the top windows would have been able to see the blue fields far away.

I turned in at the fish and chip shop and stood waiting for the fryer to finish the next shoal of cod. I leaned my arms on the warm silver counter and saw, between the sauce bottles and the Box for the Blind and the old jumbo glass-and-chrome pepper pots, Bella, unsmiling, talking earnestly over a table to

118

Father Garsington. She held his hand across the table. They each had a couple of rock fish in front of them and a mountainous heap of chips. Father Garsington's plate was splattered in blood-red ketchup and he had taken off his mittens.

So—is the picture in place, Joan?

Five months or so after my initiation to the inner workings of The Shires, the call came to Belgravia. Two babies. Mrs Djinn arrived on her worn soles at my door and together we picked up Bella when she stepped off her bus from beyond the tracks. At The Shires Mrs Djinn got out of the car in a business-like way and disappeared inside the house and Bella got out hesitantly and hung about at the gates, smiling. There was a long pause.

Father Garsington appeared. 'Hullo, my dear, hullo, hullo,'—very hearty to Bella. He strode past her. 'Good day, good day, good day,'—to me. He stamped with cold feet, puffed white mist like a dragon. Pink finger-tips thrust out of his mittens grew as purple as his mouth. 'Just the first touch. The first touch of autumn. Ha.'

Two children came quickly down the path, each carrying a soft white bundle, and Matron followed behind to arrange them all in the back of the car. Mrs Djinn came down the path next, almost languid with good sense. She carried a file and some brown envelopes and got in beside me. Bella went round to sit in the back of the car but one of the girls was fat and it was clear that someone must be left behind. 'There's no room for Bella,' said Mrs Djinn.

'No room,' said the Chaplain. 'Oh dear.'

'You're not essential, Bella,' said Mrs Djinn, 'I've never known so many auxiliaries as here. There's none of this in the Public Sector.'

'Oh, I'm not a bit essential,' said Bella, smiling.

'Walk on the Common?' asked Father Garsington, 'I'm just off there. Goodbye, my dears. Good luck. God bless.'

But the two girls were leaning towards each other lighting up cigarettes and dropping ash in the shawls. Inside the shawls the babies' heads were like hazelnuts.

'I'm sorry, dear,' said Mrs Djinn. 'We can't have smoking in the car, it's not safe.'

There was muttering.

'Come on now. Put them out. You'll set fire to something. There's the ash-tray. Come on. Give the baby your whole attention.'

A baby gave a little sound.

'You see? She doesn't like the smoke, dear, put them out. You can have a good smoke when we get there. Turn here, Mrs Peabody, it's round this crescent. Yes. Just stop here a minute. I have to do a little recce.'

The babes and the girls and I sat in silence. The sweet warm smell of the babies was like baking bread. It mingled with the remains of the cigarette smoke and then with alcohol. In

120

the mirror, I saw one girl take a swig from a mini bottle of something and pass it over to the other. The first one then put the bottle back in her bag and they each looked out of the windows. The thin girl said, 'It's a lovely area.' The babies slept on without a dream.

'Fine,' said Mrs Djinn. 'Just drive up to the front door, Mrs Peabody, and then go off and park—there's a place in the mews and follow us in.'

When I joined them on the top floor of the house, up three flights of quiet, deep-carpeted stairs, the girls were sitting side by side on upright chairs. They held the babies like professionals. Djinn sat alongside, examining her notes. When I came through the door the fat one looked up, frightened, but the thin one looked out towards the window and the sky. We waited, none of us looking at the babies, and then the woman in blue with the white cuffs came in and said, 'Thank you, dear, Dianne first. One at a time. We don't want any mix ups,' and she took the baby in a scooping movement like the executioner swooping to tie the condemned man's hands. In the doorway she passed another, tweedy woman who came forward with a glorious smile saying: 'Kimberley? Isn't she lovely. That's right. Last look. Give her a kiss, dear,' and was gone.

The babies were gone and the young girls sat like naked ones, their hands loose. They looked at each other rather slyly and the thin

121

one grimaced. The fat one looked about her, very cool, pursing up her mouth.

'Cigarette, dear? That's right. You've done very well.'

'Can we go now?'

'In just a minute.'

We waited about twenty. One of the girls got up and walked towards the window. 'Don't look out, dear, just a minute more.'

A door opened and shut, somewhere in the house. Another door opened and shut. Soon the tweedy woman put her head round the door. 'Overjoyed!' she said to the girls. 'Quite overcome.'

We all got up to go. As we got to the door the thin girl turned and looked back into the room.

On the pavement they asked for their luggage at once and would not let us take them on anywhere. The fat one said, 'We're going for a drink in a pub.' The thin one said, 'Look. Here. Here's the box of presents. It's her box of presents. These is the presents she got sent by everyone. We forgot them. She's got to have them. There's dolls and teddies and that.'

Mrs Djinn said that she would see to it.

'It's only right,' said the thin one. 'I'll go back with them.'

'No—leave it to us.'

'I'll take them in now,' I said, 'I promise.'

Mrs Djinn turned away.

'OK then. It's only right.'

Both girls looked up at the windows of the

house with their expensive silky curtains. They lit second cigarettes and went over to the pub while I went up the steps with the box of presents. 'Yes, I suppose so. Come in,' said the uniformed woman who was also smoking now. 'Maddening. It's far too late. Put them there. It'll have to be Oxfam.'

'The first thing the new parents do apparently,' said Mrs Djinn when we were alone in the car together, 'every single time, is to take all the baby's clothes off and dress it in new ones they've brought with them. It's interesting, isn't it? A symbolic act of some kind—nobody suggests it. They leave all the things it came with behind them. New nappies. Everything. They often just drop the old clothes on the floor. A terrible waste.'

'Are the babies—those babies—still in there?'

'Oh no. They went off half an hour ago. We make sure they go first just in case the mothers hang about to get a look. Mrs Peabody, it's a wonderful thing we do, you know. There's an awful lot of nonsense talked. You're looking a bit white. Let me tell you I go through this now without a qualm and I've discovered it is the best way to help the girls. I know that what we do is right and my experience gets through to them. In every case we are giving three people—at least three people—the chance of a better life: the baby, its mother and some poor barren family. These girls haven't a clue, you know. The cruellest thing you can do for them is get emotional. We had a Matron once and the night before the babies went off it was like a funeral parlour at The Shires. Head up, Mrs Peabody! They're children, far from home—if they have a home and they can make a new start if they're bright enough. Half of them are too silly to take the pill. Those two will have another next year, you know.'

'I wonder why?'

'Very poor memories, Mrs Peabody.'

'Yet it seems hard.'

'Life is hard,' she inevitably said, and took a big piece of what looked like duster from her sleeve, blew her nose and polished her glasses. 'Drop me off at Harrods, would you? I always get a pound of bacon afterwards. It's beautiful bacon and no more expensive than the supermarket.'

After I'd dropped her I turned the car and bashed its wing and then set off for home. Along the Fulham Road I saw the fat girl walking with her suitcase and some plastic bags. She walked with a bit of a roll, as if she was still pregnant. She looked watchful. When she reached a bus-stop she stopped and stood reading the list of numbers of the buses. I drew up alongside and said, 'Look hullo. Can I really not take you home? Or somewhere?' and she said, 'No you fucking can't.'

That was the end of me at The Shires.

*   *   *

'Eliza, dear,' said Anne again. 'Eliza—don't go into a trance. All we have been saying is that we do so wish you would get yourself something to *do*.'

'Anne, I have something to do. I have The Hospice.'

'But only in a menial capacity, Eliza. You're not professionally qualified to be with the Dying. You're not medical or psychological or anything—*and why should you be*? You've been a very senior Diplomatic Wife for years and years and no chance of having your own profession. We thought—well I thought—that you need something quite different. Something light-hearted and creative. And you know you'd feel so much more self-respect if you earned *money*. Honestly—it's so much *fun*.'

'My dear Anne, I couldn't possibly write books. There are far too many already. Why should I spend hours all by myself in a room writing books just to amuse some people I've never met for a few hours on an aeroplane before they get pulped? I mean the books get pulped. They have a shelf-life of six weeks most of them and a good thing, too. They're like package puddings. It was in the *Guardian*. There are dozens of novels spewed forth, most of them tripe and all the poor authors thinking they've started out on an immortal career. Might as well masturbate. I don't mean yours,

125

of course.'

'Eliza! Well, but you could write something Sociological. Or about all your travels with Henry. Or good children's books, as I do.'

'I couldn't write books for good children.'

'Eliza! I want you to do something. I want you to come to my Creative Writing Class. There's a writer above the norm coming to address us. Well, as a matter of fact it's Lancaster Forbes, and you can't say that he gets pulped.'

'I'm afraid I haven't...'

'Oh please,' she said. 'I know you'd love it. You like people so much and it would do you so much good. Those little notes you used to write were all so vivid, somehow, and we miss them. Lancaster Forbes would bring you to life again.'

I thought, Poor little lamb. That's what I thought, Joan. All the boys at Harrow and that blowsy girl at Cranborne Chase and the dinner cooked by the Philippino and George only at home when there's been a row with the girlfriend in Hong Kong.

'How's George?'

'Oh, I told you. He's away. He's always away. I'm used to it.'

'Do you miss him?'

'Well, actually' (very bright) 'actually you know, Eliza, I *don't*. I don't miss him at all. Since I began my own career I'm not emotionally dependent any more, nor entirely financially dependent, and I do think, belonging to a Feminist Group...'

'*Do* you belong to a Feminist Group?'

'Well, of course I do. How could I not? You don't think I'm like the rest of the Road to you, Eliza? How could a woman writer feel alive at all otherwise, in today's world? Professional women have to stick together. If we are ever to take over.'

'Do you—do you think you may some day take over from George?'

'Oh, George is *super*. He's a superb husband, Eliza. No infidelity or anything like that. And personally I don't think sex is any the worse for being infrequent, do you? Rather better, really.'

She turned quite purple during this speech. It had been drawn from her by torture and brainwash. I remembered what Dulcie Baxter once told me, Joan, about the last-but-one Philippino coming banging on her door at two in the morning because George had been on the creep towards her attic apartment. Lonely, good Anne.

'I'll come to your class,' I said. 'When is it? Next Tuesday?'

'No, today. Could you come today?'

'Life is precipitate. Yes, all right.'

'Oh *super*. Oh, I do feel glad about that, Eliza. And today's a super-duper day because Pixie Leak will be there.'

'Pixie Leak?'

'Pixie Leak. She won the Queen Mab award in '82 and the Tulsa Golden Golly. She wrote in America first—*Your First Bra* and *You Don't Have To. Terribly* good and outspoken. Not imaginative fiction, of course. She's not poetically cast. But a definite authorial voice. I wanted to have them on the bookstall at St Saviour's but the Vicar was against it and even Nick said that some of the old ladies might get upset. The organist was adamant—he belongs to The William Temple Society—and there was some shouting. I do think Nick's a bit of a fossil, don't you? I mean, for his age. And he has tiny children who are going to need to meet issues like this before long.'

*   *   *

When she had been gone for some time I came to myself and wondered whatever I was up to, for I had taken a bucket of water and Fairy Liquid to the Aga. I had gathered up all the marigold plates, and they were standing in the plate-rack, shining clean, and I was swilling over the floor with a cloth. This in turn seemed to be leading to the working surfaces, window-ledges, windows, curtains. I took the curtains down, washed and hung them on the line. The steps to the garden weren't looking too good so I poured a bucket of hot water down them and attacked them with a hard brush, tripping backwards and falling down with what I

128

realised was exhaustion. Pleasant exhaustion.

Round the edge of the world something looked at me. A very distant, scarce-remembered relation—happiness. Like frightened, struggling Anne, happiness had slipped my mind since I had been persuaded that the world is composed entirely of super-women now, like you, Joan, in your brave defection. More anon, anon, anon—

Your admiring, searching,

separate friend, E.P.

March marches on

Dear old J.,

Continuum, continuum.

I dressed carefully for the Creative Writing Class and stood in the window, waiting. When Anne's car drew up I could see the bulk of another person beside her and Anne's head turned towards it, nodding up and down in earnest conversation. She began to leave the car with firm tread but then put her head back in the car again and continued to talk, one arm conducting music in the air. She turned and looked up at the house like a general squaring up to a hard campaign.

'Just ready.' I was all smiles and she looked relieved, I suppose because I was in a dress and not the usual dressing-gown or zip jacket. 'Eliza, lovely! I keep meaning to say—what amazing earrings. This is Pixie. Pixie Leak.'

The substantial form in the passenger seat—I'd sat myself in the back—did not show by a tremor any awareness of me, but stared ahead. 'Pixie—Eliza Peabody.' Maybe there was a sound, though it might have been only the creaking of clothes. I could not see her face at all, nor yet her hair for it was covered by a yachting cap. Shoulders were encased in army-surplus, painted with camouflage, and a leather jerkin. We proceeded down Common Side and turned in at a beautifully painted Victorian house facing the Common and otherwise surrounded by vast gardens. Steel mesh covered all the windows and the eaves held the usual alarms. A bell beside the oaken door was held steady by a vertical bar of barley-sugar wrought-iron fit for the entrance to some castle keep. It reminded me of the sinister Chinese houses in Penang where everyone's afraid of the chop. 'Are they Chinese?' I asked and was rewarded by blankness.

'She's married to a very successful QC,' said Anne. 'He could have done very well if he hadn't gone into Building Contracts.'

'He doesn't seem to have done too badly.'

'I mean,' said Anne, 'he will never be exactly the *crème de la*. It rather shows in the light fittings. I mean, he makes a frightful lot of

130

money but they know none of the right people. He's very musical and she's a bit highbrow. But *awfully* nice.'

A wisp of Philippino answered the bell's clang and the three of us trooped into a drawing room which could easily have doubled for a ballroom or the site of a mid-term investiture at Buckingham Palace. Twenty or so very well-dressed women were sitting easily about in cheerful communion. Rather apart, behind a coffee table sat a small, despondent man. It was exactly like a meeting of the Wives' Fell. in which another Eliza once had ta'en delight.

'But I thought it was going to be something to do with a college?'

'Oh no,' said Anne, 'I never said that. It's pretty high-powered all the same. The seated man is Lancaster.'

'It sounds like one of Shakespeare's *Histories*?'

'Hush Eliza. He's very shy—and terribly sensitive as a result of being abused as a child.'

'How awful. But can he bear to talk about it?'

'Talking about it and writing about it have saved his sanity. He feels he has a mission to prepare people for the Thatcher World.'

'I'd have thought most people here subscribe to the Thatcher World.'

'Oh, not when it comes to child-abuse, Eliza. Nobody here could countenance child-abuse.

131

Please give us that.'

'But does Mrs Thatcher? I shouldn't think she'd ever have had the time. Aren't her children rather loyal and well set-up?'

'Of *course* Mrs Thatcher didn't practise child—really, Eliza. You know exactly what I mean. But child-abuse must be brought right into the open. All over the world. Children must learn where danger is likely to strike and in the present political climate where could they learn better than in children's books.'

This seemed to me a mystifying statement and made Pixie Leak produce a sudden and enormous clearing of the throat. I felt her eyes on me. I said, 'Yes. Well. I suppose *Snow White and the Seven Dwarfs...*'

'Well exactly. Precisely. You have hit it. The Attachment Dynamic and the Concept of Ego Strength. It is all a question of perceiving and recognising reality and dealing with unpleasure. The child must become aware of the sin of others.'

'*Snow White* was C. S. Lewis's favourite film,' I said, rather to fill a silence. 'He and his brother used to go on Saturday afternoons.'

'Well, exactly.'

'Yes, but they were both about fifty.'

'Eliza,' said Anne, 'do be careful. There are some very bright people here.'

'C. S. Lewis was very bright.'

'Be quiet at once, Eliza.'

Pixie Leak was being whisperingly

132

introduced now to the women nearest her in the semi-circle of comfortable chairs. They all nodded and smiled widely as she glowered about for something with a straighter back, then climbed out of her jerkin and the army-surplus to reveal a gigantic T-shirt with Hard Rock Café inscribed across the front. Her face above, as she settled with forward-thrusting brows, was grim. Below the T-shirt were knickerbockers, yellow socks and bright brown brogues. I was amazed to find that the brogues sent through me a pang of pure love and I found myself thinking of my beloved Girl-Guide Captain long ago. I said, 'Anne—do you think—have you ever thought I might be queer?'

'Oh Eliza—*please.*'

Cups of tea were being passed round (Royal Worcester, Lapsang Souchong) and the little table was moved nearer to the waiting speaker who then placed his notebook more centrally upon it. Then he picked the book up again and, foolishly, the tea-cup and saucer, too. He found that if he held the notebook in the same hand as the saucer he could drink from the cup. We watched with respect, while all kinds of bits of paper began to fall out of the notebook and a number of women began to crawl about the floor picking them up. A retarded child who had been sitting quietly on the floor near her mother suddenly burst out laughing and blew some raspberries at everyone and Lady Gant,

133

sitting behind me, said, 'She ought to leave that child at home. It's very upsetting for everybody to have to see it.' Pixie Leak gave a sigh and the woman whose house it seemed to be, whose husband didn't know the right people, and who was dressed in rich brown silk jersey for which you should really be very thin indeed, went and stood beside Lancaster Forbes and smiled, brilliant-eyed, for silence. For silence at once.

Oh Joan. What good women. So concerned about children. So experienced. How efficient they all are, every one of their children at this moment safely at school or with its nanny, beautifully managed, secure. Each child in a little while will be gathered up from school, taken home to a prosperous shining house, tea ready on the table, supper in the mike. Oh, all these women with their well-washed hair, hand-made sweaters, sun-tans from second homes in Corfu or Unknown Tuscany. And good, you know. Not decadent, jealous, spiteful, cruel; few of them drunks, hopped up on amphetamines, or damped down by tranquillisers. All of them obediently divorced from nicotine, all keeping their appointments for cancer scans, dental check-ups, cholesterol counts and their diaries in sensible order for Ascot, Hurlingham, Covent Garden, tickets for Glyndebourne and the Tennis. Rich they are, rich fawn and dull, like marrons glacés. But good. Serious about Bridge, a bit heavy on the gin—but otherwise blameless, blameless. How odd that, when the story goes that women now are dragged down often to suicide by full-time marriage and parenthood, here are these survivors sitting well-groomed, good-looking, confident, articulate (how well brown-silk-jersey is talking) and having the time of their lives. They are the organisers of complex social lives, several houses and maybe a central-London apartment belonging to the company; blind-eyed when necessary to the other woman who may use it, too; and linchpins of their husbands' careers, as their children get themselves about the world to foreign friends in Mexico and Peru at an age when their grandparents were still being taken for short walks in the park.

I looked at the women, at the speaker designate, at Pixie Leak pulsating from her throne and thought, It's no good, this is not my tribe. My trouble is that I never knew my tribe. I've always been on the edge, just hanging about. Nowhere. And I've never faced it.

I could not understand one word of the talk that now followed. Lancaster Forbes spoke in a weary little voice as if at any moment he might burst into tears and in a vocabulary that was new to me; but this may have been because I found it hard to concentrate after the first few moments when he dropped his half-full tea-cup on the floor and brown-jersey crept forward on hands and knees with a damp cloth, rubbing vigorously first the carpet and then the speaker's feet, then the legs of his little table and now and again, at her whim, making dabs at his trouser-legs and even lap. When she had crept back, the retarded child crept forward and flung her arms round Mr Forbes's knees and made some high-pitched hooting noises. Everybody smiled affectionately at this except for Lady Gant, who made a noise like a demented horse, and Mr Lancaster who gave the child a nasty shove and made her cry. Most of the audience however were polite and very disciplined, and as the talk drew to a close and Mr Forbes took out a handkerchief and scrubbed at his face and hands—the room boiled with central-heating—there was a flutter of clapping and exclamations of pleasure.

Anne Robin then moved the vote of thanks. She had not introduced the speaker, she said, because everybody in the room knew him (the retarded child cried 'Whoops') and respected him so well (Pixie Leak cleared her throat again at this and flung the knee of one knickerbocker over the other) and there could be no family in the land that did not know and love him, too. There were many autograph-albums in the room, she knew, waiting to be presented to testify to this, and a number of paperbacks everyone hoped that he would sign. She knew that Mr Forbes would not mind (he gave a skimmed-milk smile) and now it was her pleasure to thank him for his very interesting talk, assure him that we would all now be brushing up our ideas on the ego and the id, sibling politics and psychological proximity, and to say that he had kindly agreed to answer questions. There was the customary, English, thoughtful silence then, and Pixie did another fling of the legs.

'Our speaker will of course understand,' said Anne, stoutly, 'that this talk has been a very *rare* treat, for we seldom, as full-time wives and mothers, hear much about the *theory* of children's literature.' She looked rather desperately round at Pixie who closed her eyes. 'Usually children's writers—and I'm afraid I am one of them—start writing without giving thought to the *theory*. I myself came late to this group which was formed by those so interested in child-psychology that they had decided to write books themselves. We are a group who meet largely to discuss the work that has emerged from our findings—little stories that support our views—and also of course just to talk about whatever comes into our heads, which is when the nitty-gritty *really* takes place.'

'But,' she went doggedly on, 'there is someone here today we are glad to say *well*-qualified to take up some of the speaker's points and even perhaps' (she looked glaringly and commandingly in P. Leak's direction) 'query some of them?'

But P. Leak was smoking a very loose-looking cigarette with tobacco hanging out of it like hairs from a nose. Her head was thrown back, her eyes closed. At the mention of her, Lancaster Bumblebee had sunk down into himself in order to consider his teaspoon.

'I was wondering,' I said, and everybody jumped. Some of them looked round and several whispered together and nodded and smiled encouragingly. 'I have been *wondering* why it is that we are really here.'

Lancaster looked quickly up, then down.

'I mean, *is* there a theory of children's literature? I thought it was just books children liked.' My voice faded before their stares. These women after all lived (Joan) with children every day. 'I've always thought that children do the teaching really. That's why I'm a bit scared of them.'

'You'll see what we mean in a minute, Eliza,' somebody called, kindly. 'We're going to have a chance to stretch our minds. Soon we are going to *perform*.'

'Let's see,' said Anne. 'Yes, four of us I think. We are going to read aloud from our works and then Mr Forbes and Pixie Leak— *whom I am proud to say we have inveigled here today*' (glare) 'are to comment. Pixie, as most of us know, is the winner of the Elfin Goblet, the Cow and Calf Ewer and the Queen Mab Shield and in her private capacity is a dear friend of many of us and lives in East

138

Molesey. Pixie.'

Then Lancaster Forbes stood up knocked over his table for the last time, muttered that he was sorry but he had to go and catch his bus and made for the door in leaps, with brown-jersey rushing after him, flapping a cheque.

There was understanding, kindly laughter.

'*Terribly* shy,' someone was saying. 'We were so lucky to get him. He's so busy. You know he thinks every morning, writes every afternoon and in the evening thinks again. It's the basis of his canon.'

'I wonder who does his shirts?' I asked, but nobody listened.

'And only ten pounds and expenses. And so *frightfully* good. You'd never think anyone so small could have written *The Video-Nasty Man* and *The Sex Machine*.'

'Grizel adores *The Sex Machine*,' said a limpid girl in apple green. 'It's cathartic, isn't it? The girl's initiation in the ceremonial killing of the mother of the tribe. Pre-Communist. Well, pretty well pre-everything.'

They all began to speak at once about politics and the inevitability of the oligarch but I kept my mouth shut because of what Charles had once said. A Philippino with sad eyes came in with a tea-trolley stacked with wonderful lemon and orange shortcakes and home-made chocolate brownies. Fresh hot tea.

Folders and clipboards taken out of hiding. 'Chocolate cake?' somebody asked Pixie, who

139

opened her eyes and began to eat hungrily with a cake-fork. 'I'm afraid this is all going to seem very amateur to *you*,' the apple-green girl said, and Pixie licked her fingers. She was seated rather close to me. Too close to me. I looked at the nice brown brogues again and was troubled once more for I found that it was Henry and not my Girl-Guide Captain they reminded me of. Henry's shoes. His dear shoes. His always-lovely shoes. The ones that I had waited for, looking out of the bowed windows of St James's Street, at an old-fashioned confident world with big clean handsome men going by.

Here I was, in this strange clique, listening to a story about a family of centipedes. It was a perfectly acceptable story—but behold all these educated women listening to it like the word of God! Centipedes, I thought, and gave a yell, for there was something crawling across the back of my neck. It was Pixie Leak's hand. 'Have to go,' I cried. 'Forgot something.' And, like Lancaster, I fled.

*　　*　　*

Outside was a bus-stop and a bus coming. I flung myself aboard. At that time of the afternoon there was scarcely anyone on it and I climbed upstairs so that I could ride between the branches of the sycamores along the Common's edge. There was only one other passenger, sitting in the front seat, too, across

140

the gangway from me.

He was a boy, about ten years old and his chin was on his chest. He had silky hair and the back of his neck under his red and black striped school cap had a heart-breakingly beautiful cleft in it. I wanted all at once to kiss it, then thought that perhaps nowadays that would be called child-abuse. He might report me. Well, so he should. We hadn't been introduced. He'd sock me one.

The boy was reading steadily, page after page of a comic, and as he read, his feet in red and grey woollen socks kicked and swung, kicked and swung. When children stop swinging their legs they're grown up. He stopped and looked at me, then went on reading. After a while he began again, swing and kick, kick and swing. The pages of the comic were lovingly turned and turned. When he gathered up all his things to get off the bus, he looked at me again and gravely raised his cap to me.

Oh, all the different kinds of love—

April 12th

Dear Joan,

You see the date. A month of silence.

I left you in March with the words 'the

141

different kinds of love' and I have nothing better to offer now. I write from habit only.

Nothing has happened. Nothing but long grey days. I stand in the window a great deal. Nothing has happened since the razzle-dazzle of Oxford, the interesting anthropological behaviour of the Creative Writing Class, except rain. Rain and rain. Soft and soaking. Deeply seeping. Whispering night and day, all our lawns of Surrey green as Ireland and we in Rathbone Road as grey as ghosts. I stand watching the rain and contemplating the silence of God.

What to tell you?

So many kinds of love.

Rain.

Yesterday, my dearest Joan, I stood looking out at the road and saw two people standing on the pavement gazing up at the house next to mine, the house where the glamorous pair have touched down, she of the hair made of golden snakes and the figure for the catwalk. She is the martyr of the Road, goddess of the watery smile, of the perpetual headache, who pushes her two small children maniacally about from morning till night, spending her life with them at every sort of class and play-group, too busy for one word of chat, one breath of friendship. Her face is pinched and fretful and she has the air of the true template for the one-parent family.

Not so. A husband, a fleeting figure, is to be

seen daily, leaping down the steps and into the Porsche and away. They smile at me sometimes, these people, but they do not know my name.

That house has never been a lucky house and, though it is the same pretty 1860s architecture as the rest of the Road, nobody stays there long. It is a giant sentry-box, well-proportioned, with handsome front door of royal blue. Bronze and purple glass lamps from some Sicilian palace or Parisian bordello are hung on either side of it. The glamorous couple have added a new wing to the far side of the house, with half-sunken garage that opens its mouth in welcome to the leaping Adonis each evening when his car turns the corner of the street. A statue of Ceres stands on a plinth to one side of the door, a sheaf of the earth's fruits showering from her shoulder. At Ceres' feet the babies' toys lie in a scatter down the steps and often stay there for days, the golden serpent girl being too tired to pick them up and the husband holding his head too high to notice them. The babies are dressed in designer clothes of soft leather and hand-stitched lawn, always marvellously laundered or pressed, or perhaps always just new.

Although the babies cry rather a lot and there is some slamming of doors, I never hear through their walls any sounds of adult activity. There seems to be no domestic help, no socialising, no entertaining. The evenings

143

are unnaturally quiet. These birds of paradise are dropped down among us obviously very temporarily, destined any day for the apartment in Dockland and the big weekend country house outside Salisbury. One day perhaps they will talk about the quaint cottage of their early years—if the marriage lasts long enough for any of its years to have been early.

For there's some tension. The other night for instance a window at the back of the house was thrown open while I was with the dogs in the garden and a nasty black thing was flung out, very solid, about the size of a dark pork-pie or a small rugger-ball. I thought, this is a grenade. I was frightened by it and there was something about the shadow-figures in the window that frightened me more. Some hatred, some distress. I saw the Adonis crash down the window-sash and jerk the curtains together. There was no explosion.

In the road outside the front of the house, now, this small man and woman stared up at the purple lamps and the statue. They were smartly dressed, the man in a long black coat that looked as if it came out for funerals, the woman in fur-lined suede and carrying a square Italian shopping-bag of quilted leather, stuffed with parcels. No umbrellas. The rain soaked down and down but they did not seem to mind. They stood nodding like marionettes.

The man saw me. He touched the woman's arm and together they made for my front door.

144

'Mr Deecie,' he said as I opened it, 'pronounced as in Washington.' 'Washington, Mrs Deecie. Mr and Mrs Deecie,' said she. 'We've just come down to see Deborah.' 'Deborah,' said he, 'Deborah is our daughter. Next door. Pleased to meet you. Peabody? Now that's a good Northern name.' 'Northern name,' said Mrs Deecie. 'We're from Leicester which is not exactly North, not what *we* call North being from West Yorkshire in the first place, but it's getting on the way. It's in the right direction.' 'Direction,' said her husband.

They took off their coats and we all trooped into the kitchen and I hung the coats round the Aga to dry.

'Now that is kind,' said Mrs Deecie. 'It was a sunny day in Leicester.'

'Sunny as anything. Well, we stepped on the coach. Unpremeditated.'

'... itated,' said Mrs Deecie. 'They're very comfortable and they give you an unspecified number of paper cups of tea and the usual facilities. Rather cleaner than any we've encountered on the trains. We've just got an hour or so before the return journey begins, but it looks as if she's out.'

'I'm afraid that Mrs Deecie is right there,' said Mr Deecie.

'Just to see the grandchildren. Well, we don't get so many chances, being so far away. A sudden whim, or you might call it a fancy. Deborah always so busy with her career in the film and modelling world and Ivan flying about everywhere—Australia all the time. Australia, Mrs Peabody, is absolutely nothing to Ivan. For Ivan it is like Runcorn or Port Sunlight. All the film-work on location. Do you think I might ask if I could use your toilet?'

'You'll know Deborah of course,' said Mr Deecie. 'Lovely girl. Just while Mrs Deecie's out of the room I'd like to say that Deborah means a very great deal to her mother and that's the sole reason we've come. For me, I'm happy with my garden and I'm not saying the marriage wasn't a bit of a relief. I sit here in this chair today entirely to please Mrs Deecie.'

'I'm afraid Deborah may be in London today,' I say.

He looks mystified. 'But I'd call this London. Isn't it? We speak of her as living in London, though I must say it took long enough from Victoria for it to be somewhere else. No we haven't been to the house before. They've not been here that long. Mind, we've heard about it. Lovely house. Nice position. Though I'd not imagined it being only terrace property, I have to say. I'd been fancying something in its own grounds and maybe a pool.'

'But we think we have very big gardens here.'

'Oh well, not by Leicester standards I have to say. Mrs Deecie and I have opportunities for brussels, runner-beans and particularly nice onions, apart from the patio and the fish and a small but by no means shameful herbaceous. I

146

can see, mind, that this is all very well set-up and a good neighbourhood and the statue's a bit above Leicester. It's the children she misses, Mrs Peabody, I'll just say this if I may before Mrs Deecie comes down. Mrs Deecie would like to see a lot more of the grandchildren. She knits them little things of course all the time but it's not the same as fitting them to the child, and you never get much of a letter. Deborah rings birthdays and Christmas and she lets them speak on the phone to their Granny. But, look at it this way, Mrs Peabody, if a child can't put a face to a voice ... Do you know, if Ivan was to pass me and Mrs Deecie in the street I don't suppose he'd recognise us. Not his own mother-in-law. It's the film-world. It breaks family ties.

'Well, yes. She did bring him once to Leicester before they were married. I imagine it was at about the time they were beginning to think about an engagement because they dropped in at Leicester on the way down from Scotland where they'd been holidaying together just the two of them in the modern way—not that I'm saying there was anything wrong in it, Deborah being so well brought-up. She's always been used to temptations too, being so—well you know her, Mrs Peabody. You see what she is. A true beauty.

'Always was. No two ways. A beauty from the start. It was a sore trouble to her and to us too as a matter of fact. She didn't ever know

147

how to handle it, the looks. Her mother's a beauty of course, but more in the Elizabeth Taylor style. I'd say, well I've always said, Deborah is more after the Jane Fonda. When she was a teenager it was different again, mind. She was the Marilyn Monroe then, slow and weepy and she could have run to fat.

'We had it all, Mrs Peabody. All the troubles—the anorexia and the over-eating. We never had the drugs, though. Maybe that was because we never had the boyfriend trouble either. She was too beautiful for boyfriends of her own age, it always seemed to me. Frightened them off. And she was no talker—nothing like her mother and me; that isn't our failing. But her mother was very proud of her always, and not at all averse to this Ivan for being an older man. Mrs Deecie has always liked to regard Deborah as her friend as well as her daughter. That's how she's regarded her. And Mrs Deecie always loving babies, this has been the extra blow. Not seeing them.'

He steamed gently like a steady kettle above his coffee-cup, and when Mrs Deecie came into the kitchen, dry and tidy and her face newly painted, he rose to his feet and didn't sit down again until she did. 'We've been talking about Deborah, Vera.'

'Oh, she's a lovely girl. You'll know her well, Mrs Peabody?'

'I'm afraid I don't. We've hardly spoken. We

148

smile of course.'

'That's the London way,' said Mrs Deecie. 'You'd think it would have taken Deborah a bit of getting used to but she was never a chatterbox even in Leicester. Very shy.'

'I sometimes wonder how she ever had children she was so shy,' said Mr Deecie.

'Now Frank.'

'She had those babies all by herself, Mrs Peabody, without her mother anywhere near her. There's character there. She's not just a pretty face.'

'That is true, Mrs Peabody. She never asked for me or needed me near at all. I was disappointed I'll not deny it. What mother wouldn't be? But after all those teenage troubles it should be looked on as brave, not wanting me.'

'Now she never said she didn't want you, Vera. You mustn't put words into Deborah's mouth.'

'She never said anything,' said Mrs Deecie. 'Nothing. Well, between ourselves, and I wouldn't say it in Leicester, she never even told me she was expecting either time—even the first one, born prematurely after the wedding. I expect she knew I'd be nervous for her. I used to get very nervous in her bad years around seventeen. And before that. And for quite a time after when you come to think about it.'

'But it was never drugs, I've been telling Mrs Peabody, Vera. We never had that dreadful

149

problem.'

'She just couldn't get up. Lay in bed with her eyes shut and her hands over her ears.'

'It's so usual,' I said. 'Or I hear it is.'

'Just seemed so strange really to Frank and me—I mean, with those looks and such a nice girl. Well, we had to send her to a nerve-home for a bit. It's where she met this theatre person who took her off to London.'

She stopped and laughed and stirred her coffee.

'We mustn't bother, Mrs Peabody, Vera. We mustn't tell tales out of school. What I want to know is what the nanny's like. What we naturally feel is that if only Mrs Deecie was nearer, Deborah would have no need of nannies. Mrs Deecie would be "Nanny". That's what is said for "Gran" in Leicester. Mrs Deecie is the natural "Nan", yet the children don't even know her face. It's hard on Mrs Deecie.'

'Never mind Frank. So long as they're happy. It's just you remember your own, and those days—all those years. I expect you'll know what I'm talking about if you've had your own. The way they used to love you. We'll have to go now, Franko. We call him Franko, Mrs Peabody, on account of his Spanish appearance. I have it too, though we're not. We're English. In my view Deborah going blonde is a big mistake and wrong for her Latin complexion. When she was young she was after

150

the old Audrey Hepburn style. The chickenpox changed her. It took away from the skin.'

'It was a very terrible chickenpox, Mrs Peabody,' said Mr Deecie. 'I don't mind telling you that I prayed on my knees for her, though out of the bedroom of course. She was hot enough for brain-damage. Mrs Deecie cried—not of course so Deborah could see her—she kept bright before Deborah. Mrs Deecie is a wonderful woman—no, I shall say it, Vera, you are a wonderful woman. We sat up four nights together with Deborah's chickenpox and she was so bad the doctor gave her a little touch of opium. Deborah looked at us with such love then—I'll never forget—and when she was better she said she'd never felt as wonderful as she did with the opium. We didn't let on locally about it, our doctor not being universally liked. Rather after the *avant-garde* style and being very dusky. I must say that it was after the chickenpox, after the opium—what? Yes. We ought to be getting along, you're quite right, Vera.'

I said, 'Oh do wait. I'm sure they won't be long. At four everyone is usually home from nursery school.'

There was a silence and Mr and Mrs Deecie sat with bright smiles.

'Fancy. School already,' said Mrs Deecie. 'They'll be professors at this rate. I wonder what schooling they can have and scarcely out of nappies? Well, still in them, last time I saw them, on account of this famous child-care book they all read now, written by one of these one-parent families. Whatever do they want a nanny for if they're at school all day?'

'It'll be for the picking-up and the school-run,' said Mr Deecie, 'because of Ivan's position. A nanny will be expected in the film-world. It's the *de rigeur*.'

'Oh, couldn't you stay on for the night? You could stay here if there's no room...'

'Oh no, she has all these dinner-parties and social functions and we wouldn't impose. And—Franko, you go off upstairs and then we'll be off, we mustn't miss the coach.'

She got up, crossed to the kitchen door and closed it after Frank. 'Just so I can say one thing in private, Mrs Peabody, and I don't want to tell tales, like I said. It's very bitter for Frank. Very bitter. I'd never say it to his face or let him know I knew, but the wedding was very bitter. Well maybe you were there?'

'No. I really don't know Deborah.'

'Well, just between the two of us I think it was probably more Ivan than her and because of his friends being so important, but we were told, Franko and I, that it was just a registry office and no reception Ivan having been married before and there was no need for us to come. It would be just a few minutes and they'd rather see us in Leicester later and take us out for a meal. But I'm afraid that wouldn't do for Frank, and I must say I was very disappointed, too. Frank said right out, "Deborah, I'm coming to the marriage of my only child however small it is and quiet." So after a bit she said all right and told us how to get there— right across in West London. We changed ready for it in Leicester and came down on the fast train with reserved seats and then in a taxi, over six pounds. We were far too early and we had to stand for hours, a cold raw day and blowy with grit, the other weddings all coming and going. Mrs Peabody, you could write a book! Those weddings! Some dressed to the nines and champagne corks popping in the street and professional photographers, and some just slinking in and sliding out. One poor little bride, she even got left behind as the bridegroom and his friends walked away— laughing and nudging at each other and this little one trotting behind him by herself with a funny smile—a poor little face all pancake and eye-shadow and not even a pretty frock. She didn't look unhappy though, even with her husband in front being slapped by these ones in leathers, off in the direction of the pub.

'Well, at last here's Ivan and Deborah and their party. It turned out to be, well I have to say it, an enormous crowd. It had been gathering up all this time all down the street, we'd been seeing it. People all dressed very unusually, the girls in wide Ascot-style hats and little leather skirts up to their thigh-tops. And the men! So ill and awful they looked, hair all greasy and balding and a very bad indoor colour to them all, like pewter. It was the Media. That was the first time it really came home to us she was marrying into the Media-world. She and he arrived together in the white Porsche and he was in a white suit and she was in almost the same white suit and her hair up in a knot on the top of her head like she had it for dancing-class age of seven, but not so tidy and not of course in the elastic band but a draggly white ribbon like a boot-lace. And she appeared to us, Mrs Peabody, like a haunted skeleton, but the crowd said, 'God, what a looker,' and other common things that made us aware that in that world she's considered at the top. And Mrs Peabody, they were both smoking as they got out of the Porsche and she had a smile that her father labelled as "relentless"—he has a turn of phrase.

'She saw us as she passed. Her father was smiling as he does, and Deborah said, "Hullo Mum, hullo Dad." Well, she couldn't miss us, being properly dressed. Mr Deecie is always properly dressed and he'll tell you that in twenty-five years he hasn't seen me without my earrings except in bed, if you'll pardon me. I had matching hat, coat, bag, gloves and shoes taking a tip from the Royals. In tangerine. Franko was dark suit, very white shirt, new, and a tangerine tie, to tone with me. It was just as she'd said, a very fast ceremony, just a few minutes, and afterwards—we'd not actually managed to get in the room for the ceremony but stood out in the passage—afterwards she gave us both a kiss. She said, "See you next week then, Dad. Mother." Ivan didn't say anything till she pulled his sleeve and then he said, "Good of you to come."

'We couldn't get a taxi away from the registry office so we walked down the street to a main road and the traffic was at a standstill there, too, and every taxi taken. I said, "Frank, we should get something to eat round here, there's lots of little places," but he said no. "No," he said. "I'm not taking you just anywhere. I'm taking you to the Cumberland Hotel." The Cumberland being the place we'd stayed the first night of our honeymoon. "It's the Cumberland or nothing," he said, "And we're going by taxi."

'But there was no taxi. Five minutes, ten minutes—no taxi. Frank said we'd start to walk, so we walked—me in my high heels after all the standing—and we crossed over a terrible corner for traffic and nearly got ourselves run over. We found we were walking towards Kensington Gardens and we passed the road-end where Princess Margaret and all of them live, and then, just nearby, was this wonderful hotel and all kinds of very good cars driving up and people hurrying in and laughing and I said to Frank, "Look there's that girl in the cartwheel hat," and Frank said, "And there's that man with the make-up on his face and the earrings."

'Then I said, "I thought I saw Ivan." Then we both saw there was confetti galore and a flick of white that was Deborah. I saw Mr Deecie's face then, Mrs Peabody. I said, "Well, it doesn't matter. We'd not have fitted in."

'I said, "Come on now, Franko, we'll go to the Cumberland and have a wine and steak lunch, the two of us," but he'd lost heart and we didn't. We had a salad at the station.

'On the way home in the train he said, "It's the finish this, Vera. I'm not a hard man but it's the finish."

'I couldn't think of a word to say. I kept trying to take his mind off by pointing things out to him from the train window. He never spoke. And he never spoke when we got home. He just sat looking at his tea. I said, "Have a whisky, Frank, it'll make it better," but he didn't. He lay in bed that night and whenever I woke I said, "Are you awake?" and he said, "Yes, I'm all right." But he wasn't. We don't ever mention it—never since.'

'But he's come to see her today?'

'Oh, it's true what he said. He's not a hard man.'

Frank asked if they could step into my back garden—he'd been looking out on it from upstairs—to take a look at the back of Deborah's house, and I helped him put his head through the weak place in the fence. He didn't mention to Vera all he saw next door—

156

the climbing-frames and swings left out all winter and all the mud and weeds. 'Very nice swings and slides here, Vera, and there's that doll you sent, sitting up in a window.' When Vera went tiptoeing ahead back to my kitchen door I saw that Frank's face looked sharper, rather sick. He said, 'Mrs Peabody there's a dead tortoise in that garden. Horrible. Birds or something have been trying to pull it out of the shell. Like stretched black liquorice. It's all torn and crawling. They sometimes don't winter over. A warm day they'll come up too soon and then—weak—the birds ... I don't care that the children should see it. If I could only get to it with a spade.'

He said at the gate, 'Thank you Mrs Peabody. If ever you're in Leicester...'

'Leicester,' said she. 'No thank you. I'll take the presents back in my bag—Ivan gave me this bag from one of his trips in foreign parts. I hope what we've said today can be private between us? I don't know what came over us. I feel very grateful and pleased we came. With such a person as a neighbour, she'll not come to harm.'

They had hardly turned the corner, heads near together under my umbrella (it came back to me by return of post) when Deborah came swooping up the hill in her Peugeot 105 from the other direction, and bundled everyone out and towards the house. She smiled crookedly

157

at me. She looked tired.
So.
Nothing has happened Joan.

With love,
Eliza

May 1st

Let me describe to you The Hospice, m.d.J., for I don't believe you ever saw it. It's a longish, lowish sort of house that stands at the end of a wooded track in the deep part of the Common. It was once called Caesar's Farm because it's supposed to have been built on the site of a Roman encampment. A fairly romantic notion, but who knows. The nuns thought very little of it, and changed the name to The Hospice of St Julian. Julian for Julius, and there St Julian hangs in the hall above Mother Ambrosine's desk, the holy lad with the golden eyes. St Julian the Hospitaler, St Julian the patron saint of watermen and minstrels, the saint of the passing show, of the Fair. The saint who put a leper in his own bed and was told by an angel to cheer up and be happy in married love. Oh, he's the man for me.

Barry thinks he looks a sulky sort of cove. 'Like a sullen cream bun,' he says. But I gasp at his beauty. Piero della Francesca. The great eyes don't follow you about the room. They never look at you, but out of the window, over the Common and away. Away to the waters of the Common and the Fair, the Fair, the Fair.

Well of course the Common's why we all came to live here, isn't it? Our Common love, ha ha. From the big roads that slash it on the London side you wouldn't think anything of it—just a round field with some grand houses standing looking at it, and a pond in the middle where we all skate in winter and fly kites and sail boats the rest of the year. Vigorous men in shorts bounce up and down on Sunday afternoons before galloping off on long-distance runs, and there's usually a horse or two with well-mannered people on board, touching their old fashioned black riding-hats with their crops. There are always dozens of dog walkers, mostly women on their own, calling out, 'Artnoon,' to each other. There's the little antique shop where you can pass the time of day, and there's a row of wisteria-strangled pastel cottages, fine furniture showing through double-locked windows, burglar alarms set at the ready. There's the seventeenth-century farm-house that's supposed to be stuffed with Rembrandts and there's the pair of thirty-foot wrought iron gates a coach and horses rattles through each night at eight o'clock, though I've never seen it. The gates lead to a new close of houses with

159

pink and peppermint courtyard tiles. The coach stops on the tiles before a house that hasn't been there for two hundred years. Ha.

But duckie-doo, dear Joanio, beyond the pond and the patios and the golfers in their yellow jerseys, like wandering bananas, the wild part of the Common begins. Remember the sweep of bracken—nearly half a mile of it? Did you know that a French duchess used to produce plays in a glade in the middle of it? Pastoral parties for the French émigrés. Marie Antoinette shepherdesses wandered down the rabbit-paths in silken pinnies, carrying ivory crooks, down to the green scythed stage. The leathery fish-bone bracken nearly met over their heads. Tinkling laughter, lemonade, sugared cakes, footmen in wigs. French farce. Deep, sleepy country then, silent as Shropshire.

Now, even louder than when you left, Joan, you can hear the traffic. You can hear it anywhere on the Common now, tearing east and west across the London counties, comforting as ships' engines, thundering along. We pay more for living near the Common now and the nuns have to pay more still to let us have the privilege of dying on it. But we still love the place for itself. It's not just the city-dweller's snob gold card, the chance he has of pretending to live in the country.

I met Old Bernard once on the Common, cursing and swearing under his breath, cracking his broken fingers, the Auschwitz number tattoo hidden beneath his shirt cuff. 'You all play at being country gentlemen,' he shouts on bad days, 'and, by Christ, it's over.' But he walks on the Common almost every day and cycles slowly about on it early in the mornings.

The Common has a presence and a spirit of its own.

Beyond the pond and the coloured cottages, Joan, remember how the woods begin. Remember how the ground drops down and the trees rise and thicken. Through the trees, paths straggle, turn and dip under hanging branches, and bring you out to grassy places with butterflies and brambles and streams with bits of logs slung across for bridges. You can walk for hours seeing nobody but the odd flasher. Or you can walk through the woods, a mile or so, and out of them again into long avenues of park-like trees. You probably never went this far, always being so busy. If, like me, you had lived here for a long time, you could have watched the trees grow and change their nature—flourish, age, droop, recover, fall. They fell some of them in what looks like their prime.

I knew a tree, Joan, a birch. It stood beyond the spring. It never grew tall. It flickered and swayed. When it was young it tossed its hair. I used to wander about on the Common then almost every day watching the women with the children and the lonely, unappetising-looking men. For the likes of me they had put a seat near the trees. On the seat was a very expensive brass plate saying *In memory of James and John, the sons of thunder, two Sealyhams who for many years were happy on these Commons.* Classy that, the plural. Classy the brass. It got nicked like they nicked all the brass lettering off the War Memorial. Old Bernard walks by the seat cracking and crackling his tortured hands. We are used to him.

'These Commons.' Where's the other one, the other one—the Common of the golden boy, the passing Fair? Hush. Wait. I think we'll get there in the end.

Now, that lovely tree grew more and more beautiful. Its bark thickened and turned to gold and pewter flakes. The leaves turned first to green and then to white confetti—from silver coins like the sun on summer water to October sovereigns shaking against the autumn sky. The gold discs were scattered around in the frailest twigs on the metal branches. Then one day, it was gone.

I stood by the seat. Gone Joan, gone. The tree had gone. There was turf over the hole, neat as needlework. If you scuffed your feet about you could just make out a few white chippings in the long grass. The tree had had its knock on the door at three o'clock in the morning. Everything tidied away. Miss Ingham came by, all cardigans and wraps and her pockets bulging with the roots she pinched. She said, 'How very upsetting.'

Someone had seen the signs of mortality in the tree and spared it a lingering death.

There are still badgers on the Common, Joan, and foxes. Do you ever think of them, among the tigers and the crocs? There are better flowers than there used to be, now that we have all become such a nice bright Green, and the cold spring still rises and flows down through the trees to feed the mere—the best water in Surrey, says Marjorie Gargery, passing paper cups of it around among her children. There's always someone standing in the pine trees where the spring rises, always some old tramp with purple lips. Often that queer little jogger dressed in black. You often see him about in that slinky track suit. He never looks at me but he knows that I am there. I sometimes think he might murder me. It would happen in fiction. The Roman soldiers at the spring would have made short work of him. I think of them, dipping their feet in the water, and their Naafi mugs. I think of them shivering and wishing for Umbria and the land of Piero della Francesca, except he hadn't then been born.

Well now, this pure and ancient trickle, Joan, flows not so far away from a metalled narrow road marked 'Private' that leads to The Hospice. One mile and a half, and down it one day I come a-Maying and find Mother

Ambrosine at her books.

'Good afternoon, Eliza. You are looking very wild.'

'I walked. Maybe I took a bus part of the way. Then I walked. From the other side.'

'Through the woods? You walked all the way through the woods? My dear, you've walked miles. Miles.'

'I'm not an old woman, Mother Ambrosine.'

'But, my lamb, it is pouring with rain. It is raining like the Monsoon.'

Mother Ambrosine is solid and sure. Her face is smooth and brown. Her eyes are brown and bright and clear. She looks completed. It is a face familiar to me but never usual. It is a face with which you do not compete. There are lines about the eyes, across the brow one thread. More lines about the mouth. But no bags. No pouches. She travels without luggage. Her ears have never been pierced and her hair has never seen an electric drier or a scented shampoo. It's short and springy beneath a little cap that is the residual fin of what for centuries in her Order was a huge and yacht-like veil.

Stout shoes beneath the desk, support-tights, knees well apart beneath the dark serge skirt, and she is scratching under the residual fin with a leaky biro. Or was. She has stopped. As I approach the desk the biro is brought point down and begins to rap the blotting pad.

'. . . to the skin,' she is saying. 'At once to the

164

Laundry. Take off those clothes.'

'I can't run naked through The Hospice.'

'We'll find you something. What shall we do with her, Nick?'

I see, for the first time, that the Curate is sitting in her office, Nick Fish the committee man, my high-Protestant priest. He and Mother A. have been sitting talking together, sitting quiet together, Anglican and Roman, talking and thinking. St Julian above their heads stares on and I examine my fingernails. They have begun to look unfamiliar lately.

I fear Mother A. and Nick Fish. This silence between them. This stillness holds within it the awaited grief. I have seen Mother A. of course many times at a death but a Hospice (Joan) is not what they sometimes make out—a brave, hearty place; though it's no bleak house of corpses either. It was to try to find out something about death that I came here in the first place, as I dare say by now you will have guessed. Only domestic work it may be, but there are few secrets in a kitchen. We've all wept in The Hospice, Joan. We're not always jealously thinking of heaven. Death, they tell you at funerals—which are hellish things, Joan, and I can't stand the people who pretend they're not—death is 'just like stepping into another room'. Yeah, who says? Who's been there? And which room Joan? How are we going to shape up to turning the door-handle to find out? I have seen Mother Ambrosine, the warrior Queen for God, distressed and shaken by death, and if it were not so there would be no strength.

And now, here's Fish-the-Committee in his scruffy cassock and woolly hat and gloves, working away at a rosary and making sure not to look at me. So my Lord and my God I am right and it is Barry. He is gone.

'Barry's been asking for you,' says Mother A., 'Quickly get dry and go and see him.'

'How is he?'

'Back in bed. Weak. Not so bad. Barry,' she says to Nick Fish, 'is still here. He is in love with Eliza.'

I say to Nick, 'He is twenty-two years old.'

Fish absorbs this information unsmiling, and twitches. He can't stand me. Upper-class-rich-bitch-never-done-a-day's-work-in-her-life. But I watch him putting holy charity together as he lets go the rosary and gets to his feet. I see the dirty trainers and boyish draggly shoe-lace. I see the inside of his head—*no* NO. Please God, no. Don't let this happen. I will my soul, or whatever it is that forces on me these visitations, I will my eyes not to see the jelly within the bone and the bone's soft marrow and the cells that make our juices, cells so temporal that they flow away like the foam on the quay that was all that was left of the little mermaid in the tale. She faded downwards from the head. Off with her head. Blink. Swallow. Better.

Nick's taut face is back, and I see the expression on its surface and the effort he is making as a Christian priest dealing with poor dotty Eliza. But how can he ever give comfort if he can't conceal the clock-work, the cuckoo clockwork going on within his head?

Yet it's hard to trust a mask, and if you arouse hostile feelings maybe it's better to know it, even if they're in a priest. Cock-a-snook back, maybe? Cockasnook. His brain is saying (*no don't look; look away*): Eliza Peabody, oh my God, not her again. The mad woman. Needs a shrink. What's Mother Am doing, letting her in here?

'Hullo, Eliza. Nice to see you. Sorry I had to go the last time we met. We must have that talk some time.'

* * *

Joan, The Hospice laundry! It ought to be the subject of a preservation order. It lies in the cellars above unexamined remnants of the centurions, and it looks as if the nuns moved their equipment into a wash-house ready made: a temple of steam and heat with runnels in it laid down by Roman fingers. The washing-machines whir, the driers thump, and there are nuns working with electric irons and starch, sleeves rolled up and faces shining. Above their heads, rows of sheets hang like heavy flags.

'Eliza!' Sister Mildred is smoothing a

167

shroud. 'Will you get those clothes off while we dry them and I find something warm—not this—to wrap you in.' She hands me a hot hairy blanket.

I sit beside the washing-machines and watch the clothes slosh and pause. Pause and slosh. Gather momentum. Faster and faster they go, and away into an ecstasy of Dervish whirling, out of control. I'm always reading novels where the behaviour of a washing-machine is considered similar to an orgasm. A contemporary image. It will date. But I try to remember—Is it? Was it? Watching the whizzing bed-sheets I decide I never knew.

'So, what's the matter?' asks Sister Josephine. 'Depths of gloom, dear?'

'We'd better hear the worst,' says Sister Anna.

'I was watching the water go round.'

'Well now, and that's interesting.'

'And thinking of sex.'

'Sure and we think of nothing else, and champagne every day for breakfast. Now then—have you had anything to eat this morning?'

When my clothes were dry I dressed again ('Love her, the earrings'll be getting the jumper in a twist.' 'Don't tell her to take them off for goodness sake. Aren't they Barry's pride and joy?') and went up to the kitchen for coffee. I didn't remember having eaten anything for some time and I felt better for a slice of fried

168

bread and a couple of sausages. Then I remembered the dogs. My walk in the rain had taken hours. I must feed them. I must take them out. But first I must see Barry.

He was asleep, lying straight, the sheets as fresh and shiny as when they were new, or still in the folds of the bath-house.

'Barry. Me. Eliza.'

No reply. Oh, the skin. The raw cracks.

'It's the Queen of the Tambourine.'

Not a flicker.

I sit by him and hold his hand. I examine each clean blue nail. The clock ticks. Outside the window it looks to be the saddest weather now.

*　　　*　　　*

Nick Fish stands by his car and appears to be waiting for me. '*Oh*-kay,' he says, going round to the passenger side, opening its door, coming back to arm me in. That's one of the new things people have started trying to do—to arm me about. 'Lift?' he says. 'I'll take you home, Eliza.' That's something else. 'Eliza.' Nick Fish always called me Eliza of course, but now it's the butcher, the baker, and the dry-cleaner. Madness is a great leveller.

'Home?' he asks.

'Yes, please, I have to feed the dogs.'

'Nice dog of yours. I wish we had a dog, we have almost everything else. It's the expense. I

169

see yours on the Common. Often by himself, I may say.'

'It's in his breed. He's a natural wanderer. I can't keep him in. He's like an eel. I do try.'

'Oh-*kay*. Don't take off,' he says. 'I'm not blaming you, sweetie.'

'Sweetie' is new. Sweets to the sweet and barmy.

'He's been better since he had company. Since we had the other dog wished on us. We have two.'

'Two?'

'One's Joan's.'

'Who's Joan?'

'Well, for heaven's sake Nick, *Joan*. You remember Joan. You've been here five years.'

'Eliza, I do not remember Joan.'

'Oh well—I suppose you can't remember everyone. She lives—she lived—opposite me in Rathbone Road. Number thirty-four. Very good-looking. Carefree. You *must* remember her. Everybody knew her. Over a year ago she took herself off all of a sudden—left the children and the husband. Shocked the Wives' Fellowship. Look, Nick, you must remember Joan. People like Joan don't just get forgotten.'

'It's a big parish, you know. I'm only one priest in it. I'm not even the Vicar. If she was such a free spirit and so carefree I probably never heard of her. Church-goer was she?'

'Oh heavens, no. No more than I am, now.'

'Really? I'm sorry, Eliza, about that—we

170

really ought to talk. But you can see why I've not heard of your Joan. I can't get round the lot.'

'It's a pity you couldn't. Still—she's all right now. She learned how to look after herself. She threw out all her fears and miseries—they were there under the cheerfulness, that's why she got a peculiar leg—and she began to make her own decisions. I admire her enormously. She was a ruthless and decided woman.'

I went on for a while and all at once he swung the car off Caesar's Lane, stopped the engine and put his face in his hands. All in one go.

'Nick—heavens, Nick, what is it?'

'Could you shut up? I need a moment.'

'Are you not feeling well? It does hit you suddenly sometimes, doesn't it? It does me. I was sick the other week just after I'd shown a visitor the garden of the house next door. Quite suddenly. I don't even know who he was really, just someone who had come to see them next door and they were out. I was just suddenly sick. What is it? Is it The Hospice? Something at The Hospice?'

'No. Never The Hospice.'

'What then? What is it, dear Nick?'

'If you could just stop *talking*.'

After some time he said, 'Well, it's Vanessa.'

Long silence. It was warm in the car. I rolled down my window and bird-chirrups came in and the swish of the fir trees tossing. A little shower scattered down on the bonnet from the

171

wet branches.

'My wife. Vanessa.'

'Vanessa is . . .'

'Look, Eliza, don't start again. *Vanessa.* A very decisive woman. Et cetera.'

Silence. I looked at him in his woolly hat and he took off his glasses and wiped his eyes with his duffle sleeve. I took the glasses from him and dried them on my handkerchief. I gave him back the glasses and he put them on and sniffed, so then I handed him the handkerchief. He sat staring out at the rainy lane and I put an arm along the back of the seat behind him and stroked his neck above the clerical collar. I like necks. He put the handkerchief in his pocket and said, 'Have to get on,' and started the car. '

On the road over the Common he said—snappish again 'D'you mind? I just ought to look in at home before I take you back to Rathbone Road. Vanessa will be worrying.'

So we turned up at the clergy house forecourt, more puddles than gravel, and he left the car and leaned in through his front door and I heard him shout, '—in a few minutes. Taking poor Eliza home.'

There was a flurry from within and Vanessa came bounding past him with a face of wrath, leapt in her car which was poised ready for her, and roared away.

'Oh hell,' said Nick Fish. 'She's furious. She's got some meeting in London. Lord, I'd no idea it was so late.'

172

A child appeared. A baby, just beginning to stagger and wearing a nappy and a vest. Another child, a girl with a very direct look, appeared beside it. She seemed about seven or eight—I'm hazy about Nick's children. We've all helped out when Vanessa's been away but mostly by sending food. I had not actually met them. The girl took the baby's arms from round Nick's cassocked knees and it squealed and thumped her. 'Au pair's day off,' said Nick.

'It's all right. Goodness me, Nick, it's perfectly all right. I can walk home. It's no distance at all. I've been walking all day.'

'It's not so much *you*,' said Nick. 'It's not so much *that*. I have the Youth Group. There's nobody to leave the children with. Vanessa must have forgotten.'

'She didn't,' said the girl. 'She's furious. You promised. She'll stay late now. She always does when you forget. It's a matter of principle.'

'That'll do. Have you all had supper?'

'Yep. I got it.'

'Well,' said I, 'I'll go now. Forget me. I'm the least of your troubles. Thanks, Nick, for the lift. Half-way.'

'I wonder,' he said looking me over. 'Eliza— could I leave you here with them for a few seconds? I'll just nip round to the Youth Group and explain. They can carry on alone for once. I'll have to nip round to St Cyprian's too and take them some stuff for tomorrow and if I cut over the Common again I might get Mike to take over at 7.30. I could be back by eight—say 8.10.'

'I'll stay as long as you like. Of course,' I said or heard myself say, and, Let's see if he'll risk it, I thought. A mad nanny. Well most of them always were, they say now, one way or another.

'Could you really? Would you, Eliza? Do that?'

'We don't need anyone,' said the girl, seizing the baby and glaring. 'We can manage on our own.'

'But I'd rather like it,' I said, and Nick held the door for me. It had a huge paper face stuck to the glass looking out. A balloon from the mouth said, 'Hi!'

'I'm here,' I said to the girl who had a flounce like her departed mother.

'There's tea,' said her father, 'or something. I'll promise not to be long.'

'Stay for the Youth Group,' I said. 'Stay the whole time.'

'Dad-dad-dad,' wailed the baby with outstretched arms. Nick paid no attention, 'This is very kind of you, Eliza.'

And he was gone—a car screeching and grinding in the thin gravel once again—and I walked towards the sitting room followed by the huffy girl and the baby yelling full-tilt. The house had a rich and earthy smell that reminded me of long ago farmyards. I passed a cage full of rustling straw, a large bubbling fish-tank full of what looked like spinach and another cage, very fruity, with mice. I walked through an open door into what seemed to be the main room where seated at the corner of a table stacked with parish papers and crumby plates was the boy I had seen on the bus.

He was pushing along an old-fashioned fountain pen but rose at once, at once recognised me and (my goodness) held out his hand. He might be eleven, I thought, but not more than twelve. I'm not much good at the ages of children, but I'd not think he was twelve. He said, 'I'm Lucien, hullo. Sorry about Timmy. He'll shut up.' The girl was bouncing the baby up and down on her arm, or trying to, for he was wriggling and pressing his face at her, open-mouthed, to bite her chin. Between the bites he was engaged upon a purple roar. 'I'm Eliza,' I said, 'ELIZA PEABODY,' and the boy did not laugh at Henry's awful name.

'I saw you on that bus.'

'Yes.'

The girl screamed as one of the baby's fingers went in her eye and she began to cry, too. She flung the baby on the sofa, still roaring, and I lunged out and fielded it before it hit the ground. Its mouth was still a cave but for the moment it had reached a silence, gathering up for the next bellow. I stood up. The warm little child was surprisingly heavy. It was also very sticky. The bellow did not come.

175

'That's a terrible noise. Terrible,' I said in what I hoped was the voice you use. 'I don't know when I've heard anything like it.' (There was something very like it going on on the sofa.) The baby, pop-eyed, slowly unarched its back and lay limp in my arms. It stared so hard at me I wondered if it was about to have a fit. Babies once were prone to fits. They might yet be. And this other one on the sofa—it was perfectly possible, it seemed to me, that her eye had been put out. There arose squeals of agony.

'Shut up can't you?' said the boy. 'For heaven's sake, Amanda, how old are you? Eliza's terrified.'

The girl's toes drummed with fury at the floor. Face-down she continued to scream though on a lower note.

'Take no notice,' he said. 'She does this to all the au pairs.'

'I'm not an au pair,' I said, flattered. I liked the 'Eliza'—he wasn't the butcher who'd changed to it when I started posting the liver instead of the letters in the post-box outside his shop—'but, I'd better tell you, I know nothing about looking after children. I shouldn't really have offered. You'll have to help me.'

'No problem. None of them do. They get caught. And they're all hopeless.'

'We get awful Church ladies mostly,' said Amanda, turning and staring at me with two tearless and undamaged eyes. She considered me. 'Look at Timmy.'

The baby, its mouth still hanging open though growing smaller, had reached out a round hand and stretched it to my face. I said, 'Timmy?' He squirmed and levered himself about in my arms until he sat upright, then he leaned forward, reached for an earring and patted it. He pushed the earring until it swung and all the bells began to tinkle like a Tibetan hillside. He gave a crow. A most delightful happy crow. He smiled at the earring with merry eyes.

'Now you're for it,' said Lucien.

'He's found your earrings,' said Amanda. 'He's crazy for earrings. He eats them. He's eaten dozens of Vanessa's.'

'Do you call your mother Vanessa?' I asked and thought, What a question. You don't have to get beyond the face on the front door to know they'll call their mother Vanessa.

'She does. I don't,' said Lucien. 'A bit Sixties.'

'What do you call your father?'

'I call him Father, she calls him Daddy.'

'I call her Vanessa because she likes it,' said Amanda. 'She ought to have what she likes. She works hard and gets no thanks for it like Nick—like Daddy—does. Nobody drools over Mum-Vanessa. She hasn't got any smelly old ladies.'

'That will do,' said Lucien and I together and regarded each other with approbation. I

177

noticed that the baby was cramming its mouth with bells.

'Oh heavens, Amanda, help!'

'It's all right,' she said. 'I'll scoop them. They've not gone right down his throat,' and she fished with a finger while the baby roared. 'There's two here. I think I've got them all out. How many's missing?'

'I can't see. They're on me. Is there a mirror?'

Amanda and the baby, who was still taking distant hopeless swipes towards my ears, were struggling together now side by side on the table where Lucien had put down his pen with a sigh.

'I'll count. Amanda, get him *off* her. One, two, three—seven on the right and—oh Lord, only three on the left. Two we've found, so two have gone down.'

'Oh no!' Amanda looked stricken. 'They're awfully sharp. They're as sharp as Vanessa's tin mobiles were. I'd better ring the doctor. No, 999's quicker, the doctor's hopeless. He doesn't believe us any more.'

'Don't!' thundered Lucien, and baby and sister were silenced. 'Amanda—look first, and I'll look. Get on the floor. Look under the jumble. Eliza, look down your front.'

Amanda flung jumble about and said, 'Well, here's one,' and I looked down the front of my shirt where a bell rested on the ridge of my bra.

'Panic over,' said Lucien. 'Now Eliza, while Amanda shows you where things are I'd better get on.'

'Where things are?'

'To bath him. He should have been bathed hours ago.'

'I couldn't help it. I had the supper to get. And find Vanessa's notes. I'll bath him. Come here.'

'I shouldn't,' Lucien warned as I gladly handed Timmy over. 'She'll drop him. Accidentally on purpose. She does. It's attention-seeking.'

'I don't.'

'You do.'

'I don't. And she can't, anyway. You can see she can't. She doesn't have a clue.'

'*Thank* you, Amanda.' I grabbed the baby back and made for the stairs.

I blanched a little at a tank of terrible newts at a turn of the landing. This made Amanda laugh. 'Look in there,' she said with malice, opening a door on a wall of cages full of little velvety things scuttling about. 'They're chinchillas—going to make us a fortune.'

Apart from the cages there were other walls of books, and tables spilling with papers and on the floor more books and papers in tottering piles. 'It's my grandmother's stuff,' said Amanda. 'She's a widow in India. She says the books would get eaten where she is, so we have them.' In the bathroom there seemed no room for anybody, so tight was the space between bath, basin and WC, and again books everywhere. 'All Gran's,' said Amanda. On the walls of the passage between its bedrooms, wherever there were no books, there were posters, and beside the bathroom door a big crucifix at which the baby took a swipe.

'Does your grandmother come here sometimes? I mean come and help?'

'No. She doesn't get on with Vanessa and Vanessa can't stand her.'

'That's a shame. I don't think you should have told me that you know. It's rather a private thing.'

'No it isn't. Everyone knows. Mum-essa says it's better to have these things in the open.'

'I'm not at all sure of that.'

'*Aren't* you?' She looked at me as if, after all, I might hold some interest. 'You ought to bath Timmy now.'

'Bath,' I said to the baby who now lay still across my knees. He gave me a lingering, personal smile, 'Oh! he smiled at me.'

Amanda leaned against the bathroom door-post, swinging a foot.

'Oh Amanda, he's beautiful!'

She came in, put the plug in and ran the taps.

'Oh—isn't that a bit deep? It looks a long way down.'

'No. It's fine. Just drop him in.'

'What now? Like this?'

'Well, take his vest and breeks off. Go *on*. Don't be silly.'

I slowly lowered the watchful child who

180

opened out in the water like a flower. 'Oh, he's floating! Amanda—can I let go?'

'Of course you can. Of *course* you can. He won't drown, not even him. He's nearly a year old. He's been sitting up for ages. He can pretty well walk.'

The baby began to beat the water with open palms and sop everything near and far including my nun-dried skirt. He gave a crow like whooping-cough, 'Oh,' I said, 'Look, look, Amanda. He's laughing at us,' and Amanda shoved herself off the door-post, came in and leaned heavily against my side all of a sudden. She began to manoeuvre her finger like a knitting-needle through a piece of my hair.

'Are you African? You've got lovely hair. Like little orange bed-springs.'

'I think the baby must be very forward,' I said as Timmy squeezed the soap in the direction of a rubber duck and killed it dead. 'Isn't that rather advanced?'

'He's got terrific co-ordination,' she said. 'Yes. Actually he's very advanced. He's a bit marvellous. He's more advanced than any baby we know.'

'I think you are all three rather advanced.'

She ran to the top of the stairs and called, 'Lucien—she didn't know you could let him float.'

'Well, don't go away, that's all,' he shouted back.

181

'Help.' I shrieked. 'Amanda, he's eating it. The soap. Is it allowed? Oh heavens, is it poison? Oh God he's drowning,' for the baby had taken a slithery sideways glide, clutched wildly about him, grabbed at some garments hanging above the bath to dry and sunk beneath the wave.

'*Drowning*,' I screamed, and Amanda fished him out tangled in what looked like some of his father's Y-fronts and a vest, wrapped him deftly in a towel and laid him again across my knees. 'Rock him and shush him,' she said. She put both her arms round my neck. 'You are so *funny*,' she said. 'You're the funniest we've had.'

We put him in a pod-like outer covering of woolly stuff over a macintosh parcel stuck down at the edges, very plump and neat. I had never seen a baby's private parts and was rather embarrassed by them because they looked so huge. I wondered if there might be something abnormal about Timmy.

'What's the matter?' asked Amanda. 'Haven't you seen that before?'

'Well, no. Aren't they a bit out of proportion?'

'No. Pretty average. They're a bit like kidneys, aren't they?'

'Amanda!'

'Well they are. You don't know an awful lot do you? Yet you're so pretty.'

She lifted him up and then down over the cot

side and between us we arranged him for the night, pink, clean and peaceful. No pillow. No covers.

'Can he sleep like that?'

'Of course he can.'

'No blankets?'

'Of course not. Mum-Vanessa doesn't like things covered up. It's for health. He needs his sucky thing though,' and she produced from some evil corner a rag covered in congealed food which the baby grabbed like an old drunk in a bar spying his whisky. He thrust a corner of it in his mouth with one hand and let the other wave slowly about above him, as if giving Benediction.

'He'll be a bishop.'

'Vanessa says she'll shoot him first.'

'Doesn't she like bishops?' I knew of course that Vanessa was a conventional clergy wife who wanted no part in her husband's work.

'No, Vanessa's an atheist.'

'Oh, I see.'

'It's hard on Daddy. In a sense,' she said, stroking Timmy's face as she hung over the cot side.

'Well, I'm sure you ... What about Lucien?'

'He's agnostic.'

'I suppose Timmy's a Communist?'

'You are *funny*. How could Timmy be a Communist *yet*? Anyway, Communism's over.' She called down, 'Lucien, she thinks Timmy's a Communist!'

183

'And what about you, Amanda?'

'Oh, I'm Christian. I'm going to be a Woman Priest. Vanessa's really pleased. And if you don't mind,' she added, 'I actually ought to be going to bed now.'

'She ought,' called Lucien. 'She's not nine yet and it's past eight o'clock.'

'Do I—? Shall I—? Help you to bed?'

'No thanks, I'm too old.'

'Would you like a story?'

'Oh yes. I'll call when I'm ready. I'm sleeping here in Timmy's room, by the way. Granny's stuff's filled up mine.'

While I waited to be called I went downstairs to the kitchen and began to clear up a bit. I did this and that. A little more. A little more. There was an ancient, salty smell rather like Venice and I wondered if it would be taken amiss if I started a good clear-out. The dish-washer was nearly full up with dirty dishes. There was a big saucepan beside the cooker I wondered if I could squeeze into the dish-washer with the rest. 'Shall I start the dish-washer?' I called to Lucien.

And then I screamed.

In the saucepan something moved. It scrabbled at the pan sides and lifted a fleshy head. The rest looked soft and purplish and old as time.

'It's only the terrapin,' called Lucien. 'It has to be kept warm till the weather's hot enough for it. Isn't it awful? Eliza? Eliza—are you

184

all right?'

He came to the door, 'It was the size of a 10p when we got it. It's growing and growing. We don't know what to do with it. Oh Lord— sorry. It does get to some people—but it's only an animal, you know. Poor thing—think of being it. Look I'll get you some tea. It's just the noise its claws make, you know.'

'I promised Amanda a story.'

'Stop shaking. Don't worry. She'll be out cold.'

'But it was only a few minutes ago. I promised.'

'Well, just you go and see, Eliza,' and I ran quickly away and up the stairs.

He was right. Amanda of the scowl and flounce had cleared a space for herself on the divan and lay thumb in mouth clutching a small lion. She was wearing a garment of a hideousness similar to the baby's and was twisted in an uncomfortable-looking knot. But nothing could detract from the serenity of her face, the two arcs of black lashes lying on her cheeks. The baby watched me watching her and sent me a further Episcopal salute, and sucked his cloth.

'All right?' said Lucien downstairs beside the tea-pot. He had laid out yellow cups and saucers on a space at the sitting-room table end. Around them were many used ones. He had black eyebrows, silver gold hair, dark blue eyes. I thought, Oh, what a man you are going to be, then remembered that women shouldn't think like this any more. But perhaps I'm old enough to admit to taking unquenchable pleasure in men.

'There's some muesli,' said the future heart-stopper, 'if you're hungry. And a bit of marmalade. We don't eat much in the week.'

'Really?'

'No. Vanessa says we don't need breakfast and we get a good dinner at school. The baby's still partly breast-fed of course. We do eat a bit of supper.'

'What about—er—your father?'

'He gets stuff all round the parish. Vanessa gets a good meal at work—she's a child psychologist. But I expect you knew that.'

'You're an unusual family.'

'Are we? Indian or China?'

'Well, China. Lovely. No—no marmalade.'

'I'd think we were pretty usual. There's crowds like us around here. Nick wants us to move somewhere poor. He's a very good man, my father, you know. The trouble is my grandmother's paid for all our private education and it's supposed to be hard for us to break away once it's started. We're irreparably brainwashed, Vanessa says. If you were hungry we could get some fish and chips.'

'I think someone should be back soon.'

'They won't be. Shall I nip out?'

'Lucien, no. I really think not. I can't go for them and leave the baby alone and I certainly

186

can't let you go. It's getting dark.'

'You talk just like my grandmother. Yet you look so young.'

I glowed.

'And terrific. You look very terrific indeed actually. I could ring a friend with a bike.'

'And what would you do for money? Fish and chips are expensive.'

'My friend might have some and there's plenty here. There's The Society of the Risen Christ.'

'I beg your pardon?'

'In the blue cardboard box in the hall.'

'Do you regularly steal from the poor box?'

'Yes. I put in an IOU, signed. It comes out of my bank account at the end of the month.'

'Lucien—let me see your homework. Isn't it about time you went to bed, too?'

I picked up the exercise book and read the pages of flawless handwriting. Everything looked perfect.

'It was a push-over. It's grott, though, having to use ink. I'd give a bit for a word-processor.'

'You'd have to.'

'I keep on at my grandmother about one. I've the Latin next. Can you do gerunds?'

'Are you on gerunds already? I've rather forgotten.'

'No prob. I'll manage. D'you want the *News*?'

He switched on the television set and I

187

watched the antics of the hysteric world as he set to work. Northern Ireland, the Lebanon, South Africa, Bangladesh. Bangladesh underwater again. Bangladesh! Good heavens! There in a crowd of faces, backcloth to horror, I suddenly saw you, Joan. I saw you.

'It's Joan!'

'Joan who?'

'It's my friend, Joan. On the *News*. In Bangladesh.'

'That's where my grandmother is. We're always seeing people we know on the telly. We know more on than off. Hundreds of bishops. They used to come and stay here once at Conferences, the Third World ones, but they're not so keen now we're so crowded. They're not into fish, tortoises and so on. You'd think they'd be keen on wild-life wouldn't you?'

'No—but I did! I saw my old friend. I haven't heard of her for a year and a half, nearly.'

'Did she look well?' he asked politely.

'She looked,' I said and wondered what it could possibly mean to this precocious and most rational child. 'She looked very usual.'

'Some of my friends are very usual. I wouldn't mind not seeing them for a bit.'

'Have you finished the gerunds?'

'Yep. Well—' he folded away his books, replaced the top of the pen, carefully arranged everything in his briefcase and set it in the hall

188

with cap and blazer beside it, '—I'll just clean my shoes,' and he carried them into the room, set newspaper on the table, smeared on polish and seriously, unhurriedly, brushed and polished it away. He created an island of order in the room. He was a trim craft in a tattered ocean.

'That's it.' He eased back the lid on the polish tin. 'I think it all went very well, don't you—the evening?'

'Yes, I do.'

I had the notion that I had been married to Lucien for many years; a good marriage but to a very much older man.

'I hope you've enjoyed it. Oh—someone's back.'

In flew Fish. He seemed amazed to see me. 'Oh, ah—Eliza. Very nice. Yes? All well, Lucien?'

'Going to bed. Fine.'

'I've brought some fish and chips. Want some?'

'Great.'

Lucien disappeared to the kitchen with his greasy packet and came out again with it plus a length of kitchen roll and a bottle of vinegar. He started up the stairs, ''Bye Eliza. Come again.'

'I suppose he always says that,' I said to Nick at the door, eye on the second package in his hands. It is odd that nobody ever thinks I eat,

189

even though they all go on about how thin I am.

'Says what? Oh yes. Yes, he's quite polite. Should I—?'

'Of course not. I can easily walk home, I've been walking home all my life. I hope I've made the grade?'

'Grade? What grade is that, Eliza? I hope they didn't do you in?'

'No.'

I could see through his heavy eyes a memory struggling: Eliza Peabody? The one they say's gone off her nut. God knows what Vanessa will say. Well, her own fault, she didn't arrange anyone else. And nothing's gone wrong.

'It's really *very* good of you,' he said. He was confused. I was behaving so normally and looking at him, I dare say, lovingly as he shifted his oily fish-and-chip package from hand to hand. It looked nice and hot. He looked hungry and cold.

May 14th

Two weeks, m.d.J., since that evening.

I have spent much of them at the window. Nearly June. What a summer coming this year. The lilacs and the syringas and the roses already some of them full out, the grass long and silky and full of daisies—I don't know where the gardener went but it's all the better

190

without him.

But I haven't been looking only at the Month of May, Joan, I have been watching for the family of Fishes. Every car that zips by, I wonder whether it is taking Amanda to the high school after dropping off the baby at the minder's. Every black and red cap I see on any boy, I think must certainly be Lucien's. Every pram has Timmy in it, every pram-pusher is the Fishes' au pair. I have conversations with them all. I ask them all to tea. I bake a cake and get ready to walk round with it. I stop myself. I won't go back to that. The cake-making of the Church of England woman, the running between each other with pots of jam. I've tried it. It has failed.

But I went to Church again on Sunday, hoping to see at least one of them. I was trembling as I went in, like an old virgin in love with the priest. I fell to my knees and tried to pray but could not get away from the shouts and conversation going on at the clergy house. 'Come *on*, Amanda, we're late.' 'Well you don't have to go. You don't believe in it.' 'We have to—for Dad's sake.' 'What about Ma's sake?' 'What's Ma doing?' 'Feeding Timmy and reading an essay.' 'Who's doing lunch?'

On and on it went, the life of the Fishes in my head. Not one of them turned up at Church, not even Nick—it was an unknown priest with an ambling grin who kept getting lost in the service and gave a sermon about the place of

191

the United Nations in the future of Europe, which seemed a pretty small one. Instead of listening I thought about Lucien and Amanda, sitting beside me in the pew, and Timmy beatifically good in my arms, stroking my face.

So yesterday, when it had been very bad all day and it had come to evening and grown quite dark, I left the dogs and with a secret smile and a dark coat set out walking to the Common and towards the clergy-house. It was quiet along the almost empty road and I slid in through the wide gates, one off its hinges, kept to the rhododendrons along the scruffy drive, made a quick dash past the glass front door and stood concealed behind the ceanothus outside the living-room window where shone the only light in the house.

I stood very still, back from the window, flat to the wall. Discovered, and where should I be?

Soon I leaned sideways, turned my head and looked in to see Nick writing at the table among the chaos and Timmy asleep and very large upon his knee. Nick was writing peacefully. A cat was sitting on the window-ledge looking out at the night. It looked at me with distaste, jumped down and stared hard at the study door in silent command. Nick got up, holding the baby and the pen, let out the cat and stood brooding in the middle of the room. I thought, Oh lonely and sad. I saw him sigh, hitch up the baby on his shoulder, wonder whether to take him upstairs and risk him waking as he was put in his cot, saw him look longingly back at his work. The room about him was unkempt and dismal, colourless and scruffy. The twentieth-century setting for the tormented Anglican priest.

He looked up all at once and listened. Then Timmy woke and pointed at the window, and I thought, Oh Lord they've heard me. What shall I say I'm doing? Just calling? It's nearly ten o'clock at night. I must run away. But before I could think about how and where, round the corner swooped Vanessa's car and parked right beside me at the other side of the ceanothus. Both car doors flew open as the light went on over the porch and Vanessa, eating something large, half-wrapped in paper, and Lucien, doing likewise and carrying a big cardboard box, ran forward to the glass door, laughing. Nick appeared with the baby.

Nick said 'You're late. Was it good?'

'Wonderful,' said Vanessa putting her arms round him and the baby together. 'Superlative. Big Macs. We've got the programme. Here—in the box.'

'Is Amanda up?' asked Lucien. 'Wake her up—there's a Big Mac for her.'

'Did you like it too, Luce?'

'Great. Great third act. Ma cried.'

Nick looked down at Vanessa smiling and put his arm tight round her shoulders and kissed her hair. 'Watch out for Timmy,' she said, 'Don't let him eat burger.' They all went laughing indoors. A moment later Nick crossed to the window and drew the curtains across and somebody turned on some loud music.

*   *   *

So then I stepped quite noisily out of the flower bed, Joan, and walked right up the middle of the clergy-house drive, crunching the gravel, jaunty and light. The Common when I reached it looked very black, the road along it much longer than when I had walked it less than half an hour ago and very ill-lit—a lamp-post only every quarter mile or so. I passed the old Pound where the stray sheep used to be gathered and then I took myself diagonally across the grass to the pond where a glitter of light spread in a long extending triangle behind a nocturnal duck. No sound but the traffic's far-off roar.

There were dimmish lights from some of the great houses on the perimeter of this part of the Common. I watched for the coach and horses at the wrought-iron gates but it was past eight o'clock so I'd missed them. A warm summery wind was blowing and shaggy clouds swam over the London-lit red sky. I walked down Hill Street into Rathbone Road and stood by the fridge eating the cake I'd made. It had icing on it and a cherry. The dogs watched me, desperate.

'*All* right,' and I found the leads. '*All* right.' I

sang and hummed about. I set off down Rathbone Road again, my nightly patrol around the block.

*　　*　　*

Each paving-stone I know. Each lighted window I know. Evening after evening I walk thus—pausing and calling, stopping and waiting. First I stand before Deborah's house and salute the magnificent rocking-horse that stands in the window. No lights there tonight, but I know the flare of the nostril, the blaze of the eye, the ear pricked to the distant drum. I stand and stare from dark into dark until I can make out its prancing shape. Not long to the Fair. Not long to the Fair.

At my feet on the pavement is one of the children's toys made out of Vera's knitting, left out of doors. The dogs sniff at it. I sit it on the balustrade of the steps where it leans its flat head.

Some of the houses are flats now. Young people in sexy clothes stand about in basements. Expensive tiny television sets glare. Pine cupboards, stainless steel, sheaves of dried flowers. The broad back of a pregnant girl. She touches glittering taps with yellow plastic gloves. Farewell the Sixties drama of the kitchen sink, for the Kitchen Sink is now Art. The floors are made of pale or bronzy cork. The girl turns to crush garlic in a pestle and

195

mortar. Light falls on a bottle of Italian oil. Her boyfriend, man or husband is ironing his pink shirt.

Higher up the street, and here are the Gargerys, one on each side of a plastic-topped Fifties kitchen table talking seriously over mugs. About the walls hang posters, pegboards, certificates of merit; a piano, well-used, its keys concave with practice. It was her mother's, and the tune goes on and on. The darkened windows on the floors above conceal each a sleeping Gargery child stuffed with knowledge. As I watch, the windows all burst open and the children fly out of them and away, five Chagallic embryos. One clutches its little blanket, another a suitcase labelled 'Anywhere', one is baying at the moon. Take comfort in the cocoa, beloved Gargerys, while you can.

Not far along the road and we're at Anne Robin's mansion. It's an older house and she's grander than any of us. The light is still burning in her study. She's hard at it, creating rabbits. Above is the lighted window of the new Philippino au pair. Eastern music twangs. Solitary Anne blocks up her ears as she seeks for childhood again in the empty nest.

Up behind me now comes the little black jogger, light on his feet. He never speaks. He knows it's me. He passes each evening, but he never speaks. He's somebody's lodger.

Here, opposite my house, the house of the

childless and admirable Baxters, Dulcie Baxter in full view at her desk, marking examination papers. Her beautiful white hair springs up from her head enraged by what it sees on the page. I cannot see her face for the lamp shines down, but I seem to see her firm, judicial stance. Tick, tick, cross, she goes. She doesn't look up, perhaps to avoid the sight of Anne's light. She despises Anne with almost Johnsonian thunder, hardly keeping her voice down even when they are in the same room drinking the same hostess's sherry. 'Why are we all so proud of Anne Robin? Any of us could write that stuff.' The pen is the extension of Dulcie Baxter's school-ma'am fingers, her dedicated critical mind. She is reliable, over-worked, Girton, proudly uncreative. She wishes there were only dead authors. Living ones are beneath her attention. Even dead ones shuffle naked and anxious before her. Shakespeare trembles. Once, somewhere, long ago, surely some little thread of poetry touched a nerve of Dulcie Baxter? One wonders. Tick, tick, cross.

And up behind her tiptoes old Richard with a cup of tea. He sets it reverently beside her, and she nods.

I turn along the High Street and all the little shop-windows. There's an end shop that has a flattering old mirror set in the wall that has brought comfort to me over the years. But tonight I have a mazy look. I turn left. Down

197

the line of little cottages I go, the servants' cottages of the big houses a hundred years back. A woman with a grim pony-tail is playing a violin through double-glazing so that there's no way of knowing if the music matches the passion of her widow's face. She's alone. I watch for a bit to see if she'll explode into little bits—stars and comets that stick to the ceiling like wet confetti. She did this for me last week. Then on, and round the corner I go towards home, towards the retentive darkness of the Church.

But the Church is blazing with light, and as I look, amazed, I am filled all at once with thoughts of Henry. His Church alight so late and quite without his authority—however could he bear it? He, the good Church-warden? I know all at once, too, that there is some mystery about Henry's departure to Dolphin Square with its pellucid pool, its face shut to the river, its sinister underground car-park, some mystery that I ought to be able to solve. It is perhaps something that everyone knows but I.

Now it is getting towards midnight. The little block of expensive flatlets to the west of the Church's west door is all in darkness. Across the road the artless-looking woman who is always being burgled and sits up late with a cudgel in her lap, even she is in darkness. Nearby is the house of the woman who gives little fork-lunches with her friends, to talk of their salad days, and at night pads off clink, clink with a bag to the Leather Bottle—she is in darkness, too. Glaring in on all of them in their beds are the six long windows of the north transept. The wide window of the south wall blazes down on the block of flats.

St Saviour's is one hundred and fifty years old, built as a chapel of ease for the parish church which had proved to be too small for the intensity of Christianity at the time of the Oxford Movement. It represents one of the dying breaths of the Pre-Raphaelites when the Brotherhood was grown rash like Picasso in old age running about with pink toilet-rolls and making them into sugar-pink doves. Our windows are mostly coloured splashes of glass so garish that through the Thirties there were petitions to have then taken out. War came and the windows survived. The raspberry-red robes, the purple camels, the orange palm trees scarcely rattled when the land-mine hit Rathbone Road. Here they still shine.

*　　*　　*

And tonight, this dark night, Joan, they shone indeed. They blazed their kaleidoscope of tall slabs, basted with lead like the wrong side of an embroidery, across the black streets. As I drew near, I heard the sound of the Church organ.

I stepped inside the porch and stood. Joan—I never heard such organ playing in my life. The fabric of the building vibrated. The camels and the cacti and the rainbow saints shuddered with awe and joy. Boom, boom the music surged and rolled, ever louder, ever more tremendous, more fearful and more solemn. The dogs began to whimper and whine. They dragged on their leads. I stood there shaking and exalted with an almost sexual shuddering. Winding the two leads over my hands, I dragged the dogs towards the Church door and tried to turn the handle, but it was locked.

The music now rose higher and higher as I shook the door and I sank on my knees with my forehead on the big iron ring of the handle and I felt the Church inside fill with music as the sea is filled with tides, as a glass filled convex to the brim. The music passed through the door until I was filled up with it, too. It flooded me. I took the dogs home and ate another piece of cake, and a small pie.

Then, Joan, I knew I must go back. It's all very well to receive a religious experience but one must relate it afterwards to the world of every day. I had to know exactly what had been happening inside the Church. It was my duty as a sidewoman. I had not done any pew-dusting for weeks—no one had noticed—so there was every reason for me to be there and nowhere, I think, is it written down that we shouldn't do our Church-work at midnight. Off I set again, alone, and found St Saviour's now in darkness and quite silent. I took the key from its place inside the south door, above the noticeboard, behind the loose stone, and I wondered why I had not remembered it was there before. Had whoever it was who had been playing, used it? Locked himself in with it? Only just put it back?

The key did not feel just put back. It felt cold, as if it had been in its little damp grave a long time, yet the only other key, except for the Vicar's, is always in the clergy-house. A third was once with Henry. Perhaps it is now with whoever his proxy is—I've never asked. Perhaps it lies on Henry's still no doubt meticulous, fastidious desk-top in Dolphin Square? Your Simon had a key once you may remember, Joan, when he was doing his first organ exams, but that was several years ago. I remember that Simon used to practise at night. There were complaints about it.

Inside the Church I felt about round the door for the light-switch to light me to the vestry, but couldn't find it, so I felt my way down the dark side-aisle. In the vestry I found the lighting-panel for the whole Church and switched on the one marked *Chancel*.

The organ when I reached the chancel was locked, its hood pulled down, and I walked over and felt the cushion which did not seem to be at all warm. I looked up at the silent silver pipes with their swallows' nest slits. It was unbelievable that the glory I had heard not half an hour ago had sprung from this cool plumbing. I had dreamed.

No music now.

But there was a fumbling, a sudden clatter far away down the unlighted nave. Someone was moving about. I called out, 'Oh! Hullo? Is someone there? Hullo?'

Silence.

I had to get down through the nave to leave the Church. If I switched off the lights from the vestry I'd have to walk down the nave in complete darkness. I looked hard at the shadows. Utter silence. Blackness.

'Hullo?'

Silence still.

I went to the vestry and turned out the lights and began the walk down the side aisle, my hands feeling out in front and only the slightly lighter panels of the drained windows to help me. I went at first slowly and bravely, then faster and faster, looking defiantly into the dark.

I felt very weak when I reached the south door again and I turned and shouted into the nave, 'You can't fool me. There isn't anybody there.'

There was silence, and then the whole Church began to ring out with laughter and I ran stumbling away. I heard it, high, triumphant and mocking like an idiot child. The door banged behind me and I ran across the road, down the alley and into the sleepy street.

I lay in bed.

It was one in the morning.

I slept a little but kept waking, first with echoes of the music, then with echoes of the laughter. Then I slept and dreamed.

I dreamed of a child with outstretched arms and the confident girl, Amanda, and the dignified boy. The boy stood at a table of books and addressed me on stern matters. Beneath the severity he seemed just, though not particularly kind, I knew that he spoke for my own good but I could not hear the words. His lips moved but it was a faulty track. 'Tell me, tell me,' I begged and I was calling it out as I woke again. There was a light in my bedroom. It went out.

I have moved my bed, Joan, oh long ago, trying to deny, to negate this business of beds at opposite ends of the room. I had first piled Henry's bed with things and covered everything with dust-sheets. Then I had sent all the things to the jumble and Henry's bed to Age Concern. My own bed now stands alone, in the middle of the floor. I have removed the carpet and of course, long ago, the curtains. I lie now each night as a corpse with no need of bedside light or night-table. I lie afloat now, all Danae to the stars. The centre, ceiling light is a bulb, shadeless.

The window frame grows against the

moonless night. I hear the wind in your tall trees across the road, Joan, and in my own tall trees behind me, in the back garden. Otherwise, all so quiet. Dogs asleep in the kitchen. I begin to drift.

Then the beam of light springs across the room again. Up, round, down, gone. A torch.

There is someone in the room, Joan, and I am standing, before I realise it, in the window, and my heart is an organ-pump. Thump, thump, thump—I feel for a curtain to cling to and there is none. Thump, thump. I clutch the window-frame.

The light comes again and it is not a torch-beam in my own house, Joan, but one in yours. The light is coming from across the road. Up, down it goes, switching about in an upstairs window. For a moment it lights the plasterwork doily in your bedroom ceiling and the chandelier of painted lemons from Sicily via Peter Jones I was never brave enough to copy—and all cobwebs now. I see flashes of your house, flashes of you, still brilliant with colour and life—your royal blue stair-carpets, your marble urns with the undying ivy plants, your eighteenth-century, broken, French torchères upon the wall. Your enviable snook at the road's good taste.

All black again.

There is a burglar moving from room to room in number thirty-four, Joan, and so at once I ring the police.

And then, dear Joan, away I go again, across the road in my dressing-gown and slippers—and a tweed hat for it is not warm now. I walk swiftly, quietly through your garden gate, round the side of the house past the ballroom and the piles of frail gold chairs, to the back. Standing on the terrace, I watch.

Nothing to be seen inside the black windows at first but then, from the hall, the torch-beam again. It gets nearer. A flash, long, dizzy, urgent around the drawing-room walls. I move close to the windows and stand among the weeds and the faithful, untended chrysanthemums and dahlias. I look in.

On goes the torch again, and I see Simon. He has propped the torch upon the hearth and it shines in his face as he busies himself with paper and sticks and a box of matches. The flame on the lit corner of a firelighter takes hold of the sticks and he begins to arrange with the tips of his beautiful fingers little pieces of coal. 'Oh, Simon!'

I knock on the window expecting him to jump out of his skin but he continues calmly making the yellow fire before slowly turning his gentle Galahad face to me. He smiles, gets up and crosses to the French doors where I stand, and I see his lips are saying, 'Eliza.' Then I see that the lips are not Simon's after all, nor yet is the face, nor would Simon ever wear this slippery black track-suit, as a hand like a brick lands on my shoulder, and the police are here.

Not only here, but at your front door on the street side of the house, Joan, and at your side door by your coal sheds and beside the gardener's loo. A police car has crept quietly into Rathbone Road packed full of stalwart disagreeables. Silently but not secretly, for, from all around in the Road, there move other figures in assorted attire. Here are Gargerys and Philippinos and frantic-eyed Dulcie Baxter with ink in her hair. Do I see Isobel Ingham wrapped in a shawl? And the pregnant girl with the laundering husband? Only Deborah's house is dark, its blue door shut. The statue of Ceres isn't giving a toss.

'Eliza, oh Eliza!'

The inhabitants of Rathbone Road move towards me as a policeman marches me forward towards them. 'Oh, Eliza, whatever are you doing *now*?'

They are so persuasive, the inhabitants of Rathbone Road, so articulate, confident, authoritative, highly educated, resourceful, strong, commanding and rich. They polish off the police presence before I have even begun to try to explain myself to it, even to see its face. The police-car is gone. Marjorie Gargery is running with a cup of tea and somebody else with an extra coat. Isobel Ingham goes off without a word and doesn't look back as she passes through the high door in her wall. Everyone else—not the pregnant couple who stand apart, a little embarrassed—but everybody else urges me over to my own front door. And oh, good heavens, here are the Baxters coming out of their house with hot-water-bottles, and it seems they are to spend the night with me.

'I'm perfectly all right. I have Simon. Simon will stay at number forty-three tonight. It was only Simon. I can't think why he didn't simply ask for a bed over here in the first place.'

But they have got me into bed (the buggers) and Dulcie seems to be hauling mattresses about so that she may sleep on my floor. 'Now Eliza, you can't be alone.'

'Look,' I say, sitting upright, swilling tea, crunching biscuits, supremely wide-awake. (I don't feel tired. I have not felt tired for months.) 'Lincoln biscuits, very nice, Dulcie—I'm sorry. I was woken up by a light shining in on me. I went over and found that it had only been Simon breaking into his own old home.'

The Baxters were both there, side by side at the foot of my bed.

'Simon?'

'Joan's Simon. He must have been down in London from Cambridge and missed the last train. A concert I expect. I heard him playing in the Church earlier. You know—like he used to. He was wonderful. I sat in the porch listening.'

Now they are seated side by side on the end of my bed, the two Baxters, shifting their thin bottoms about.

'I must be mad—I knew he had a Church key. I didn't connect. When the torch-beams began to play all over me, I didn't connect. I rang the police before I went across and found it was only Simon. But, before I had time to come back here and ring again to say it was all a mistake...'

'Eliza,' said sombre Richard Baxter of the prudent, judicial lips, hair on end in scant but tidy tufts. (How wise of him to become a judge. It's a head already half a wig.) 'Eliza, let me ask you one question. Where do you think Simon is now?'

'Well I hope, I very much hope that someone is looking after him. That house must be freezing. Nobody's been near it for months. I never see Charles there now. Or at all. Sarah's in Oxford...'

The Baxters sit in thought and I start to climb out of bed to go and look for Simon, hungry and alone. Four Baxter hands are raised to press me back again.

'Dulcie, Richard, could you find out about Simon?'

Two kind Baxter nods.

'There's my spare room. Poor boy, messing with firelighters. He needs looking after. He needs his mother.' I had a flash of fear though. I remembered the natty, cruel little face that was no more Simon than it was Tom Hopkin.

'Yes,' they say, watching me. 'Yes, Eliza.'

Now all at once my eyes are heavy. There

must have been something in the tea and I'd like to fight it. I haven't needed sleep for months. I haven't really slept since drunken Christmas night.

May 29th

D.J.,

And I wake to hear a telephone conversation going on in the hall. At first I can't think who is in my house. 'Very,' the voice is saying. 'Very. Yes. Called the police. I think it is essential. Yes.' Then I drift again and wake again. Dulcie Baxter with a most slipshod tray of breakfast is lurching about the room, looking for somewhere to put it down. She blinks through her spécs. The ink is still in her hair. I am overcome as I remember the goodness of Dulcie and the events of the night. I spring up in bed and cry, 'Oh, Dulcie—you look so tired.'

'It's the end of the Mock,' she says, 'it is the worst time.'

'But you *never* make fun.'

'The Mock. Mock, mock, mock. "A Levels." Marking. This is the worst year we have ever had in the history of the school. The worst papers I've ever seen. Of course it's twentieth-century stuff they set now, most of it.'

'Really?'

'Well, enough. They all choose the recent authors.'

'Don't you like recent authors?'

'I'm afraid not much. It's all stuff we could all of us write if we could be bothered, the modern novel. And modern poetry in particular.'

'You're very good still to be taking it on.'

'Oh, they're very short of people. Young examiners won't put the hours in. For the pay. It has to be someone with plenty of time.'

I think of my time in its plenty, and nothing done. She plonks the tray across my knees and the marmalade pot slides and slips and spills. She walks about the floor trampling vigorously my shed garments. I am troubled by them. They ought to be over a chair. My dog arrives and lies on my knickers. Dulcie shoos him off. Dog growls and she looks as if she's going to give him extra homework. She looks about my bare room for something to do, needing curtains to draw back.

She stands at the window, facing the road.

'I've telephoned Henry,' she says, 'I'm afraid you won't be pleased, but Richard and I decided last night that Henry ought to know about you.'

'Know what?'

'That you are frightening us all. That you are clearly very unhappy.'

'Did you get through?'

'Yes, he was just about to leave for work.'

'But did you get *through* to him? You'll be the first for a long time.'

'He's coming to see you. He'll be here this afternoon.'

'Well, I'd better get up.'

'No, no Eliza. We want you to stay quietly where you are today. I've brought the Mock across and I shall work in your drawing room and bring you your lunch to bed. You need a rest.'

'What is there for me to rest from?'

'Eliza, oh Eliza.'

'I know, Dulcie. You've sent for the doctor.'

She blinked. Her eyes through the hard-worked tri-focals turned to fried eggs.

'So you heard the phone?'

'Not really. I didn't know who it was. But it's what you would do. Perhaps you're right. Who's coming? I've never had a doctor visit the house. Even after the hysterectomy.'

'I've sent for Richard's doctor. Dr *Sepsis*. He's an old doctor Eliza. Very experienced. He doesn't do much nowadays, but Richard has the highest respect ... He was awfully good when Richard's mother died. And his father. *And* his cousin, come to that, in Merton Park. And he was marvellous when Sybil Etheridge died and poor—you know, the man from down the hill with the Airedale. When he went.'

'Do his patients ever get better?'

'What? He's properly qualified—very highly

211

qualified indeed before the War. His father
used to live in Anne's house, or it may have
been Isobel Ingham's. It was a doctor's family
before the Great War.'

'Can he get up the stairs?'

(Oh Barry, Barry—just wait!)

'Oh, he's very spry. I'm not sending you
some young psychiatric type, Eliza. No—we'll
see what Dr Septimus has to say.'

'Septimus?'

'*St Thomas*, Eliza.'

'What, where he was or what he is?'

'Eliza, just let me get a bowl of water and a
flannel and then you can have another sleep.'

I examine the bowl and flannel for soporific
elements and watch my rose-geranium soap
grow soft and pale round the edges as the water
cools about it. I loathe pink. I loathe *pink*.

In the end I take it out of the water. A
Christmas present. I'd never have bought pink
for myself. One pound thirty they cost. The
green ones—mint—are lovely. I sit squashing
it in my fingers, feeling rather sick.

What's Dulcie up to? There are dreadful
noises going on below—snarls, woofs and
smashing crockery. As I slip into sleep again I
feel the soap slip, too, out of my hand. In the
mists I hear a bell and Dulcie's voice.

In further mists I hear a second ring and two
voices coming nearer up the stairs, one Dulcie's
the other a sort of wheeze with pauses. At
length Dulcie comes sailing in carrying the

earthenware pot I keep for old lettuce-leaves for the compost-heap. It is stuffed with yellow roses. 'Look what's come for you. What a bouquet!'

Beloved Simon.

'And here is Dr Sepulchre.'

(You know it's funny, Joan, I can't get the hang of the way Dulcie Baxter speaks, I'm glad I'm not one of her pupils. She's got something of Sarah about her, making godfather sound like father.)

'Here's the patient, Doctor, and I shall leave you alone.'

And he looks quite a nice old thing. He has the usual half-smile they fix on with the stethoscope. Sometimes you see it at The Hospice though not often, Mother Ambrosine choosing her doctors as carefully as her helpers and, if I dare say so, her patients.

'Ha,' he says. 'Hullo there.' (Well, what can they say?) 'Not well in the night I hear?'

'It was not a—not a very usual night.'

'Not a usual night, eh?' He is feeling about in my neck glands. 'Open wide.' Gleaming a light down my throat, he seizes one of my hands and inspects the nails then, seeming unsurprised at them, he flings back my bedclothes, whips out a hammer and hits me on the knee. My foot hits him obediently back. 'Excellent,' he says. 'Excellent. Sorry my hands are cold,' and he begins to press me in the stomach. He continues with things of this nature and then

213

sits with bowed head for a considerable time. I wonder what it is that he has found.

'There's a big bar of soap on the floor,' he says.

I can think of no reply.

'Ah,' he says at last, and very sadly. 'And how old are you, Mrs Peabody?'

'I'm fifty-one.'

'Ah fifty-one. Menopause going all right? Everything drying up nicely?'

'I had a hysterectomy at thirty-one. That's the scar.'

'Ah, the scar.' We both look at the huge purple zip-fastener across my lower regions and my tired stomach, once so taut and golden above it. The skin above the scar hangs poised like the overhang before an avalanche. You'd have thought he might have noticed.

'I believe I knew your father,' I said.

'Really?'

'Long ago.'

'Ah, long gone, long gone. Now I do congratulate you. Well done, well done.'

'For knowing your father?'

'For getting rid of the good old nursery-furniture, my dear. Best removed when no longer needed.'

'What a perfectly horrible thing to say. What a foul phrase.'

'What? Ha?'

'I was thirty-one.' Then I added, 'Fuck you.'

'*Now* then,' he said. 'Tell me. How many

children have you, Mrs Peabody?'

'None.'

'Ah, I see. Some trouble? Was there malignancy?'

'No, we were very fond of each other then.'

'I mean—er—my dear—did you *want* children?'

'No. Not by then. It was not possible after ... But we were both fertile.' (Why the hell tell him?) 'It was a sort of unspoken postponement.'

'Husband happy?'

'Oh, I expect so. He's living in Dolphin Square. He left me.'

'Ah, now then, I *had* heard something? Why was this d'you think?'

'I think...' And then Joan I did indeed endeavour to think. I looked straight at the old creature's eyes. How mysterious that I should feel suddenly impelled to tell the truth to the Son of Dreariness, who no more than his father cared in the least about it. I think perhaps because he had looked with distaste at the rose-geranium soap.

'I think he left me because I had become impossible. He thought that I was going mad and he probably saw it before anybody else did. It is hard to bear—someone else's rift in the soul.'

'Leaving you was not a sympathetic move.'

'No. But I think, you know, that he was frightened. My soul's rift had caused

215

another—a chasm that opened between us. The chasm only opened a few years ago, the rift years maybe ten years before that. I believe. I believe that deep down somewhere he found something that was too difficult for him. It was probably in me but it might, I suppose, have been in himself too. So he went off with a friend.'

'Ah, and the friend a younger woman.'

'No. He'd *never* do that. He's not at all romantic. He went off with a Senior Member of the Civil Service, a man. From the house across the road. The house you can see. Number thirty-four. The man's wife was my friend. Well, my acquaintance. She left her husband a year and a half ago. You can see how sad that lovely house looks. No, Henry went off on Christmas Day with a perfectly friendly congenial excellent sort of man, in a very dignified way.'

Doctor Access stood looking out at where your lost house stands lamenting you, Joan. He said, 'We lived in this road once you know. Over on that side of the road. Splendid old houses with such beautiful long gardens. I expect this side is more practical. Lot of bomb-damage over there. Of course I was away at the War. I must have a talk with your husband, Mrs Peabody. I think he must be made to come and talk to me about you before we decide on the next step. A consultation or two. Nothing very urgent.'

'How like your dear father.'

'What? Now there's a place I could recommend. Rather expensive but excellent for complete rest.'

'But I don't need a rest. I'm never tired. What I want is a revelation.'

'Now, alas, that is not in my power. Who doesn't? Who doesn't?'

'I need to understand the nature of sanity.'

'Mrs Peabody, this is a little outside my sphere but I believe that if you comprehend a notion of sanity...'

'But I'm not sure I do.'

'If you think yourself mad, then, to be blunt you are most unlikely to be so. That's what my textbooks used to say anyway. Of course, I'm old-fashioned.' He sighed deeply and his face hung like a crag. 'Just my opinion of course.'

'You look, doctor, as if you don't find life very rewarding either.'

'Rewarding? Now, we're not here to talk about me, are we? One does one's best. That is the only reward. I think you know we all ask too much. I remember my Indian servants before the War. Poor as dogs. Life expectancy thirty-two. Happy all day long.'

'Really?' I saw the flies on the boy with dying eyes, who was head and torso only, in the mud of the bank of the Brahmaputra outside our house near Dacca.

'And such good health available for us *all* now. When my old father was first a doctor
217

here he used to go round in a horse and trap, or on his feet, walking between patients, and all he had to offer when he got to them was a kind face and a bottle of coloured water most of the time. People died or recovered, as they do today. But all so much happier now.'

'Penicillin?'

'I prescribe it rarely. Even without it—so much splendid health. Yet all these nervous breakdowns and everybody depressed.'

'I work at The Hospice at Caesar's Farm.'

He looked up with a totally different face. 'I didn't know you worked. You're medical then? Dulcie should have told me.'

'Oh, only the washing-up.'

'I see.' He looked relieved. 'Well, my dear, I shall be in touch with your husband and my secretary will be writing to you. And don't worry. You seem very fit to me. This confusion is a wretched business. It's the age, you know, the age. Even though all the little bits and pieces were nipped out long ago ... We must think of all the starving people in Ethiopia, mustn't we? And of Buchenwald and Belsen? Of the atomic bomb and of terrible cancers?'

'I don't think that that would make me happier.'

Not hearing me presumably, he took a quick, worried look across the road again at your house and said, 'And above all, we must keep jogging along.' He patted my hand, slid on the soap about six feet across the room and

218

fell flat on his face.

'Jesus laughed,' I informed Dulcie who came bouncing in with a glare as if it was all my fault. She gathered him up, ushered him out and they went off downstairs. I nipped out of bed and watched from the window as he loped down the path like an old turtle, his head waving about in front of him feeling in front with his creepy claws. He slid slowly away in his car, past Old Bernard who today, as every day, was zig-zagging up the road on his heavy bicycle. Two grim-faced men, one who used concentration camps as moral fodder, the other who had known one.

May 30th

Humpty-Dumpty piddle and pie,

Soon after you arrived to live in Rathbone Road, dear Joan, I spent a day with Old Bernard that I have not forgotten. It revealed much to me. First, it revealed to me the duplicity of the sainted Miss Ingham. A note from her had come through my door. She was then—as now—a woman I saw only occasionally to smile at. We had scarcely spoken. She wondered if I would do her a favour. Every year, she said, she attended the Chelsea Flower Show with Old Bernard, as his guest, his poor wife Lola being unable to go about much. This year she, Miss Ingham, was beginning to feel that she too was unable to stand about. Would I very kindly go with him instead?

The Chelsea Flower Show, Miss Ingham said, was the big day in the year for O. B., the only time he now ventured into central London. He certainly could not go alone—too old—and, as I knew, he had few friends, being so outspoken. She had her Fellows' Tickets which meant that we could go on the least crowded day and afterwards Old B. always took her to lunch at Peter Jones. He would be delighted to do the same for me. What a kindness I would be doing, she said. The C.F.S. was the last spark in the old man of his lost Bavarian childhood.

I rang and said I wasn't sure if O. B. liked me much. He seemed to regard me only as the one who had knocked him flying with my car door. Miss I, speaking faintly and with pauses, as if simultaneously doing something else—prodding at seed-trays, examining her whiskers—said that everyone had knocked Old Bernard off his bike at one time or another. She had suggested the outing to him and he had seemed very happy.

We went padding down the hill, then, the two of us, Old Bernard and I, to the station where O. B. made a great performance of buying the Underground tickets.

'D'you have a card? It's only one pound fifteen if you have a card.'

'A student card? Goodness, no.'

'No. A pensioner's card. Have you a *pensioner*'s card yet?'

'I'm not sixty, Bernard.'

'No,' he said dismally, 'maybe not.'

We sat side by side, joggling along the District Line, Old Bern cracking his knuckles. I said that I hadn't realised he was a gardener.

'I'm not a gardener.'

'But you go to the Show every year?'

'Miss Ingham is a forceful woman.'

I could see it was going to be a long day. 'Perhaps,' I suggested, 'we should split up?' We had reached the Chelsea Embankment and had joined the hurrying happy feet. 'I could look at the flowers and you might . . .'

'I shall be among the furniture. The garden seats.'

'We could meet here again at say, twelve-thirty.'

'That's too late. They'd have given us up and we'd have lost our table. Peter Jones is a considerable walk.'

'I don't really mind missing Peter Jones.' To tell you the truth, Joan, I couldn't imagine Old B. in any kind of restaurant and certainly not among the pastel tints. 'Couldn't we just have a snack, here at the cafe?'

'I don't eat out of doors. The flies here are diseased.'

221

'Diseased?'

'From the spraying. The sprays they use on the flowers. This place is a death-trap. We breathe poison into the lungs. That's why I never go near the flower-tents. The roses are all spray. The gladioli pure ethylene.'

He sat down on a cruelly bright, tobacco-coloured garden seat and stared at some polystyrene urns and a statue of Pandora letting all the troubles of the world out of a polystyrene box at her feet. She had a join all down her sides and over her head like an Easter egg that would fall apart if you tapped it. I went round the flower-tents trying not to breathe. 'But they smell absolutely wonderful,' I said when I found him again, looking at gold-fish and lotuses in a pool loud with a hose-pipe-engendered waterfall. 'They smell only of heavenly flowers.'

But he was abstracted.

We made our way up Lower Sloane Street where I met, among the afternoon Flower-Show-tramping-feet, Duffy and Dilly Fancy-Baker from Wallis and Critch before they were bought up by Klein and Woo, who shrieked and embraced me in the usual way (a light-year-and-a-half away, dat ole Eliza-girl) and asked if Henry and I were going to Glyndebourne. Old Bernard stood bleakly with his long cuffs hanging, looking at the road.

In the crowded Peter Jones lift he revived

and seemed at home, gaining confidence and a little cheerfulness when people began to whisper and fumble about, prodding buttons for the right floor. He called loudly, 'Fifth floor. Fifth floor. We want the fifth,' (it turned out to be the fourth) in a resonant voice, and marched me towards a window table.

'Have what you like,' he said. 'She pays.'

'Miss Ingham pays?'

'Yes. Don't ask me why. It pleasures her.'

'I thought Miss Ingham said ... You mean she gives you money? Like a boy?'

'Oh yes. *I'm* not taking you out.' He laughed long and loud, a harsh laugh that made heads turn. After it, he sat smiling, the smile I get from him when he stops and speaks on the Common and talks about the Lamb of God.

Now all this happened, Joan, when I still felt God to be on my side as well as at my side, and I was hand in hand with Him. I said, 'Bernard, I expect that it is very difficult for you to like us in Rathbone Road even though there are quite a number of Jews there. It must be very difficult for you, very annoying, and you would have been a lot happier in Hampstead. We have all had very much more constricted lives than you, but we cannot help it.'

'You can all help it. Hampstead is neither here nor there. To the middle-class English the Holocaust might never have happened—look at them all, eating their lunch.'

'We can't help not being Jewish.'

223

'You can help your self-absorption. Introspection.'

'You don't tell me Jews aren't introspective?'

'I'm not talking about Jews. Jews are irrelevant to this conversation. Let's forget the Jews.'

A woman came up and asked if the spare seat at our table was free and I thankfully removed my handbag from it and she sat down. Old B. turned to the window and gazed at the sky.

'How beautiful it is,' said the woman, 'this part of London.'

We all three looked down at the tops of the trees moving gently in the square.

'Like Paris. The last romantic bit of London to look like Paris. D'you know the little bit where the bus goes round to Passy?'

She wore a black hat from another age—Leghorn straw, its veil pulled over her face and tied tight round her neck with a narrow, black-velvet ribbon. Pale brown splodges on the skin. She wore the oldest black coat I had ever seen, most beautifully made, but cheap black net gloves. Under the gloves the fingers were heavy with diamonds and the veins on the back of the hands were pumped full of purple ink. They stood up in blebs and knobs under white make-up. Her head nid-nodded as she undid the veil. She said to Bernard, 'I'm afraid I heard what you said. I don't think you ought to speak of the Jews like that.'

Bernard munched.

'You remind me of one of my late husbands who made Jewish jokes. One of them ran as follows. One man says to another, "My new house is all right but it looks out over the Jewish cemetery." The second man says, "You're very lucky, where I live they're still all walking about." This is the sort of joke that only a Jew may make, just as only the blackamoors are permitted to say "niggers". Don't you think? I'm very clear about this. I have a friend close to the Queen Mother who says Her Majesty feels exactly the same. We—you and I—have to be so careful.'

Old Bernard began to eat his lemon sole.

'Fish,' said the woman, 'fish. Now that is something the Jews understand. Nobody cooks fish like a Jew. I always think of that in Church when we have the Feeding of the Five Thousand. I don't think, by the way, that there is a Jewish chef here, do you? There's something in it you know—it has been scientifically proved—this talk of fish making brains. The Jews have plenty of brains. One quite grants them that, even though it does seem odd how many managed to get caught. Excuse me, my dear, but are you one of the Terry family?'

'Terry?' I asked.

'No—not the chocolate people. The *Ellen* Terry family. You have something of the same

225

hair. Of course red hair in a woman is often Jewish, though I'm sure Ellen wasn't. She would be Church of England.'

Bernard munched.

The woman ordered and ate a little omelette and got up to go.

'I eat a little omelette here every day. There is nearly always someone to talk to. I hope we may meet again,' she said to me, casting a glance of disapproval at anti-Semitic Bernard. 'I live in a very nice bed-sitting room in Royal Avenue. Once I lived in the whole house and many members of the Terry family came to see me frequently in the old days. And several very Jewish people too.' (Another flash at Bernard.) 'Excuse me, but you have smudged your arm, your wrist. How dirty London has become. I need fresh gloves every day.'

Bernard unbuttoned his cuff and laid his arm along the table and we all three read the number inside the wrist.

'That reminds me of something, too,' she said, 'but I can't remember what. Something very nice. I know it well but my memory is failing. Could you tell me what it is?'

Old Bernard and I said nothing. I felt it was not for me to say and Bernard was chewing his apple tart.

'The world grows more and not less mysterious as we grow older,' she said. 'I look back on simple, happy years, not least the wonderful days of the Edwardian London stage. All the Terrys—Gielguds, Trees. Such *Hamlets*—Gielgud a non-pareil. *The Merchant*. Alas—not an easy part but—I must go now. I do hope you didn't mind me taking you up about the Jews. You see, I can remember Mosley. Such an attractive man. Not unlike a member of the Terry family. But so dangerous.'

She turned, took her bearings and set off over the wide floor of the restaurant, feeling precisely with her stick. After a few steps she turned and said, 'Oh, I have remembered. Your numbers on your wrist remind me of my grandchildren. We all once went for a Continental summer holiday on a lake shore. There was a little club for the children. To show they'd paid their entrance money their little wrists were stamped with a number. Then they were allowed the swings and slides of the fair. They so loved the stamp coming down. 1939—that wonderful sunny summer. We all so loved the old Germany. It made us feel close to our own Royal Family. I always thought, if only someone had adopted Hitler as a little boy and sent him to a good English public school like some of those fine African leaders who were loyal to us for years. But the idea is impossible, isn't it?'

*   *   *

Bernard stood strap-hanging home on the

crowded tube. He hung by the other wrist. Across the carriage, through the forest of gardening pamphlets everyone was carrying, I could see the old white arm clutching up at the rail. Tramping back up the hill home he said 'Ach—the inconsequence. The studied eccentricity. The inability to reason. The irrationality. The shortness of memory. The pride in new poverty. The lack of the once-transparent smear of imagination. The unshakeable security. The remains of the Churchillian myth of the British bulldog, a most detestable animal. It is a terrible ignorance. The great fact of this age is The Holocaust. Only The Holocaust. It can never be forgiven or forgotten. I am not talking about race. I am talking about evil. Nothing else matters—yet what do you any of you care or know?' He raised his arms up and outwards to the road, 'Stagnant, unawakened, calm, criminally comfortable, fifty years on.'

I said, '"Never *understood*" not "never forgotten". It's not that we forget. And we can't help not being Jews.'

'It must *never* be forgiven.'

'No, I suppose not. Nobody not Jewish dares to forgive, Bernard, I know. Well, I suppose.'

'"Suppose?" "Suppose?" All this good-mannered caution. Understatement. Morning mist and cricket. And flower-shows.'

'Oh, Bernard, you're antique. She was

228

antique too. She was a coelacanth. That sort of thing has gone. She was History.'

'But I am History. I am antique. I am the ancient of days—a wanderer. And by God, I am still here.'

'Come on—you've been forty years in Rathbone Road.'

'My mind is far away,' he said. 'So much as is left of it.'

'Give my—remember me to Lola,' I said at the gate. 'I hope she does—is better.'

'You should come and see her. In my country everyone would be calling on her daily.'

He crackled his knuckles as he stood waiting for Lola to unlock the door and I went on and walked on the Common for fresh air. On the way home I made a detour to the old parish church and sat in it for a time looking at the hanging crucifix above the rood-screen. I wondered if I could manage forgiveness if I were Old Bernard since I could not manage forgiveness even in Rathbone Road, and how Jesus would have got on, watching the children being sorted for the ovens.

Two talkative women came in and started cleaning. They ran a cloth over the Red Cross knight who lay on his marble tomb, legs crossed to show he'd sliced some Saracens; member of the local great family, long defunct. God looked down on the lot of us and for perhaps the first time I saw the suffering of His silence. The smallness of our prayers.

* * *

'Well,' said Dulcie, breezy and restored, for there had been a long muted discussion with Dr Seneca in the hall—some women get almost sexy in their conversations with departing doctors—'well, I gather there's no reason at all why you shouldn't get up, so I'll leave your lunch ready on a tray. After lunch you might rest in the drawing room on your long chair. Then at three-thirty Henry should be here.'

'Henry?'

'Richard and I spoke to him this morning. He has appointments and then a luncheon but will come out here to see you straight afterwards.'

'Whatever for? I'm not in any state to talk about a divorce today. I feel wrung out.'

'We told him he ought to see you. Also, Eliza, we wonder—have you no relations? Is there anyone—?'

'Relations? I've only a cousin. Whatever—?'

'Just an idea of Richard's. He thinks that you ought to be in touch with a close relative if possible. If you have one.'

'Annie Cartwright? Whatever for. She lives in Canada or America or somewhere.'

'Canada or America,' said Dulcie, 'have you her address? Is there any way of finding it through Directory Enquiries? Only of course

230

with your permission.'

'She's married. She's called Annie Grucock. I suppose that might make it easier. Why on earth—we haven't met in fifteen or twenty years. Oh, except once for an hour at a party in Washington. We don't get on. We're nothing to each other.'

'But she's your next-of-kin.'

'Henry's my...' But then, Joan, I understood. If the divorce goes through, Henry will no longer be my next-of-kin. And if, between them all, they are to deposit me in a mental hospital it will have to be Annie Grucock who signs on the dotted line, a task she will be ready, nay eager, nay utterly unsurprised, to be asked to perform.

'Don't you ever bring Annie Grucock here,' I said and flung off the bedclothes, rousted for my slippers. 'That's all, Dulcie. Thank you very much for being so kind to me, getting the doctor and the breakfast and lunch and the tea last night with the sleeping tablets in it and even for ringing Henry, though I hope he doesn't come and don't expect him—but just keep clear of Annie Grucock.'

'I'm afraid,' she said, 'that Henry may already have rung her. We had to mention it to him. I may say he became very vague and silent.'

'If she turns up I'll send her across to you. And to Anne Robin. To Gant and the Gargerys and Nick Fish—no, not to Nick

Fish, he has good children.'

'I don't believe she can be so ...'

'She is. I was at school with her. She was The Harrogate Rose.'

'Oh, my dear—school. You'll like each other now. I find I get on frightfully well with girls I didn't care for at school.'

'I wouldn't risk it. Not Annie Cartwright-Grucock. I was brought up with her. I'm going for a bath. Have you fed the dogs? Go on, Dulcie, take the old Mock and go home. Finish all you have to do. Because if Annie Cartwright's coming there'll be nothing done in Rathbone Road until you've put her in her first-class carriage home again. With bouquets, champagne, hot-water-bottles and several people's husbands.'

'You are I suppose recovering,' said Dulcie, 'if recovery means you are becoming unrecognisable. You sound—well, you sound rather common.' And she flung off.

I opened the window and watched her cross the road, talking with some dignity to Lady Gant. I leaned out and threw a swear word at them and Gant looked up at me as if she'd swallowed a scorpion. I listened to the cadence of the oath upon the noon-day air. I sang;

> 'In't it a pity
> She's only one titty
> To feed the baby on?
> 'The other old dangle

232

Got caught in the mangle
And now there's only one.'

Gant wears a hat. It's because of the tumour on her head. It sticks up. George Orwell had one, too. People noticed it when he raised his hat. It stood up tall. Lady Gant, a Trojan of a woman I much admire, keeps her hat on. Poor Orwell, stuck with the etiquette of his times.

'Poor little bugger,' I sang,
'He'll never play rugger
And grow up big and—'

Dulcie turned, after urging Gant in through her front door, on the top of the steps. The steps are flanked by twin lions for Richard's family is heraldic. She called kindly, 'Leave the dog, Eliza, I'll see to him. Rest.'
'Is there enough food in for them?'
'There is enough for *him*.'
I said, 'I'm not giving Henry dog-food. He's going to a luncheon.'

Later

Joan oh Joan
I scribble in the bed and the white sheets float about the floor and the biros keep running out.

Bath. After Dulcie had gone, the great white virgin, I lay in the almond oil suds and watched my face swell and contract in the Victorian taps. I looked along my skinny body, half a century old: the purple ridge, the appendix scar, the blotches of the old-fashioned vaccination marks on my thigh, but all still serviceable enough. A body not much noticed since the womb. Unused.

What might it have looked like? If I had married a man who thought sharing a bed important? Fat and flaccid? Covered in stretch-marks and Appalachian ranges? I've never seen a stretch-mark and don't know what it looks like. I have never seen a contraceptive pill. I have never seen pot or hash or heroin. I've never actually examined a condom, and still feel they are rather secret, nasty things.

Bosoms. Scarcely there. They might, I suppose, by now be hanging like old leather bottles? The children saying, 'Mother's letting herself go. Such a shame.'

But I'd have looked used.

I thought of the saints, the ones whose bodies were discovered at death, and centuries after death, sweet-smelling, unlined, supple as lads and girls, wafting with daphne and the scent of pomegranates. Pristine, like St Julian for God. Annie Cartwright, no saint, will smell all her life of double strength *Ma Griffe*, so long as it is expensive enough.

When my parents died, Joan, I was taken in
234

by my mother's sister who was married to a mill-owner in the green soft boggy country outside Bolton, Lancashire. I had been staying with them when it happened. I was six. Annie was their ewe-lamb and she was eight. The four of us had been very quiet. My uncle had already been able to retire from his profession and the mill clattered peacefully away down the dale, looked after by managers. My parents, a tear-away pair, had been on their first holiday together since their War-time honeymoon. My father had been in Changi gaol since the fall of Singapore. They were killed in France in their hired car. A lorry smashed into them from a side turning. It was my aunt who broke the news to me and she was stern about it.

My uncle went out of the room. When he came back my aunt went upstairs to her bedroom. My uncle sat in his leather chair before the big, brass fender. Do you think of a pot-belly, Joan? A plebeian head on a knitted antimacassar? Of homely Lancashire vowels? The Southerner's image of the North? Wrong. He was a gentle, thin and thoughtful man not unlike the figure of the Red Cross knight on our parish church tomb. He spoke gently. I knew that he suffered for his sister and that he suffered for me. I knew that Annie, their daughter, sitting on the fireside stool with her rosy lips pouted out suffered for me not at all. I knew that she was jealous of her father's pity.

235

She sat on her hands and looked down at her polished shoes and taut socks that came three-quarters of the way up her firm calves. She asked if she could do her sewing.

'No, not now.' My uncle lifted a hand from the arm of his chair and stroked my head.

'Then I'll go and ask Mother.'

Soon she was down again and sitting with a little bit of canvas. She stitched white petals with pink French-knotted tips.

*   *   *

We went to the same school for a time in Harrogate, Annie and I, but then she went on to another school with a fetching uniform—straw hat with pink and grey ribbon, pale grey dress, white gloves, shell-pink lawn blouse. It was not that she had had to leave the first school but that she was artistic, my aunt said, and couldn't concentrate on what didn't interest her. She rebelled against learning by rote.

Before I went up to Oxford, Annie was about to leave yet another school—her finishing school in Switzerland. She had set out there the previous year, in fur: a creamy fur coat with darker, toffee-coloured fur collar and cuffs, and a fur hat. She had a stolid presence with bulging, treacly eyes but an innate self-confidence and poise that nothing could shake. Soft, wet lips. And she had the

236

advantage of having no shoulders and the consequent air of frailty. The neck sloped down to soft Botticellian arms, pale little hands, all at variance with the strong jaw. Her self-confidence was based on her knowledge that men on seeing her wanted to wrap her shoulderlessness in their arms and at the same time felt comforted by her obvious possession and understanding of a good deal of money. It was an assurance that showed her a match for her fortunes, that the cheque-book inside the crocodile handbag (she would go to Italy now and then solely for the handbags) could conquer the world—or the parts of the world she was aware of. She could see no parts of mine.

She seemed complete, Annie Cartwright, at twenty. There were a great many men after her—young men being watched cannily by parents galore at the functions of the local Conservative Associations of Lancashire and West Yorkshire. It seemed to me unnecessary that she should go away anywhere. She seemed in the golden lap of the world for keeps.

'Won't you miss her?' I asked my aunt.

'She has to go. All her friends go. I like a finishing school. I was finished myself.'

'She seems finished already.'

My aunt looked to see if I were being nasty, decided not (wrong) and said, 'A finishing school teaches a girl how to sit in a chair.'

Annie and her husband Basil Grucock came

· 237

to see me once at Oxford and she sat beautifully in her chair in my lodgings—a knockabout tall house where we were left much to ourselves. Basil seemed less comfortable and kept getting up and pacing about, looking at his Philippe Patek watch which had been her wedding present to him. I should say *tried* to pace about for it was the time when I had released myself into squalor. Old tights and bras and half-eaten Welsh-rarebits lay everywhere on the floor. My bed, with grey sheets, was not so much unmade as unmakeable. This was my second year—my first year of tweed skirts and polished shoes and college hall-of-residence was done. In the middle of this, my most beloved room, the big gesture of my life so soon to be denied, there was a table, and on the table jam-pots, wine bottles, a pair of the man of the moment's trousers I was mending and a space cleared for papers, text-books, notes, pens and an unopened packet of condoms. They were for show. They never were opened. Somebody took them away.

Annie's long silk legs, her French silk suit, her complex curls, her drooping, glossy mouth, her vacancy, her little cigarette case with an 'A' on it in diamonds, dumbfounded all my acquaintances as they put their heads at intervals round my door. 'Oh—I'm sorry.' Open mouths.

'How do you do?' Basil walked forward

heartily to each of them. 'My cousin Annie. Her husband Basil,' I said to their hastily backing-off nods. Her slow smile.

As they were about to leave, Henry arrived. He was not the man of the moment. We had just met. I remember that I covered the condoms with Sweet's *Anglo-Saxon Reader*.

Seeing someone in a clean shirt, Annie came to life. Unwinding herself, getting up most beautifully from her chair, she approached him, paw held out like a present. She gave him a long, long stare. Oh, Henry's wonderful twenty-two-year-old looks! And, when she had gone, his amazed eyes.

'Who on earth was *that*?'

'My cousin.'

'*Your* cousin!'

And we both laughed and laughed. To my surprise Henry went over to the door and locked it. I put the alien trousers hastily out of sight. He came over to me and said, 'You are full of surprises.'

'She's the only relative I have.'

'You must be glad. Wherever has she been?'

'Being finished.'

'It can't have taken long.'

Now, in the bath-taps, I see the Oxford twilight. I close my eyes and get a breath for just an instant of the Oxford spring. I feel Henry's grave chin on the top of my head and my amazement when his hands began to move about my bare back.

239

That, however, was where they stayed, for he left before long in a hurry and that night dropped through my door a terrible note. 'I think we must be careful. We have only just met. We must not do what we might regret.' I felt humiliated. I tore it to bits.

But the next morning he was standing outside the gates of St Hilda's as I came from a supervision, and a warm April wind was blowing his hair about and he asked me to marry him. Knowing, knowing, knowing that this was the right thing to do, I said yes at once.

Annie didn't come to the wedding. I didn't tell her. We asked only about ten friends. I sent her a postcard on our honeymoon in France, and we laughed about her now and then. We sent Christmas cards for years but then stopped.

And now one of the hands that had moved over my back and done no more—nor for a long time after marriage come to that, for he was as hopeless at love as I was then—one of those hands was about to sign the document that would put me away, unless of course it had already signed the one that said he had no further responsibility for me, nor for anything of mine; in which case the hand that condemns me will be the little pink paw of Annie. I see the pink shells of her nails as she slowly writes her name. After which, the clean quiet room, the pills, the dutiful visits of Rathbone Road for a while, the couch. The separation of body, soul

240

and spirit from my dear world. Still my dear world.

'Hang on to God,' says Mother Ambrosine, so I hang on to the towel-rail—I can approach no nearer. I try to pray.

'Courage,' I tell the toothpaste. I do my teeth, I brush my hair, I look in the glass. I look, as usual, most wonderfully well. The mad seldom seem to catch things. You don't see mad people with tiresome colds. They don't seem to get the flu. The skin goes, and there are headaches, yet not even these afflictions have visited me. Oh Barry, Barry, sanest of men. Sores about the mouth, sores between the fingers, pus around the eyes, bones a cage wherein the bees could make their honey. Out of the weak shall come forth sweetness even mingled with the smell of decay. Thin, thin hair. Oh Barry, my love, my child.

And here am I, lean and lithe with health, shining with un-physical fever. For there is something burning in me, flowing hot through the map of my veins, rapids clattering along and searching for the sea. I'm an old central-heating system that never conks out.

Why am I permitted no release into sickness?

Faster, faster, says the Red Queen. Roll up to the Fair. Oh, roll on the Fair.

As I cross from the bathroom to the bedroom I see from the landing that Tom Hopkin is talking to dear Simon in the hall below. Tom needs his trousers mending. I must

241

hurry and dress.

But they have both disappeared when I am ready to go downstairs. I look for them everywhere. Then I get out the silver tray and the rose-bud tea-service—inherited from Bolton, Annie's late wedding present, now I come to think of it. Remembering the quiet stone house in the green valley I add sugar-tongs, silver milk-jug, sugar-lumps and a lacey plate of those very nice biscuits that are getting to be rare—the ones with coffee, lemon and chocolate stripes which Henry and I both like. I see that my newly bathed fingernails have tiny flowers growing out of them, ten little arcs, fresh and blue, like miniature speedwell.

The dogs are still. The house is very still, too. Through the back windows of the drawing room I see that there are still lacquer-red shoots on the dog-wood. I walk the length of the room and observe the Road from the other end. In your front garden—oh Joan!—oh, if you could see the lilac blossom and the fat cream tulips. If you could see the dark red cherry tree toss and shake and feel the wind catch up the petals and throw them like a wedding at old Isobel Ingham drifting home.

I open the front door on it all. The warm wind blows all the papers off the hall table. (No note there from Simon or Tom.) Standing on my top step there's the aching smell of the sap of spring and the nectar welling. Colour is coming into the soil. There's a rose or two in bud, frilly pansies with astonished expressions at their early call. You'd wonder at yourself today, Joan, for ever wanting to leave us.

Concerning June 2nd

But oh my dear, dear Joan,

It had not been only the wind getting under the hall rug that I had been hearing with my door wide to the daffodil pollen, it had been the dogs. They rushed and scuttered about. I went and sat on my chaise-longue beside the tea-cups and thought of Bolton, my six-year-old self handing round the little sandwiches. But tip, tip, tap of claws. Snuffle, snuffle—very tactful, out in the hall. One of the dogs—my Toby—at last comes in and stands in the drawing-room doorway and looks at me, head askew.

'Walk?' asks he.

'Yes. Later. After tea. He won't be staying long.'

'Oh well, OK,' says Toby, dubiously, going out. I hear him take a run or two down the hall stopping short with a skid at the door-mat, waiting to be told to come back. The silence, the cunning silence of a dog ready to slide out of your reach and go off on the march. I ponder the difficulties of women with afternoon lovers who have a dog in the house. It is a predicament not touched upon in (for example) the television drama. Why worry about the wretched dog? He's never been run over yet when he's been out on his own. The police know him—always very friendly about him. 'Genius of an animal, Mrs Peabody. Safer than a human being. I've seen him look to left and right.'

Nevertheless.

And I'm not sure of your truculent beast, Joan, slinking and scowling about the High Street, 'OK, kill me then. Don't bother to brake. Why should I care? It's a dog's life. Oh dear—near thing! Almost through the windscreen. Better be off.'

I might be prosecuted. One of these animals could cause death. Think if they should cause the death of a child.

And I see frenetic Vanessa screaming behind the wheel, foot hard down on the brake-pad, eyes closed, 'A *dog*—a bloody *dog*!' and all three little Fishes scattered like rain-drops in the road with the number 9 bus bearing down. Amanda screaming—'Mum-Vanessa—Timmy's *dead*.'

So, off I go, carrying leads to look for them both. I leave the front door wide for Henry, who should be here in a minute, and Dulcie is watching. If a burglar comes instead of or as well as Henry she'll be there, though her head does not look up as I pass now, quickly along

244

under her window. The open door will reflect my genuine readiness to see Henry again and also show that I don't mean to be long. I'll no doubt catch up with the wretched pair at the top of the road.

But I don't. I cross over the main road and search round the dust-bins of the Little Greek. No dogs. At the edge of the Common I scan the terrain, but I can see no loose dogs at all today—all trot to heel, politely sniffing each others' hind-quarters. Nothing roves. I drift for perhaps half an hour, then home again.

Now the front door is shut. Dulcie is not to be seen at her desk. Out of the sitting-room window of my house the faces of the dogs regard me over the sill. They become wild with emotion, spring about in hysterical attitudes, disappear, reappear, bark like fiends at the wrong side of the front door. 'Henry,' I call through the letter-box. 'Hullo. Eliza here. Just had to go out for...'

But Henry's coffee-cream BMW, I now see, is not in the road. Through the letter-box I see no sign of him—hall table still bare of notes. Oh well. I had better go in. Why ever not?

Because I can't. I haven't a key. I didn't take one.

So I walk casually round to the side door and the dogs are magnetised around the inside of the house in the same direction, kicking up Hades. At the side of the house all is bolted and barred. I try the door at the end of the path that

245

leads to the back garden, and find it bolted, too.

Now this door is never locked, so possibly a burglar has passed this way, despite Dulcie. He has made off through the back garden sealing himself off from his pursuers or, oh dear yes, perhaps Henry did call, and in a fury he has secured his abandoned house on all sides and has left again. Even the ladders are round at the back and I can't get to them. It is becoming rather cold out here without a coat and the nectar and the scents of spring are not so balmy.

I stroll.

Gently, carefully, not looking anywhere in particular and certainly not anywhere near Dulcie's bowed head, I stroll. What do I seek? A strong, large man. A strong large man with the introduction to a ladder and who is on my side. Oh, how this Road still seems to be peopled with women, Joan, who live in their houses from dawn until dark.

Old Bernard appears upon his door-step. He lifts a hand in salute, arranges his bicycle-clips and goes weaving away. Lola will be in. She never leaves the house. Lola and Bernard had a daughter. I knew the daughter and used to talk to her, but she was rather remote. In those days Lola used to stand at the gate to wave the daughter off to her violin classes, and would talk. Not for ages now. They say she sits in the corner of the room always facing a door like

246

the famous picture of Beckett—the playwright not the archbishop.

Her french-louvred blinds are heavy with dust. I look through the letter-box and the photographs of orchestras and soloists cover the walls. They are curling at the edges now, most of them. I remember little Hannah (later called Felicia) so clearly now that I feel she may come round the corner of the dark hall to answer the door. Up and down the road she used to go, agonised and silent, her violin in a black leather case much too big for her.

Lola came to the door instead and, as ever, it is she who looks made for the concert platform. Tall, long neck, giant eyes, black oiled hair screwed back tight in a knob. It looks painted on like Olive Oyle in *Popeye*. She is unageing.

The house is in semi-darkness. She has no ladder for me. There might, she thinks, be one in the shed but neither she nor Bernard has been in the shed for years. Would I like to come in and see the latest photos of Felicia from Haiti? Oh yes—touring, always touring. The photograph is far from new and surely Felicia must be much older than this by now?

'How young she looks.'

'Oh, it's the life. So healthy. The wonderful audiences—and the travelling. She's so lucky.'

Lola settles herself in a corner, looking left and right. The garden taps on the window, half-way up the window. I see how unsettling the Chelsea Flower Show must have been for Bernard.

'Lola, how you must miss her.'

'No. I accepted it before she was seven. It's the price she and I both pay for her genius.'

There is dust everywhere, heaps of old clothes, empty coffee cups. Through the window I look at the little meadow blowing in the breeze. I say, 'Well, it's good that you understand. I suppose, having been a musician yourself...'

'Oh, I was never a musician. I was never allowed lessons. I was never anything. But I knew, the minute I saw her as a baby in the hospital, when I touched her little hands. I have been the vehicle for Felicia, that is all. Bernard has suffered I'm afraid. Men seldom understand.'

We sit staring at a Victorian screen covered with yellowing concert programmes.

'Upstairs,' she said, 'I have every violin she's ever played on, from the very first.'

Out on her doorstep again, and the door is shut behind me. I hear bolts drawn.

I walk on, cross the road, and as I pass the high door in her garden wall there appears Miss Ingham. She holds a small plastic bag of earth with a green sprout sticking up. We confront each other.

Now I am aware that Miss Ingham has never thought much of me. Long ago, in the days when I wrote notes to people, she thought me an idiot, though I didn't much care, being (I thought) directed by God. Miss Ingham is also way past ladders. Nevertheless, she is one of those in the road who does not now have letters an inch high emblazoned across her forehead saying, '*Here comes Eliza, the poor thing.*'

I wonder at what point those letters began to appear? Lately they have become a virus, an epidemic.

Miss Ingham clutches her cardigan about her and says, 'I was about to take this to Anne.'

'I could do it. I was looking for a ladder.'

'I can find you a ladder. Are you painting something?'

'I'm locked out.'

'Ah,' she says, 'when my lodgers come in they could help you. Or you could call the police. If you like you may use my telephone.'

'I sent for the police last night. I'd better not.'

'So you did,' she said, 'so you did. You had better come in.'

We sit on her covered verandah in basket chairs among the lemon-scented geraniums and she says, 'I expect you'd like tea.'

'I was expecting Henry for tea. It's all ready on a tray. It's a shame I can't get in. It was a nice cake. And biscuits with stripes.'

I saw her think, She's playing the child.

'Would you like some salami?' she said, 'I usually eat a plate of salami at about this time of day. It's having had Polish lodgers for so

249

many years. Polish, Latvian, that sort of thing. Very good for me.'

'I never see your lodgers.'

'They sleep a lot.'

'Oh, I see.'

'They tend to work at night. One of them is a Croupier. A fascinating life, though prurient and most unhealthy. I send him jogging but he never looks really well. He has that yellow look. But then all Croupiers do.'

She disappears into some remote kitchen and I stare out from the verandah at the huge view to the Epsom Downs, southward where the race-horses prance and life is lush. It seems quite lush here for Miss Ingham, too—the broad sunshiny terrace without, the warm secure covered verandah within, both teeming with great pots of vegetation bursting into life. A jasmine like a feather-boa floats about the glass above my head. In an Ali Baba jar there is an orange tree with glossy leaves and five living breathing fruits. It stands beside a writing desk where there is an open accounts ledger, an ink-well, a silver pen-tray, a bottle of whisky and the photograph of a beautiful woman.

'I was twenty,' says Isobel Ingham, moving slowly back across the verandah with the salami plate in one hand and a couple of tumblers in the other. 'I have lived here for fifty years.'

'We've only been here for twenty-two. Everyone else came long after us and they're always moving. It's strange that you and I have never really met.'

'Well, it's my fault as much as yours,' she said. 'I don't go about much.'

I imagine the dazzling twenty-year-old arriving in Rathbone Road. No man. Living with parents? No marriage. Odd.

'It's strange how close some of us are in the Road, and some don't know each other's names,' I say.

'It's the same in all villages. All over the world.'

'I suppose, when you came here to live, it was all very different. Very formal. Everybody keeping to themselves. Only the servants in these houses would really know each other.'

'It wasn't that long ago. It wasn't crinolines, you know. I was a petty-officer in the Navy. At the beginning of the War. Have another whisky. I was put here.'

'Put here?'

'A far suburb. My father was a member of Parliament. I chose to keep the child and not marry the father. My own father bought me this house and washed his hands of me. Better than some cultures. In the Middle East I'd have been stoned.'

'And,' I say, taking the ribbon off the salami disc, 'and the little baby?'

'Ah. In the end it never was. No—that I will not say. I lost it after three months of pregnancy. He was perfectly formed at three

251

months—little arms and legs and hands and a round, opaque head like a grub. I had him here, alone. It was the maid's day off. Nobody had told me that a spontaneous abortion— miscarriage they call it now, to make it sound neater—is exactly like a birth. One goes into labour, you know. But there is no joy.'

'None.'

'They counted mine a child you know. He is in the records at the Town Hall. I'm glad of that. My father wanted me to go home afterwards.'

'You didn't?'

'Of course not.'

'You just lived on here? No other—well, life?'

'I paint a little—not very well. I know something about flowers and I run a lodging-house. But if you mean no other lover—then no. Oh, sometimes the lodgers, especially those from the Baltic States—so attractive. And Poles—I first met Poles in the War. Very inflammatory. But no—no love. Dear me, no. That did not happen again. I took sex where I needed it—which, if I may say so, it is sad you cannot do. It stands out a mile that you are in great bodily need. But it would not be your solution.'

'You know nothing about me.'

'I know about sexual needs.'

I said, 'Miss Ingham, had you married the man you loved you might have changed for one

252

another. Lovers do. I have experience that you have not. It may be no more than changes in bodily chemistry, but then it may be more profound. You have lived in a state of romantic memory. Had you married your man, you don't know what might have happened. Marriage can be very terrible and surprising.'

Whereupon, Joan, most unexpectedly I began to weep. I wept and wept. I could not stop. Miss Ingham kept picking up slices of salami and examining each one before peeling it and placing it delicately in her mouth.

'I'm not at all sure,' she said, not (Joan) even raising her voice above my sobs and yet I heard each word, 'I am not at all sure of all this light talk of change. I think it can be simpler, less mystical. I think it possible that after many years some great event can come between a man and a woman that cannot be shared. A silence forms and begins to fester. Handkerchief?'

'You can't know. You didn't have time for secrets to form. It was all glamour and passion and renunciation. Just the top-soil.'

'Oh yes,' she said. 'We had no time at all.'

'You sound smug, Miss Ingham.'

'And you sound dictatorial, Mrs Peabody. But I have watched a lot of secrets form and fester and destroy—or come near to destroying—in the most unlikely places. Poor Anne, for example.'

'You mean George and the mistress in Hong Kong, and creeping about after the Philippinos, and everyone knowing except Anne?'

'Of course Anne knows. She's not the fool she makes herself out to be.'

'You mean, we all know each other's secrets? Unconsciously? That's not true.'

'No. But there is a tribal knowledge. In any small community.'

'I got it into my head once,' I said, 'that my husband was deranged, and once that he was homosexual.'

'Most women believe both at one time or another and usually rightly. But you were wrong on both counts about Henry. You were frightened to look in the right place.'

'However can you know? Sitting here behind that door in the wall.'

'Oh, I see him. Or I used to see him. And I see you.'

'You know,' I tried to say in my old brisk way and then felt it fizzle out. 'You know, a year and a half ago I used to talk like that—behave like you. The wise woman of the tribe. It was a complete failure. I have learned not to make oracular pronouncements any more. They did me and other people no good.'

She looked disdainfully over the Surrey plain. 'You were ahead of yourself,' she said. 'Too young. But there's time yet. The old women of the tribe have almost always been

254

the wiser. If they keep their marbles long enough. Old men forget—or tend to reminisce, and reminisce falsely and sententiously as a rule. We are often very silly in our middle years but we tend to improve—as our marriages often do. Women who survive, survive better than men. It's because our lives—our physical lives—are more dramatic.'

'Is it because Anne won't face George's—well—randiness that she writes books for children?'

Miss Ingham sat up quickly in the basket chair and turned reddish round the mouth and nostrils. 'Don't you dare patronise Anne! In her work she knows exactly what she's doing. It's in her life she is hopeless. She doesn't like to look further than her books, but that is no short journey. Her books may be ahead of her—ahead of most of us. They're a good deal more commendable than her husband.'

'Yet I do like George,' said I, 'and I can see his point. She is dull.'

'Can you? Can you indeed? And who says so? I think Anne suspects that she can see George's point, too, in looking about him. She's full of her own limitations. She's a bag of false modesty and misplaced guilt and she attracts humiliation by people who ought to be honoured to know her. But don't tell me that she needs a romance. Anne is not equipped for the torrid zone.'

'I'm sorry. I didn't say—'

255

'Any more than you are, but with you it is your great misfortune.'

I was silent.

'Do you feel better?' she said. 'On your way home you might drop this little hybrid lilium altromerium in on Anne and save my arthritis. She could do with seeing a new face sometimes. Would you like to see to yours before you go?'

I was not ready to go, Joan. I wanted to stay. In the 1930s white-tiled loo, with its frieze of little black triangles and mirror tapping from a long cord, I looked at the chaotic map of my life, my eyes nearly sunk away, my mouth a poor hair-pin. The earrings hung like dead birds. I wasn't looking well.

'You look low,' she said as I came back to the verandah, 'and that is good, for you have been looking dangerously high for some time.' She wrapped another old cardigan around herself and came with me to the gate, passing me the plastic bag.

'Thank you for...'

'Not at all. I'll send someone with a ladder.'

'They all think I'm mad now, of course.'

'I know. You are not mad. You are frightened.'

'*Never*! I'm never frightened. Don't even take that away from me, Miss Ingham. I've been fairly brave and I've tried to be self-sufficient. I have survived alone perfectly.'

She leaned forward and touched my arm and smiled, and the girl of twenty, happy about the

256

coming baby, looked out at me for a moment. 'Face what you know,' she said. 'Grow up.'

I thought, Once this was my function, handing on advice. Making people of people. I looked steadily at her and said, 'You sound like me, advising Joan. But I suppose you never knew Joan either. Nobody else did.'

'Of course I knew Joan,' said Miss Ingham. 'I was very fond of her.'

* * *

'But here comes one,' she went on at her garden door, 'much too young to have known her: still damp from his cocoon,' and she turned to where the laundering husband could be seen bouncing towards us up the hill, in either hand a plastic bag of supermarket groceries, a briefcase hooked over a stray finger.

He smiled when he saw Miss Ingham, called out 'Hi, Isobel,' and lifted the one-bag paw.

'So young,' she said. 'He will always look young. He has such a little nose. Now then—' as he went prancing by on the other side of the road, calling good-evening to me, but skirting me, not quite looking, the letters on his forehead glowing '—now then,' she said, 'Dickie—stop at once.' He sprang on for a couple of steps, turned a tight circle, came over to us and stood marking time.

'Mustn't stop. Ratatouille. Gabriella's having her check-up at the hospital. May not be back yet—blood-pressure. It's a bit of a bore. Had to take Mick with her—supper' (wagging bag) 'when they get home.'

'It can't be long now?'

'Any day. I packed up work tonight— paternity leave. Shan't be back for a month. Bought plenty of food for a week.'

'Could you help Eliza? She's locked herself out. Have you a ladder?'

'Gabriella'd know. Find out. Pronto—she's probably home,' and he passed on his way, not once having looked at me.

Joan, now and then I have my doubts about *The Ancient Mariner.* Now every wedding guest plods by and no mad eye glitters bright enough. The mad have become sadder, and however important the tale they have to tell, they soon cease trying. The tail and the tale get curled within them like an embryo. Locked within us. It gets more difficult to call out, 'Excuse me, could you spare a key?' Oh, I dare say my eyes give off a bit of glitter, but it's only what I was born with. Fortuitous, like Dickie, the-man-who-has-everything's youth-giving nose.

'In case he forgets,' said Miss Ingham, 'or in case Gabriella's time is come, you could ask across the road for a ladder when you drop this in on Anne. My Croupier may not have time before he has to leave for his casino.'

* * *

258

'It's a lily, I think,' I say to George who is standing on the terrace, looking raffish and sun-burnt from months of oriental solaria, and stirring his thick gravel with the tip of a gardening shoe. George wears the right clothes for every occasion, not of course that he gardens himself, he employs; but he counts it good manners to the flowers to appear before them in clothes they may respect. George, one feels, might walk the Common in a smock, visit The Hospice in a toga. Oh dear—I do like George. Peel off the clothes and I dare say there's not much sinew, just a smooth stuffed tailor's dummy of oatmeal canvas and little black tin-tack heads, and here and there a prickle of horse-hair with only a whiff of the wild: but I should rather like to stroke the odd hair on George. It's what he wants and seldom gets, I suspect, from his Philippinos, who all look very high-minded, or from silly old Anne, mourning flown children and taken up with *The Baby's Opera*.

George has a long, lank head and an expression of sensual desolation. His sweet, weak mouth is nipped in at the corners. Something in his looks always revives in me the distant tingle. They do not recreate it but they stir a frail string. His eyes greet every woman with appeal. He hasn't spotted yet that his appeal excites few western women now. He spends far too much time in the Orient.

'Oh, hullo Eliza, whatever's this?'

259

'A plant from Miss Ingham for Anne.' Once I would have said, '*George*! How very nice! You're home again—how lovely. I didn't *know*! Anne *must* be pleased. And how was Indonesia?'

Farewell that woman, that doddle-taffy woman. There she blows.

I stand. I stick. Like a plug in a hole.

'Do go on up. Anne's working. Well, she's in her room, I won't say working. There's some sort of crisis.'

'It's all right.' I put the plant down on the dwarf wall near the clusters of Provençal jars filled ready for the Robins' annual celebration of the giant pelargonium.

'How are you, Eliza? I'm just back. Six bloody months. Lovey—you look tired. Where are the glittering eyes? Hey—'

He comes across and puts an arm around me. 'Tears? Not Eliza! Tears? Here,' and he brings out a gardener's handkerchief thick, lineny, the colour of grass-clippings, beautifully folded. 'Whatever's Henry been doing to you? Neglecting you? Come in and have a drink.'

'I've locked myself out.'

'Then I'll send someone with a ladder. Don't be an idiot, sweetie—hey, aren't you thin? Go and see Anne while I do something about the ladder. She's having a rather bad time—well, we both are. New Philippino. *Very* critical of us she is,' and he gleams at me with a mixture of collusion, apprehension and lubricity.

'And something too terrible to describe has happened to Anne on the recent Grand Book Tour. Daren't ask for details but maybe you'll hear. Now then—ladder.'

I roam round their house which is standing open to both road and garden, but no Anne. Her supremo of a study is empty and the vase of Sissinghurst pinks droops on the desk. 'Anne?' I call. 'Anne? Hullo?' I start to wander the garden. 'Anne? Anne?'

Down near the asparagus bed stands a meaningful-looking shed and I look through its window where at a potting-bench which is draped in cloth-like cobwebs Anne sits glaring at a hose-pipe hanging on the back of the door. A virgin notebook lies on the bench, with several biros beside it and some trays of seed-compost. I tap on the glass and she turns a bleak face to me. No glitter there –but no true grief either. Take heart, Eliza, you can cope with this. Such albatrosses as she knows are chicks.

A look of disappointment changes Anne's blank face for the moment, and for the worse, but I am glad to see that it is Eliza she is looking at, not mad Eliza. No letters on that brow. She stares at me, then looks away.

The door is locked. I begin to try and make myself heard through the glass. After a time she leans forward and struggles with the window-catch. The top of the shed window tilts outwards with a painful cracking and several spiders come tearing out, falling over each other in haste to reach salt-free air.

'George said I was to look for you Anne. Sorry.' (Why was I sorry?) 'Is it the new au pair?'

Anne looks sharp for a second, then resigned. I am a loony—no point talking. She turns her face away. But I feel light suddenly, for I'd asked an objective question and George had not been simply pitying when he had dabbed my tears. 'Anne, can't you tell me? Remember all you told me that day you came round and we talked in the kitchen. The day I went to your Literary Tea. All you told me about your career?'

'Career,' she cried. 'Career,' and crashed her face in the seed-trays.

'You've been to America, Miss Ingham says. I'm sure you were a huge success.'

'What does Miss Ingham know. Oh, marriage!'

'But George wasn't with you in America.'

'I'm talking about marriage and my literary career. I'm talking about loneliness. I could never tell him ... Or the children. *Never.*'

'Well, I'm afraid I can't know about children, but ...'

'I had a terrible time, Eliza, terrible. No—not the Children's Book Tour, that was super. There were tens of thousands in the audiences and our photographs all blown up much bigger

262

than life-size round the Carnegie Hall. Even my ear was about two feet long, and we went to Boston where there's a college where all they do is children's books. They take degrees in them. Well—wonderful. Well, if you want to know...'

'I can't hear you, Anne. Your face is in the soil.'

'I don't care what my face is like. I don't care about my looks. Eleanor Farjeon was a very plain woman and so was Beatrix Potter.'

'But what *happened*?'

After an age she lifts her head, swivels sideways, drops her face in her hands and sits like a tired Catholic priest who has heard one confession too many. Outside among the asparagus fern I sink to my knees in the penitential position and lean my ear towards the refugee spiders. Role reversal.

She is still.

I wonder after a very long time if she has fallen into a fit. I even wonder if she is on some drug or other that someone has recommended in America, though drugs didn't really sound part of the Children's Book World—you never know, of course. Pixie Leak had seemed a little strange. A little tranced.

'It was New York,' Anne suddenly shrieks. 'I should never have gone to New York. I only went because they said it would be useful. Useful to me as an Adult Writer. To meet an Adult Publisher. I've sold an Adult Novel, you see, to America. It was sold actually ages ago and it's been out for months and not a single review. So they said, here in London—my editor, Bessie Bilbury—she said I ought to make myself known to the Adult World, and I did, and they asked me to lunch.'

'But that was nice.'

'They told me the restaurant and the day and the time, and I spent hours and hours getting ready so that I wouldn't look like a children's writer. I put on a big shawl like Margaret Drabble and a simple aertex shirt like Susan Hill and some thigh-length boots, and took a taxi and got there ten minutes early. I thought early looks efficient so I went in and it was gorgeous—in Fifth Avenue—shadowy and pale and only seven tables in creamy marble and expensive flowers and waiters more like Claridges than America—well, I don't have to tell you, Eliza. You've been everywhere with Henry. It's all humdrum to you, but it isn't to me. The headwaiter came up and looked for a long time in a black book—a programme thing of the reservations—and furrowed his brow.'

'He furrowed his brow?'

'Then he said, "Come this way," and put me at the best table in the restaurant, right in the middle of the window-tables, and gave me a cool little smile. There was only one other person in the restaurant, it was so early. He was at the next table and he said, "Hi—you look happy," and he was so friendly I said, "Yes, I

264

am. I'm here to have lunch with my American publisher. I'm English," and he said, "You don't say." He honestly did—spoke the words, "You don't say." Then he said, "Is this your first book, then?" So of course I told him that I'd been all over America touring and reading my works. He said, "Have you written many books?" so I told him the truth, ninety-four—I didn't say they were for children, well, why should I? He asked my name then and then he asked, "And what name do you write under?" We're all used to that from the philistine masses so I gave him the look they all get when they ask it and said with the unspoken words very clear in the air, poor fish, you're not exactly in the know are you? Aloud I said, "My own."

'So the time passed and his friends arrived and I could hear they were all talking about publishing. All the other tables filled up except mine, and I sat and sat. And the *maître d'hôtel* came up and asked if I'd like to order and I said I'd wait a bit longer, but it was now three-quarters of an hour since I'd arrived and I asked, "Do you by any chance know Miss Gobbet's telephone number?" and he said, "I do. She comes here three times a week." I said, "Do you think that I might telephone?" and he said, looking away, "Yes, you could do that." And I sat.

'And the friendly man leaned over and said, "Could we four tempt you to a glass of

265

Bordeaux?" and they were all looking sorry for me, and so kind that I could bear no more. I mean—oh, *confused*. I mean, America's meant to be so tough and ruthless and these men behaving like the most terrific *gents*. And American publishers all meant to be so efficient, never missing a trick, never muddling anything. That's supposed to be *us*. I looked at the letter in my bag and I hadn't got the date or the place wrong—oh Eliza! *Eliza!* Not bothering to turn up!

'So I went to the telephone which was by the *maître d'hôtel*'s desk and there was a dim gold lamp and a vase of lilies and the *maître d'* stood looking at me. And everyone in the restaurant could hear.

'I phoned Miss Gobbet—I mean it was *Grizelda Gobbet*. She's a legend. Oh, and Eliza! The girl on the publisher's switchboard said, "Speak louder can't you?" and I had to shout, and silence fell all over the restaurant. And then—oh—then Grizelda Gobbet answered and you could hear her eating. She was smacking her lips and crackling papers and she said, "Chrissake—I clean forgot. Can we make it tomorrow?"

'So I ran out. Right out. And there was a taxi and I stood for—oh, Eliza!—for a fraction of a second and the driver said, "Look at it this way, are you getting in or aren't you? Just *get inside*."

'So I didn't. I walked all the way back to the

hotel, about seven miles, between those canyon walls, and there were lunatics everywhere, some of them on roller-skates playing Russian roulette with the traffic, and there were other people fighting and looking like the Marx Brothers or Woody Allen—everybody *acting*, Eliza. Continental-looking people working themselves into a sweat being comedians on street-corners, sweet-talking, behaving like an opera and I reached the hotel and oh...

'I couldn't go in. I just couldn't go in. Not at three o'clock in the afternoon. What could I do there? It's failure to be back in a hotel at three in the afternoon. They look at you at the reception, pretending not to see. So I just went on walking. I walked right past and on and on until I came to a sign saying that I was near the Metropolitan Museum of Art. And I thought, well, at least I'll be able to say I went there. Pathetic—oh, pathetic, Eliza! I began to go over speeches to everyone at home. "Yes I did. I got to the Met. of Art. Yes—I only had forty-eight hours in New York and of course these American publishers work you very hard, but I was absolutely determined to get there and ... Waah!

'I went up the steps of the Museum and the glass wall of doors was locked and there was a notice saying "No strollers". All I wanted to do was stroll—I mean, what sort of a museum—? I wanted to stroll and gaze and forget Miss Gobbet and the restaurant and look at the

267

Renoirs and think of peasant France. So I tried to shout through the glass at the attendant, who carried a gun, "Could I just be allowed in this once, to stroll?" and he stared at me and turned his back. Just turned his great fat back. And then a black person sitting by the fountains, though they weren't working, I mean playing, dressed in a silver wet-suit and his hair in ropes, he said, "They're not open today, Ma'am. It's Tuesday," so I walked away. I walked all the way back to the hotel and didn't go anywhere else that day or in the evening. I had room-service and lay on the bed.'

'But didn't you—? I think this is awful.'

'Oh yes. Oh, *yes*! The next morning, Eliza, I woke up remembering who I was, and George and the children and how I am not dependent on the United States of America in any possible way. I thought about England and the Road and everything and how lousy the Americans were to us after the War when they stopped lease-lend and we were all eating whale-meat. And how they think they won the War and took over all our air-bases and then went and made that amateur mess in Vietnam and all the army went on drugs, they were so scared. So I rang her again. I put on an ice-cold voice and Gobbet said, quite easy and pleasant, "Hi, sorry 'bout yesterday. Glad to be seeing you today." I said, "I'm sorry, Miss Gobbet, but I will not go back to that

268

restaurant. I was humiliated," and she said, "Oh fine. Fine. Why don't you come round here and see the office?"

'So I went—dressed in my Jean Muir coat and pearls—and it was utterly empty. I got there a bit late on purpose, but there wasn't a sign of life in all the acres of little cardboard booths they work in—all out eating. Miss Gobbet's desk had nothing on it but her nail-varnish and a collection of cartons of health-foods. There were no books anywhere. She started looking about, not saying what she was doing, opening and shutting drawers, and after a time she found a copy of my book in the back of one of them, very shiny and as if it hadn't been opened. She said, "There you are. Isn't it great? I had a hand in the jacket myself. Don't you think it looks great?"

'I said—why am I so *polite*, Eliza?—I hoped she had liked the book as well as the jacket, since she is *my editor*. I was so sorry, I said, that it didn't seem to be selling very well.

'She said, "Oh it's just great. No, I guess it isn't selling very well."

'We went to a restaurant then, where you queued up with a tray and all there was to eat was salad and great chunks of pulped-over meat that wasn't meat and glasses of thin foamy milk and we sat at a little table where I kept getting knocked. Grizelda Gobbet *lay* in her chair, Eliza, lay back in it and sort of half-smiled and messed with her salad and started smoking.

'And she said, "So. How you enjoying New York?"

'I tried to talk to her. I did try. I tried to talk about the book—it's what I was told I should do, but whenever I did she just looked up at her cigarette smoke and the ceiling. I noticed how her hands shook all the time, just like my editor's at home, which reminded me of the masturbation scene that I'd found so difficult. So I asked her if she approved of the masturbation scene, and she looked absolutely shattered.

'"I'm sorry to have to say this," she said, "but the book isn't going too well. You know, the trouble with us Americans is that we're just not egg-heads."

'I said, "But it's only about love. You liked the book. You bought the book."

'"Well," she said, "I didn't exactly buy it, someone else did, and she's left. She was the house drunk. Matter of fact I haven't exactly read it yet. Say—", she said, "—do you have a cat? I'm a cat-lover. Do you ever think of writing a book about a cat? I live with my cat and—do you know what—I don't seem able to feel for anything like I feel for my cat. Not even for Central American politics, which is my area."

'Someone kicked the back of my chair then, it was so crowded with people walking about with their trays, and I was tipped forward and

270

nearly crashed into her face with my own, and when I saw her close, Eliza, she was so old. An old sad woman, not at all unpleasant under the mask of paint. Her eyes were quite vacant.

'She said, "Well, I guess you'll be wanting to go shopping now"—it wasn't quite two o'clock—"don't let me keep you." And that night, Eliza, I flew home to England.'

I said through the grille, 'That is one of the most horrible stories I have ever heard. My dearest, dearest Anne,' and she let out a wail, crashed from the shed and made for the house.

'Awful,' I said on the drive to George who was coming in through the gates, 'George—awful. What happened to Anne was awful. Don't ask. She'll recover. And never let the children know that it wasn't all wonderful for her.'

'Yes. I gather. She hasn't said much. I don't know why she cares about the Americans though, do you?'

'Yes I do. We were brought up to think that they liked us. It's taking time to realise they don't give a fuck.'

'Eliza—*what* did you say. My goodness!'

'Also, Anne is young and good, and she can't help having beautiful manners, and she suffers.'

'Who doesn't, sweetheart?' he said with more interest than usual. 'Oh, I love you when your hair sings.'

'*Sings*, George?'

'With electric currents. And your Eliza-eyes are black-currants again now. They are black-magic currants. I wish you'd come with me to Hong Kong.'

I side-stepped him and also Mrs Cori Aquino who was coming along behind him through the gates with a steely smile.

'Are you the woman who has locked herself out?' she asked.

And Joan—do you know, for a moment or two I hadn't the faintest idea what she was talking about. I was shaking with fury for Anne. For something that was of course nothing, that in the end Anne will be quite able to bear, to tell the world, make into a party joke and in the end all but forget—such *fury* for Anne, Joan, that my own locked sorrow, my broken soul were quite forgotten.

I walked to number forty-three and saw a house bristling with ladders. Windows stood open on every floor. A man of Slavic appearance was heaving himself over the garden door. Half-way up the principal ladder to my bedroom, as if it might have been some great, untrammelled gorilla, there hung by one hand an imminently pregnant girl. Her small-nosed husband, unafraid as he held in his arms his one-year-old baby, was calling instructions. Spotting me, Dulcie Baxter began to remove herself hastily back to her own house. Some Gargery children were talking about the fire-brigade.

The pregnant girl eased herself competently, carefully down, on the inner side of the ladder, hand over hand, tight-lipped, and fell in a heap into somebody's waiting arms. Nobody said much. It was all very orderly. There was an unspoken team-spirit. She was sensibly dusted down.

I loved England then, Joan. I had loved it in the morning and I loved it now towards evening, after tea.

E.

❊❊❊

?

Dear Joan,

It seems to me that to feel the goodness of someone is a rare occurrence. Experiencing the corporate goodness of the tribe is rarer still. In Rathbone Road all our security and worldly success is usually brought about by hard, slogging work, careful and conventional and un-eccentric endeavour suitable to the class in which we are all stuck, and the troubled knowledge that comes with the years is that we are most of us little more than holes in the air.

And yet, I think that most of us try to be good a lot of the time. We have ample opportunities to do good, and most of us take them. We give liberally to charities.

But we most of us only really know people of our own sort. We leave our five-bedroomed houses of an evening some of us twice a week to man—or usually woman—the food-stalls for the homeless under Waterloo Bridge, and we do our little bits of part-time good work. But is there one of us here, Joan, ready for total immersion? Is there one of us ready to forget his or her self-righteousness? Anything less than total love, universal love, Joan, achieves nothing. We are not angels. I don't think I know any totally committed human being— totally committed to anything. I know no St Julian.

Yet all those ladders, all those people springing about on account of one tiresome member of the tribe—it was so kind.

I found the dogs subdued. They were exhausted with barking and badly frightened by all the aliens tramping through the house.

And there was no message from Henry, no sign of him. The front door must have blown shut behind me and the dogs safe indoors all the time. My rosy tea-service still stood on its silver tray.

The phone was ringing. It was Dulcie, gulping with rage.

'*Wherever* did you get to, Eliza? Henry's been ringing and ringing you. In the end he had to ring me. I said I had left you much better, bathing before beginning to get tea ready for him. He said there had been no reply from your

274

house for hours.'

'I thought the dogs had got out. I went on the Common looking for them. I left the door open but the door slammed. When did he arrive?'

'Oh, he didn't arrive. I'm glad to say he hadn't that nuisance. He found that he had to have a very important conference this afternoon—a crisis of Government. He was very put about. Something arose over the luncheon and had to be pursued through the afternoon.'

'The dogs had to be pursued through...'

'Eliza! He was put about. He asked me to tell you that he was *put about*, not being able to keep the appointment with you.'

'Oh, well.'

'He asked how you were and I said, calmer.'

'Yes. That's true.'

'You know, you and Henry will have to meet, Eliza. Soon. You can't just sit there at number forty-three all your life spending his money and with not a blind thing to do—just there all day and half the night in that sitting-room window.'

'I have a lot of blind things to do.'

'If we had nothing to do, no work, life in this Road would be quite unjustifiable. I mean, what about all our degrees and qualifications? I know that they were some time ago but—it would be living death. My work utterly exhausts me, I'm glad to say. I don't have to do it. We're perfectly comfortably off. But it

makes the Road have *meaning*. After all,
nothing happens here—nothing. *Nothing* goes
on except the tiny events of every day, and
you're not old enough for that yet. You're not
Isobel Ingham. You can't just *be*.'
　'Yes, I suppose so. No, I suppose not.'
　'And you don't play Bridge.'
　'I never liked it much.'
　'You go to no classes. There are excellent
courses of lectures.'
　'Yes, I know.'
　'Courses of *good* lectures. With very
distinguished lecturers.'
　'Yes, I know.'

*　　*　　*

Classes. I have attended classes, Joan, not
always in this country, and have found them
very valuable. Some taught me that simply
being alive can seem very adequate. Some
taught me that working is a lot easier than
living. We all attend classes.
　Some time ago, before your time here, Joan,
or Dulcie's, or Gant's, there were the
Penumbras. You know the house. Indeed you
do. Stand for a moment at your old front gate.
Across the road, head on to you, is my house.
On your right is Deborah's. On your left, next
door to me and on my right, stands the pastry-
coloured house with the white blinds and great
empty barn of a basement kitchen you can see
276

right through to the back and out the other side, all chrome and copper and 'butcher's blocks' and old circulars tossed about the floor in the clean white dust. The house we all explain when anyone asks as 'belonging to film-people, I think, but they're hardly ever there.'

Ten years ago this house was dirty and unkempt and knocked about, unrecovered since the War. Its windows were covered by thick and grimy crocheted curtains, never washed. Blue hydrangeas bulged about in front of it, blocking off the view from the basement, straggling across the windows of the first floor, stalks black, leaves brittle through the winter turning to mulch beneath them, paddled into the path. Newspapers blew about and two tipsy dustbins, seedy comedians, rusted at the side door. There was an unassailability about the place. It seemed impervious to us and to all our standards. It had the curious effect of making us behave as if it were not there.

'They're blacks,' said Angela. 'They've been in a while. Nobody's seen them. Name like Conundrum.'

Henry said that Conundrum sounded rather Indian. Angela said, 'Well something like Conundrum. It's from those parts. Pakistani-blacks, they usually are. And fancy! In this Road!'

We settled for Penumbra. The Family Penumbra, shadows of shadows, though we

277

only ever seemed to see one member of it, 'the man', who left the house each day at eight and returned long after night-fall. He was a tall full man with a passive, greenish face and a solid plastering of close-knit hair gone prematurely grey. He walked away down the hill to the station with bold strides, gazing high above our heads. If greeted, he looked through us.

Little movements of the curtains occurred within the house sometimes. Occasionally we heard muted music, but we saw no one. Behind the house the garden was high with grass and roses, unpruned for years, flopped about in it on old posts. No one went into the garden. No one called at the front door. No milk was delivered. An old large tinny car behind the broken doors of the garage was never taken out.

Then, one day, I was in my garden at the back of the house and heard children in the Penumbra garden alongside, and felt eyes watching me through a knot-hole in the fence. Later, from the turning on my staircase I saw two women there, veiled and in black, giving sweets to a fat boy. I told Henry that they were Arabs, the Penumbras, not Pakistanis at all.

A day or so later, a ball flew over the fence and landed at my feet. There was screaming and lamentation, then silence. I threw the ball back and the silence deepened. In a moment I heard a whispered chattering and fussing as the children were bundled back indoors.

This was about the beginning of the time when I took to the distribution of little notes. I wrote one, addressing the envelope only with the words 'By hand', saying that I wished to be a good neighbour and would be honoured if they would like to come and have some coffee with me.

Silence entire.

About a month later however, the offerings began. Henry and I returned one night from the theatre to find our top step strewn with flowers and sugar biscuits and Henry said, 'Aha—Penumbra.' For we had met this before. Once, in Syria, waiting for our official residence to be ready, we had silent and almost invisible neighbours who left us gifts, gifts that increased in volume and value until they became an embarrassment and then a burden. Every evening there they were. No message. No one to thank.

'Tell them to stop, Henry.'

'My dear Eliza, it's the custom.'

The offerings in Syria had arrived in waves that seemed to have no rhyme or reason. They seemed unconnected to any religious festivals, political events, phases of the moon, or with anything at all that we were doing, though it was remarkable that whenever we went away, even unexpectedly, the offerings ceased. We asked our servants, who smiled and said that it was friendship. I did just wonder once, after a particularly lavish display which had included a large game-bird, whether our neighbours had seen us watching them one night as they dug a hole in their garden and buried a big lead casket. But there seemed little reason for them to mind. I brooded on it in my courtyard among the sweet doping lilies, my orange trees almost ready for marmalade, the water from our fountain glittering and splashing into the cistern. I never discovered the answer.

'I wish I had,' I said to Henry. 'I should have discovered the answer then. Perhaps I should call now next door, and ask outright.' But in the end I wrote a note saying, 'Thank you so much, particularly for the last present of the marigolds and the Sainsbury duckling, but I feel that we can accept no more presents.' 'In this country,' I wrote, 'we do not accept presents from people to whom we have not been introduced.' I said I was sure that the unmarried mothers at The Shires, run by our Church, would be pleased to receive the presents, especially the duck, but that they must be the last.

When I told Henry, he said, 'Oh, my God.' I said, 'Well why didn't you deal with it?' He said, 'It's making so much of it. Did you have to mention the Church?'

'Why shouldn't I?'

'It's a bit provocative, isn't it?'

The offerings stopped. The dirty house relapsed into blackness and trance and only the daily progress of Mr Penumbra down the hill to the train to London, sure as the passage of the seasons or the noonday gun of yore, proved that its heart still beat. Each day he strode away, staring over our heads at the Epsom skyline.

One day, hearing some little noises through the fence while I was in my garden, I called out a greeting in Aramaic. Then in Farsee. But there was no response. That evening we saw Mr Penumbra in his garden walking thoughtfully up and down. He must have been able to hear us talking, but he made no move. 'Funny cove,' Henry said in bed. 'Rather rough-looking. Very shabby. Those English cardigans. Looks as if he's used to wearing something better, somehow, but he doesn't really care. I can't place him. He's a gent, though.'

*　　*　　*

But when in October Henry attended a dinner at his old college, he found Mr Penumbra there, and very firmly placed indeed, on the high table and next to the Dean.

'My neighbour,' said Mr Penumbra to the Dean. 'Whose wife speaks Farsee.'

After dinner at the dessert, Henry met Mr Penumbra eye-ball to eye-ball across a silver bowl of fruit. Mr Penumbra was wearing a dinner jacket as green as his face and of very ancient design and, delicately peeling a

281

Conference pear, he said, 'Good evening,' in a slow, low, academic and slightly American-Oxford voice, 'Rather', said Henry, 'like T. S. Eliot's.'

'May I give you a lift home, Peabody?' asked Mr Penumbra.

Henry was very annoyed to be staying in the college overnight and unable to accept.

* * *

About a week later, on my door-step stood Mrs Penumbra, with no sign of an offering. She appeared to think that I knew her quite well. She was very small with pretty hands and large eyes. She was sharp about the cheek-bones, wore lipstick and was smiling. She smelled of my Syrian courtyard orange-trees, or maybe my lilies, and I felt a pang for them and for the water falling into the cistern: the slow, hot days.

'Mrs Peabody?'

'But how very nice. Do come in.' Angela was prowling and peering. 'May I get you some coffee?'

Mrs Penumbra sat daintily on the edge of her chair and sipped. Her dress was silk and short but very old and rather tight. She wore high-heeled shoes and fine stockings. On her head was a silk scarf, like the Royal Family.

'Won't you take off—?'

'Oh, no. I don't remove it. It is a

dispensation from the veil—only while we are in England. It is an honour, you see.' Then she loosened the scarf, loosened its knot, pushed her fingers under the scarf into her hair—her hair wasn't particularly clean as a matter of fact—and then she took her fingers out, smoothed the sides of the scarf and tightened the knot again. She watched me all the time. It was something I'd never seen done.

'I've lived in the Middle East,' I said. 'In Syria—Iraq. Iran.'

'In the time of the Devil?'

'Yes, I was there in the time of the Shah. But afterwards, too. We moved about.'

'A terrible regime. An evil man. We are now restored to our faith.' Again she played with the knot of her scarf. She moved her head about restlessly inside it. 'We give thanks to God for all His mercies.'

I thought of a Sheraton Hotel where Henry and I had stayed as the Shah's reign ended. The night before we flew home. The hotel was next to the prison. All through the night, precisely on the hour and the half hour, we heard the firing-squad. We counted through the hours. Five, six, seven, eight times. A rip, whiplash, crackle of shots. Quite short. Nine, ten, eleven. We lay in the dark holding hands. Gant, Dulcie, Gargery, even Old Bernard, hearken. Sometimes there is nothing to be done.

I said to her, 'Of course we're quite out of touch now. But I loved the Middle East. I'm

283

sick at all I hear.'

'What do you hear?'

'We still have friends there. And we read the papers. And—for instance the other day, outside Marks and Spencer there was a group of girls with a book of photographs. Some were veiled, some weren't. They carried a collecting box and showed the photographs to people coming out of the store. The photographs were of young men—well, teenaged boys, being hanged from scaffolds in the streets. Sometimes a whole row of them—and people in the market going about their business, or watching. In some of the photographs the boys were hanging dead. There were other photographs, with the boys still standing waiting. There were some girls, too. They were children some of them—not much older than your own.'

'The photographs were fakes. Did you give them money?'

'I gave them twenty pounds, but that was nothing. I should have given them everything I had. No regime can be good that hangs children.'

'They were only beggars, those people outside Marks and Spencer. They were English people. The photographs were fakes.'

Mrs Penumbra was suddenly gone. I came to my senses and thought, I must never tell Henry. The wife of Henry talking politics, breaking the first spider-web thread of understanding! I went to find Angela, who was lurking in the hall, to see if I had dreamed Mrs Penumbra, she was gone so fast—this was in the days when I had little trouble in this direction. I had few waking dreams.

'Angela—was she real?'

'Real she was,' said Angela, 'but I never saw anybody gone so white.'

I didn't tell Henry of the visit. I tried not to think of it. I was ashamed. I felt guilt and fright and couldn't say why. I knew that there was something worrying about the visit from Mrs Penumbra so soon after her husband had mentioned to mine that I spoke Farsee.

One evening in spring, Henry and I came home from a walk on the Common to find Mr and Mrs Penumbra, the fat boy and two small girls all standing at our door, Mrs Penumbra holding a great dish of caviar standing in an even bigger dish of ice.

The girls carried trays with toast and forks and napkins and lemons. The whole family swept into our house with us in a troupe and arranged everything on the gold and glass table, and Henry said—we blinked at the superb quality of the caviar—'I shall find some champagne.'

Then he said, 'Oh dear, I do beg your pardon. That was worthy of Eliza. I forgot.' He turned to the children and said, 'We are not Muslim you see. We do drink alcohol and with caviar we drink champagne because we think it is the most perfect wine with the most perfect food. They go together.'

'Like fish and chips,' said the boy.

'He likes fish and chips,' said one of the girls.

'He likes McDonalds,' said the other and both Penumbra parents for a moment looked furious. Mr Penumbra recovered very fast, though, and laughed. He said, 'Perhaps just tonight I might drink champagne. I dare say not my wife. Not quite.'

'No,' she said, 'I celebrate with champagne of my mind. Champagne of the heart only. It is enough for me.'

They rose to go, taking their trays, and we went with them to the gate when Mr Penumbra without warning grabbed at, clutched, then clung to Henry's hand and held it against his own chest. We saw that both Mr and Mrs Penumbra were weeping.

'We learned today,' said Mr Penumbra, 'that our son has been released from the death-cell. He has been there for fourteen months. I have worked for him and worked for him. Writing, writing. Working for our country. He is now only under house-arrest. A teacher, as I am. As I was. He is twenty-one years old.'

'It has been fourteen months,' said Mrs Penumbra. 'Fourteen.'

On their top step, as they looked for their keys and the children pushed each other about and larked with the trays, Mrs Penumbra turned and eased the knot beneath her chin.

She said, 'Thank you for your kindness.'

We saw none of them ever again. Mr Penumbra was killed shortly afterwards in the car that had stood so long unused. The wheels were unsafe, which was not surprising. The police called on us—which is how we knew; the accident had been far from home—to ask about Mr Penumbra, and if we knew of his having enemies of any kind, for the wheels looked as if all the nuts on the hub caps had been systematically loosened.

We heard nothing at all of Mrs Penumbra and the children except that they had not been with Mr Penumbra in the car. They disappeared like water down a sluice.

The house was put up for sale, was sold, sanitised, gentrified, deadened and became invisible to us in another way. To me it is like a darkness over my right eye as I stand in the window, a cataract creeping. The shadow of a shadow in this eventless street.

*   *   *

'Eliza—you are not listening to me,' said Dulcie. 'Look, do buck up a bit. Shall I come across and see you? Hullo?'

I looked round the room—the sugar basin on the tray on the gold and glass table, the sugar-tongs. I felt some old sad occasion stirring, not the Penumbras only, but dozens and dozens of times, all gone. And slow, slow nineteenth-century summers. 'I don't like it in here this afternoon,' I said, 'there are ghosts about. Can I come and see you?'

'I'm adding up marks and we're off to the theatre soon. I can't give you long. Oh well—yes of course.'

* * *

'Have a drink,' said old Richard, opening the front door wide on me and his lions. 'She's just a bit busy with the final stages. Won't be long.'

We sat with the clearest, driest sherry poured into the clearest smallest glasses, and Richard sipped. I tried to remember what Barry calls fino sherry. Hen's piss.

'I beg your pardon,' said Richard, '*what* did you say?'

'Just this—I'm sorry to butt into your evening. I expect you're just as busy as Dulcie.'

'Oh no, I clear the decks for Dulcie when she's marking papers. Clear the metaphorical decks. I never feel retired, you know, at her examination times—but no, nothing like so busy as she is. It's all pleasure for me. We discuss the questions. It's good for me,' he sipped. 'Just at present I'm giving a lot of attention to *Christabel*.'

I said, 'Have you met the new Philippino at the Robins'? She looks very fierce. By the way, George is home.'

He looked long and soberly at me.

288

'You have a grasshopper mind, Eliza.' I saw him deliberate whether to say, 'I must ask you to concentrate please on the matter put to you', in the voice he must have used for forty years in court, or whether, because I am not a reliable witness, to lure me carefully back to the subject so that I shall not be embarrassed to find that I have strayed. He took a millilitre of sherry. I wondered if Christabel was the cat.

'I didn't know you had another cat.'

'We haven't.'

'Oh I'm sorry.'

'There's no need to be sorry that we haven't a cat. No need at all. I am far from sorry. Hairs everywhere.'

'D'you know what Anne Robin was asked by her American publisher? If she'd write a book about a cat.'

'Really? I don't call that particularly interesting, Eliza. I thought she wrote about all kinds of small creatures. There aren't any hairs on your chair are there?'

'No. I'm sure there aren't. It's leather.'

'I'm sorry if there are still signs of the old cat. I really do hope not. It's what we had a long battle about. We both became very upset about it. It was dreadful to have the old animal about the place knowing that very shortly it would all be over for him. I saw to it in the end. Dulcie isn't domestic, you know. More sherry?'

'Well, yes please.'

'This is a very rare sherry.' He poured a third

289

of an inch into each of our glasses and looking through the side of his own glass, holding it high, said again, 'Not a bit domestic. Hopeless cook. At Girton it was part of her charm.'

'Girton isn't a very domestic place.'

'Ah, but you could have seen, wherever we had met, that she would never be domestic. She had a fine mind. Sharp as a scimitar. Enchanting. Far ahead of her time.'

'You were ahead of yours too, Richard. Not to mind.' I tried not to look at the layer of dust that coated everything like soft grey plush. 'How's Dulcie's hay-fever?' I asked and again saw him think, Her mind is all over the place.

'I am basically rather domestic,' I said. 'It comes and goes. I don't mind mess. Clean mess. I don't like smells though,' and I thought, This is the most pointless conversation I have ever had in my life even in Washington. I shouldn't have come. Just because I was frightened of the tea-tray.

I began to try and analyse my feelings about the tea-tray.

'Smells?' he said. 'I do hope there are no smells *here*? One thing I can't stand is the smell of cat. Especially when it has been dead for some time.'

'But, didn't you take it to the vet?'

'I mean' (he seemed to be thinking nostalgically of the death-penalty for his wife's friends) 'I mean the smell of a cat that hangs about when the cat is—oh good gracious me,

290

Eliza, you know what I mean.'

'I'm quite sure, Richard, that Christabel never smelled.'

'Christabel? Christabel's not a *cat*. It's a poem. By Coleridge.' But he got up all the same and started padding about, sniffing.

'Oh for goodness sake, Richard,' said Dulcie, pouncing in, 'I'm sure Eliza knows her Coleridge.'

'I don't, you know, Dulcie. How strange though—I was thinking about *The Ancient Mariner* today. I don't know much about Coleridge though, not really.' For some reason I then added, 'Not *reelly*.' To round things off I then said, 'Cock.' They looked non-plussed.

I said, 'Why isn't non-plussed minussed? Or just nought?'

'Minussed? *Nought*?'

'You both look minussed.'

Pouring Dulcie an enormous brandy and soda, Richard took the decision to soldier on as if I were my old self—or even Henry. More likely Henry, he used to like a disputation with Henry. 'We've been having something of a stinger in this year's Mock,' he said. ('Ha—much better,' said Dulcie. 'Needed that.') 'To do with the difference between the fancy and the imagination. Coleridge of course has the reputation for self-indulgence. Opium and suchlike. Yet in his poetry he resolutely, resolutely suppresses the fancy. He destroyed all verse that even touched the periphery of the

291

fancy, delicate, delicious though it might be, in order to let in the full flow of the deep, true, creative imagination. He was his own harshest scourge, you know. There is nothing to fear from the power of the imagination, Eliza,' and he looked at the darkening evening through the sherry glass. 'But the fancy, oh the fancy—it is a false star.'

'It must be tiring being a poet,' I said. 'Like being a religious. I'm very fond of *The Ancient Mariner* but I'm glad I don't have to try and work out how he did it any more.'

'*And*,' said Richard, turning to me his pursy face, his careful lips, 'fancy to the non-poet, after childhood, has to be cast out like seven devils. Hallucinations are not always produced by drugs you know, or by brain-disease. They are often wilfully conjured. *They are very dangerous and frightening to all.* They used to cause belief in witches. They are destructive. They can destroy the personality. Cut us off from our fellows and the real world.'

'I don't think of Coleridge as being cut off. Wasn't he a great talker? Didn't most people adore him? And when there was nobody congenial about—and even when there was, didn't he just go on talking on paper? I mean letters. How nice—I do remember something about him after all.'

'Coleridge,' said Dulcie, 'was Coleridge. I've been aware of that all day. I'm sick of him— poet or no poet. There was real lack of moral fibre there. I'm a Wordsworthian.'

I thought, Oh how I want you, Barry-boy! You and the racing track. I hate culture. I want the Fair.

'Yes?' asked Richard. 'Yes?'

'Yes what?' I must have missed a bit. I said, 'But why are you so angry, Richard? So judgmental? Judge—mental? Judges are mental.'

Dulcie said, 'Oh, don't you understand, Eliza? I know you understand. We're all so worried about you. *Hallucinations.*'

'What hallucinations?'

'Well—for example all this about your dogs.'

'Is that the time? I must go. You've reminded me. They have to go out. Joan's dog is such a menace.'

'Think very carefully,' Richard said at the door, holding the wheel of the Yale, making me wait and look in his face, his other kind hand under my elbow. 'Just think, Eliza. Think. Quietly. Don't *feel.* Now then—*dogs*?'

I said, 'But you were imagining cats,' and I saw them turn to one another as I ran down the steps.

* * *

Finding my front-door key at the top of my own steps I think, Dogs, cats—what an afternoon! Dogs, cats, American publishers, spontaneous abortions and violinists; yet Dulcie says that I must widen my horizons. I don't think I can bear anything more today.

Whatever is this?

For the garage of my neighbour has suddenly opened its clattering mouth and Deborah's car appears. It does not get gobbled up between the iron jaws but stops outside in the Road. Ivan emerges from the back seat and together he and Deborah almost lift from the seat beside the driver's little Mr Deecie, hunched like a wounded man inside his long dark coat. Ivan pauses to lock the car but Deborah yells, 'Don't do that now, you fool. You can do it later. Come here and help,' and Ivan jumps to it.

Each takes an arm of Mr Deecie and lifts him up the steps. He looks boneless, like a Guy Fawkes, and they look tall and tense at either side of him. It is a fraught, strange little pietà. Or it's a man being taken kindly but desperately towards his execution. It is one more snapshot of the day.

And Richard is here on the steps beside me once again. He is saying, 'Trouble with the key?'

He has hurried over the Road to me. I had thought that I had silenced him, forgetting that one can never silence a judge. 'Eliza,' he says, 'there is something else. Dulcie and I both spoke to Henry this afternoon and she told him very forcibly how worried we are about your health, my dear. Your loneliness. We said again that there must be someone, some near relative and that we should like to be put in touch with your Yorkshire cousin.'

'Lancashire cousin.'

'Lancashire cousin.'

'And he said?'

'My dear, he's as bad as you are. He said nothing at all as only the Diplomatic Services know how. At first he said he thought we must be exaggerating and then he said he saw no reason to contact Annie Cartwright—in fact implied it wouldn't be possible.'

'He's right. I haven't seen her for years, or even heard of her. For all I know she's dead. I think she went to America.'

'Well, we got him to say that he'd speak to you about it. He said there'd been some trouble ... in your childhood...?'

'My troubles are to do with here and now, Richard. About my bewilderment.' (I saw him think—ah! At last. Talking.) 'About Joan going away.' (A look of strong disapproval now.) 'About Henry going away. Richard, Richard—how I envy them all—all away. For thirty years I have been the one who can't go away alone. I have held the fort. I've always been the one who worries about the others. Since I stopped going abroad with him, I've been the one spending her life at the window looking out for someone's—well Henry's—return.'

There was an almost ingratiating delight on Richard's face now. (At last! She's never said so much.)

'Then the time's *come* for you to go away, Eliza. Do something of your own. You're scarcely fifty—you're a child still. What you need is a job.'

'I had a job. For thirty years I had Henry. I saw him through. He was hopeless when we married—so diffident, afraid of trying, said he was no good at languages. When we married it was made quite clear to me that Henry's job in the Foreign Service was shared between us. Diplomatic wives were not allowed any other work then. It's different now. Then it was full-time social punishment and doing the intellectual and diplomatic polite. We were Oxbridge-trained geisha girls and I was a very good one. And I was worth something better.

'And why do you say I should "go away"? Why should something black in my heart vanish because I am standing on another piece of the globe? If I'd thought that, it would have been I who went off—not Joan. I wouldn't have been the one writing the letters.'

'You write *letters* to Joan? Eliza—you know you really ought to see someone. I believe that Henry truly will turn up tomorrow. You must promise me you'll talk to him. Tell him all this. He is going to ring you again tonight.'

* * *

And he does.

Such an unfamiliar voice. Is it really Henry or a Coleridgian fantasy? A new, nervous voice and the sentences punctured by little frightened coughs. Heck, heck, heck. He has turned into an Edwardian bishop. What on earth's the matter with him?

'Henry—what's the matter?'

'Ahem, ahem, Eliza—I'm so sorry about this afternoon, ahem. Heck.'

'Not at all. I had an interesting afternoon.'

'Good. Ahem. Heck, heck.'

'There's absolutely no need for you to come here, Henry. I'm sorry the Baxters have been on to you. I'm perfectly well. Don't listen to Dulcie, she's hardly seen me for months until this week—they most of them just discuss me, they don't come and talk. Anyway, she's much too busy for everyday life—and you know what she's like about common sense. If you haven't a full pint pot of it she looks you up and down. She's been giving Coleridge hell.'

'You sound—Eliza—ahem—'

'Different?'

'Like you once were—quite funny.'

'And nicer I suppose—less bossy?'

'Well, actually, no. Rather catty.'

We both laugh and stop. We have surprised ourselves.

297

'Ahem Eliza, I ought to see you. About the future.'

'How's Charles?'

'Be quiet. Listen.' (No coughs.) 'About our future.'

'Oh, the divorce.'

A long, long silence. Then a little string of coughs.

'You need some linctus. Henry, whatever's all this about Annie Grucock?'

'I'll be there tomorrow. I promise.'

'Well, what time?'

'I just don't know. But you're not busy are you? Does it matter?'

'How d'you know I'm not busy?'

'Well—evening then. Seven o'clock. Shall I tell Dulcie? We might go on to the Little Greek.'

'With *Dulcie*? D'you think I need a minder? Why ever tell Dulcie? Anyway, they're off on holiday tomorrow to get over the Mock.'

'I thought you might like someone else there. In case you got upset.'

I put down the phone.

I thought, And what was all that about? Something. Something. He's very frightened. Does he think I'll have a carving knife ready down the chaise-longue? He is terrified of something, whatever it may be.

AND, my dear J.,

The next day was still and beautiful. I sat in the morning early at the window, watching the Road. All had fallen so quiet that as I looked at your alternate crimson and white standard roses I watched a velvet petal fall to the ground and almost listened to hear it touch. Such roses—all the better really for having been left unpruned this year. Charles always slew them. They had to struggle out of the bare wood to catch up with the year and never looked anything before August when the whole Road except for us and you were on holiday.

'Gone away.'

How many years since Henry and I have gone away? In the first years we travelled so much. Now we scarcely leave the Road. Since Henry in his distinguished middle-age has been London-based, his only trips have been flips to Washington and Brussels, and, for nearly twenty years now, always alone, the rule about the back-up of the camp-following wife being gone. Rathbone Road is the place where Henry has wanted his holidays. Like a boy back from boarding-school he wanted no bucket-and-spade country, but his own bed and garden.

Oh, all our travels. I thought of the busy, happy woman I used to be, laughing, talking, organising, setting up our official residencies.

There was the one with no floors. There was the one with no furniture, no glasses, cups, saucers, the great reception hall empty except for filth and crates and empty bottles. I left Henry then, flew back to England, placed a huge order for everything down to salt-spoons, wrote furious notes to the Foreign Secretary. Henry sent a cable saying, 'Has he resigned?' I threatened to contact the Queen. 'I shall BEARD THE QUEEN,' I wrote to Henry from London, and he sent back a little drawing. I slaved over that old shabby, shadowy house in a Syrian street. I started the garden there. My lilies are still flowering in that garden, I dare say, somewhere in the rubble and the gun-fire. Oh Henry.

Martinis round the pool in Cairo. Did I ever? Did I ever, truly, sip martini round a pool? Talk drivel? Do I really remember, in Jokjakarta, sitting for hours on the floor with the women of the harem in the dark cool rooms, listening to them talk at first slowly, then, as they forgot me, merry and careless. 'Daft,' we'd have called it at school. 'Being daft.' Then Bangkok. I tried as I stood watching your *Alice Through the Looking-Glass* roses, Joan, each on its dark and snappable stalk, to smell the East, the hot spicy blast that hits you as you step from the plane. The queer dry smell. Sweetish like dung and sun and sex.

Then I tried to be in New England again. Oh my, how I worked for Henry there—well, for myself, too. I wanted to be a success. All the huge parties, all the hard smiles. The wafts of French scent, the punishing barbecues, the idiotic dressing-up of all the surroundings as well as myself. I sent to Italy once for fireworks and to Malta for powder to scatter on the fire in winter for house-parties, that made the flames flicker in pretty colours. The superb English cook I found who had them all wild about Lancashire hot-pot and steak-and-mushroom pie and treacle pudding.

Untouched. I am left untouched by it all. Or maybe touched. It has all left me, as completely as my old, sensual life, for I can remember no more of the excitements of sex than I can remember my mother's arms, my mother's voice. All gone.

I ought to remember something of my mother. Six is not so young. They say she was so loving. In dreams sometimes there's something, but I can't remember it when I wake. Can't remember what she looked like—just now and then I catch a sort of breath of her. A lightness of heart. A running figure—long legs. A laugh somewhere down a passage. I remember my father better—Army moustache, cheek-bones, trilby hat—yet he had been away for three years.

Another petal falls on the grass. Only just June, yet that rose is almost over. Must stick the petals on again. Sleepy. Write a letter to the Red Queen. The window is open before me and

I sit. The wonderful English hot June morning. Heavy. Everyone must be in a trance somewhere. Everybody has gone out today. The whole Road. I am in a trance, too, I am falling asleep.

And the door opposite, Joan, is flung wide and out rushes the laundering husband, the man who has everything, with his first child Mick, named for Mikhail Gorbachev, under his arm. He looks a bright little boy.

The father rushes down his steps and up the steps of the house on your left, Dulcie and Richard's house. He beats upon their door. Mick wags his legs about from beneath his father's arm.

The father runs down Dulcie's steps again and into the road and up the steps of the house next door to me, of Deborah of the watery smile. There is no reply.

The father looks wildly about him, down towards Miss Ingham on the crest of the hill, then at Anne's mansion opposite. He deliberates, looks desperately over his shoulder at his open front door, then comes tearing up my steps. He bangs, he beats, he rings. 'Can you take him? Half an hour? It's come,' he cries and pushes the child in my arms. 'Hospital. Ambulance.'

'Come? The new baby's *come*?'

'She's having it now. On the floor. It was the ladder. *Now*.'

His short and fashionably bristly head of

hair, his little round nose, his Jermyn Street T-shirt, his cheeks like cherries. His utterly terrified eyes.

'You're good with kids. They all say so. Back as soon as...'

The ambulance arrives. From my top step, Master Gorbachev wriggling, I watch the dashing and the rushing and the pandemonium—and a stretcher with a mountain of blankets come jogging out, husband running behind. All is shovelled in the back, and away. The laundering husband's door has been left wide and the Road again falls silent.

The baby regards me, weighs me up, points across the road to his front door and begins to scream. I thoroughly agree with him.

I cross the road and go in. There is a push-chair thing, the seat a nest of straps and buckles and I sit him in it. He screws himself out of it. I put him back. He thunders and lightnings at me as I tie him down. I take the door keys, wheel him out, close the door behind us. In the street he roars like a lion but attracts no attention. I think that this is all a dream.

And I am full of rare delight—for I have said, 'This must be all a dream,' knowing that it is not. It is happening. This is true. I am perfectly sane.

'We'll just go over to my house, Mick,' I say. 'I'll feed the dogs and then...' I think. What does one do all day with babies? Go for walks.

Yes. I won't take the dogs though—too much. Not safe. Must give the child my whole attention.

He roars on. So loud is his roar that the dogs wince. 'D'you like cake?' I ask him. 'Cake?' and he stops, mid-roar. I cut a large slice of Henry's chocolate cake on the kitchen table. I had been too dispirited last night to put it away. 'More?'

More indeed. A second slice.

I look about for a cloth to remove crumbs from M. Gorbachev's chops. I don't like the idea of using the dish-cloth and so I look about for the rag-bag that hangs, as it has for many years, on the back of the wash-room door. It is a cherry-coloured bag and it still has my name-tape on it, for it was my school sewing-bag. Annie Cartwright's initials are on it, too—it is from the time when we were both at the same school. They are sewn upon it, very large, hardly faded, in beautifully even chain stitch. Very neat. 'A. C.' intertwined. I had wanted a sewing-bag of my own but Annie, now eight, was moving up from Sewing and my aunt said that it would be silly to buy a new one. 'You can unpick the chain-stitch if you like, Elizabeth, but I really shouldn't bother. The "A. C." will show through. It will always be there. Just stitch on your own name-tape.'

I tip the rags out of the bag, mop up the baby with the softest one, and I have a great assurance now about what has to be done.

Locking up the house, I go off with the baby and the empty rag-bag up the High Street. The bag swings, light on the handles. When we reach the Building Society I carefully manoeuvre the push-chair inside, not expertly. The push-chair kicks at someone's heels. They are the heels of Dr Sepsis, looking grave. I think he swears but realise what he says is, 'Buggy.' Then he looks a little interested. 'Mrs er?' he says. 'Getting about?'

'Yes, I am.'

'Excellent. Grandchild?'

Two days ago I entrusted to him the story—part of the story—of my barrenness. I have entrusted it to no-one else. 'Greatgrandchild,' I say, and he looks rather puzzled, but not seriously. He becomes entangled again in the chair as he leaves, remembers the soap and gives me a glare. 'Awkward things those,' says the counter-clerk. 'They call them strollers in America. It's quite the day for a stroll.'

I ask if I may take all the money out of my account. Almost all of it is left. I have separate quiet money of my own that my uncle left me. Money's never been a trouble to me, I've always managed. It's the Lancashire cotton genes. The clerk goes away and returns with the manager and there is a repeat performance of the day after Boxing Day.

'Shall you want it all, Mrs Peabody?'

'Every penny. In coin if possible.'

'We could manage only a percentage in coin.'

'Heavy coin please. Could you put it all in here?' And I hold out Annie's bag.

I am in the High Street again and we set off for the Common only stopping once at the patisserie, for éclairs. I buy seven. Bella Bentley is in the patisserie. We do not acknowledge each other. She watches me, her cake-fork poised.

Over the Common we go. Big vans, enormous lorries, queer pantechnicons are standing about near the pond. There are caravans, shuttered and still. *The Fair is coming*.

The baby squawks, and at every new squawk I hand down an éclair. Soon he is asleep and I stride off in the direction of Caesar's Farm.

Such a balmy and beautiful walk, Joan. My feet go pat, pat on the earth along the road side. So windless. Even the very tips of the delicate fir trees are still. If I stop for a moment I can hear the crackle of pine needles, as if they're on a griddle—or maybe it's the gorse-bushes beyond. There's the odd squeak of a bird. No more.

At The Hospice nobody is sitting behind the desk which is not usual. I hang about looking at St Julian. At last a nun walks by and says, 'Well now, and what are you doing here today? It's not your day is it? What a lovely boy. Now then, what are you up to, Eliza?'

'D'you think I might show him to Barry?'
'Oh no dear. Not now. It's a bad day.'
'Just for one moment. Oh, please.'
'But the child is fast asleep, and Barry's eyes are shut too, Eliza darling.' The nun takes my hand and looks clearly at my eyes. 'It is a very bad day. You do understand, don't you? You do know?'
'Just for one minute.'
'Leave the push-chair out here then.'
'Oh, but I must take the baby. I'm in sole charge of him. I mustn't leave him for an instant.'
Mick is lifted from the push-chair and I carry him sleeping to Barry's room. A nun is with him.
'Could I stay one minute with him alone?'
'One minute, Eliza, one minute.'
I sit by Barry and look at the poor face covered now with bandaged sores, the bones seem nearly through the skin. The head is bandaged too. The gummy lids are closed. Barry is dying. I hold on to the child very carefully but manage to stroke—and fearlessly and no doubt unwisely—one of the oozing, bandaged hands. One of Barry's eyes opens a slit.
'Had a baby?'
I can hardly hear him through the blistered lips.
'Barry. I want to say something.'
'Not mine. Deny all knowledge.'
307

He floats away from me. Only the joke is alive in the room. Only the joke is left in the automatically comical heart.

'I want to say—oh my child and lover—that I love you.'

'Love you back, Elizabeth.'

'Queen of the Tambourine,' he says.

*　　*　　*

The babe and I go marching on. Down the lane again we go, over the Common. The babe sleeps. My tears run down my face and fall on my hands. They trickle over the hands and down the handles of the push-chair. Some fall on the child. I take a cut through the Roman woods and we get on to rough land and then into bracken. We push on through this, leaving a rippling track. We come out among the little paths and the flowering blackberries.

Nobody about.

Rabbits, birds, badgers, foxes—all somewhere near. I want the baby to wake up so that I can tell him about them, but he sleeps on. We get to the woods above the far mere; and the stroller-coaster, the baby and the bag and I go bowling and rollicking into the trees, swinging and bumping. Down we go. We reach the mere. Still nobody about.

The mere is a strange place with black water and very bright green weed. The trees, very tall and close together, slope down all round it. It's in a hole. In the middle of the mere there's a post sticking up saying: DANGER THIS LAKE IS UNSAFE FOR BATHING.

I wonder why?

Once it wasn't. Once people came all the way out from central London to swim in this mere. Only fifteen years ago it was a place for naughty nude bathing, men only, before 9 a.m.—an extraordinary idea it seems now. A hundred years before that it was not a mere at all but a soggy stretch of ground in the woods where famous duels were fought.

But the mere is deep now. A young dead girl was found here one winter's morning a few years ago, stuck in the ice. Her hair was rayed out in icicles. Dead and frozen. A frozen water-lily. Oh, Ophelia.

Today, in the warm sunshine, there is a boat, and I take the baby from the stroller. I take Annie's sewing-bag off the handlebars and drop it in the bottom of the boat. Then I place the baby in the bottom of the boat—so beautiful. Like us all, he will become cruel. In mid-mere, rowing slowly, just a few strokes then a few more, I lift the oars out of the water and let them drip. I bring them in close, rest them along the sides of the boat. They stream with water and green weed. I have put a big stone in Annie's bag, just for certainty, and I lift the bag and throw it in the mere. It disappears at once. Gone. The boat rocks a little as I lean to look. Nothing left of Annie's chains or Henry's money.

The baby, all chocolate éclair, stirs. His eyes fly wide and he watches the water streaming from the oars above him. I pick him up and hold him out over the water and he begins to wriggle and yell. So I drop him in the water and he disappears like the bag.

I watch. Up he comes. His back is rounded over and I can't see his face. He comes up for the second time. I can only see his bottom now in its bunchy covers. I watch him a moment.

Quite soon, the third time, before he sinks back, I catch hold of him, nearly upsetting the boat. I lift him high.

I stand in the boat. I lift him high.

Water and weed stream from the child as they streamed from the oars, and there is silence like the first or the last moment of the turning world.

Then the voice of the child is loud in the heavens. He yells. He roars. He rampages. My hands support his armpits. His head is flung back. The boat rocks. His voice cracks the firmament. His legs and arms flail, hard, strong as roots.

The boat has sidled up to the bank. It shimmies over the water to the shore. Flop-slap goes the water against the sides of the mere and some loutish, truanting boys come running and shouting out of the trees and appear beside the water, quite near to us. They seem brought up short. They stand still.

They are silenced.

'It's fallen in,' says one.

'She's let it fall in.'

I gather the baby, light in my arms, still screaming, and push the stroller one-handed, past them. They seem uneasy.

'Eh—miss? Missus? Did it fall in?'

'Yes. He's all right.'

I push on through the woods, up the steep wooded slope, the baby crying, and take him on to the sunny plain of grasses up above. I think I see Bella walking by herself somewhere in the distance, determinedly smiling.

I stop, I lay down the baby and peel off his outer skin, take off my jacket and jersey and wrap him in them. Some golfers go by.

I sing to the baby. I point out this and that to him. At last his sobs begin to grow farther apart. 'Look,' I say. 'A daisy. Look, a butterfly.' At last there is the true long shuddering pause between sobs that means the worst is past. He takes a blade of grass from my fingers. Gravely he hands it back again to me. I give him the seventh éclair, but it is some time before he begins to eat it, watching me.

Then I play a tickling game, rubbing him hard all over, my hands and my clothes drying him, warming him. Secure in the pushchair, he laughs once on the way home. His drying hair curls sweetly over his head, in rings. I look down on his hair and sometimes, now and then, as we proceed, I stroke it.

And back in his own home I give him a bath, remembering perfectly all I was taught by

311

Amanda Fish. I wash his clothes and put them in the drier. I find others and dress him. Then I play with him in the sunny garden, but he's tired. He seems to need no more food. He is such a very good child. Soon now he sleeps in his cot, eyes heavy. His afternoon rest.

I sit in the pine and marble of the kitchen, watching over him, so much more beautiful than any inanimate thing—the steel, the polished wood, the black glass tulips in the white glass vases. Oh, the beauty of him! I should like a cigarette but it would be a pity for I have managed to stop. And I don't like to see people smoking near a baby. I look at my nails. I shall have to cut these pretty flowers.

At length a taxi drives down the road and the father, the man who has everything but might today have had less, goes running up the steps to my front door. I watch him from across the road in his basement. When there is no answer I see him begin to look frantic. How very emotional he is. He jumps about, then comes running across to his own front door which I've left on the latch. A moment more and he stands at the top of the staircase to his basement dream-kitchen and cries, 'Daughter!' and I rush to him and we embrace. I kiss the man with the small nose whose surname I do not know, and he seizes Mick from the cot and kisses him, too.

'You have a sister, a sister, a sister.'

'And all's well?'

'Oh, very well. Perfectly well. Not so quick as we thought at first. We were misled. There was an interval. But perfectly well, both of them. A beautiful child.'

'She couldn't be lovelier than Mick.'

'She's Perry—for Peristroika. Perry Margaret. Do you like it?'

'I think it may date her.'

The baby in his father's arms looks at me.

Holding one hand before me I feel for the kitchen wall. I edge now, most exhausted, to the foot of the stairs. 'I must go home.'

The man who has everything finds that it is time for a large, late luncheon. 'Famished, famished,' he cries. 'I'm ravenous. Has Mick been fed?'

'Yes. Rather a lot.'

'How good you are. I must get myself some nosh-up,' and crash, bang he goes among the copper saucepans and bunches of fresh herbs, the baby on his arm. He sings and twirls about.

'I really shall have to go now, Dickie.'

'How can I ever thank you?' he says and then decides to give me a present. He says, 'You're not so eccentric Eliza P., whatever they all say. You're the best of the lot. I don't know what I'd have done if you hadn't been in. There should always be someone who's at home all the time—a sort of tribal mother, isn't it? Gab and I thought we were all geared up for anything, but we couldn't have managed without you. I'd have had to stay behind and

Gab would have been furious. She's pretty Feminist you know—she doesn't believe in doing things by herself.'

'A great pleasure.'

'We never leave Mick with anybody you know. We're always being told that it's time to leave him with baby-sitters and so on, but we've never been able to bring ourselves to do it. You just can't know who you'd get. This is the very first time. I found that I utterly trusted you.'

'I must go, Dickie.'

'Mustn't keep you then.' The succulent ratatouille is purring in the mike, his omelette is growing a golden frilly edge with the perfect central wetness. He scatters soft cheese on it. 'Mustn't leave this. Tricky moment. Hate you finding your own way to the door...'

* * *

I speak to the dogs and feed them. I look in the fridge. There is an opened tin of anchovies. Fillets of worm. They lie clouded in oil. The lid is coiled back in a lethal, razor-sharp roll. Unwound it could sever an artery. Well now?

There is a piece of bacon stuck to the floor of the deep-freeze compartment, but it will not tear off. There is half of a yesteryear's tin of baked beans in a pyrex bowl. The beans have a navy-blue ring round the top. They have grown old as we that are left have grown old.

314

They linger.

Hunger is gone.

Standing at the far end of the drawing room with a cup of tea I see, out at the back, under the trees next door, funny little Mr Deecie working in his daughter's garden with spade and hoe. I can only see his white shirt and braces and the top of his dark head. He works with the concentration of years. He lifts the rake forward, drops it to the earth, makes slow careful lines, trawling it towards him. Sometimes he stands and stares at the ground.

Evening of evenings

My dear Joan,

There are still hours to go before the arrival of Henry and I sat down on the chaise-longue, the last piece of furniture in the room, the rest having long been stacked in the crowded attic. I put my tea-cup on the floor beside me and watch the sky above the trees at the back of the house. There are two humps, two rounded hunks of wood, sticking up at the open window. They puzzle me but not enough to stir and when I look again, the light on them has changed. There's a glimmer of twilight. I have slept.

So still. The immobility of this day.

What's this? I've slept again.

I strain my eyes to see in the light, that is now different again, the rosy cups, the tea-spoons, the little pearly cake-knives, the sugar-lumps, the small lawn napkins tucked beneath two small plates. Whoever set that lot up? I did? Nonsense. It was not I. I, Eliza Peabody have been used for years, programmed by the dead, by Lancashire half a century ago. By Annie Cartwright and her perfect sense of an ordered life, by her mother, by idiotic Victorian mores. By Henry?

Poor Henry. Well, I suppose this sort of archaic set-up is what he wanted. I'm sure it wasn't my idea to place bone china on a tray for Henry. Was it? Do I rather like it myself? Salami and booze for ancient Ingham but auntie's tea-cups still for the travelled experienced Mrs P. Hush. Listen.

I hear now the faraway jungle I listen out for every June, the moment of moments. The blare and the rootle-tootle ting-a-ling clang of the Common. It's back again, Joan, the inconsequent, healing *Fair. The Fair is come.*

So, full summer is come, and I close my eyes and try to catch behind the canned music of the loud-speakers and the tannoy; the shake of the tambourine, the thump and vibration of the drum.

There's another sound, another thumping sort of sound quite close to me and I see the two chunks of wood sticking up on the sill begin to

316

move urgently up and down. Bump, bump, knock, knock. They begin to bounce more vigorously as if it might be an earthquake starting perhaps, or one of the sexual encounters so dear to television.

A small head appears at the window. It is the Polish Croupier on Miss Ingham's ladder which must have been standing at the window since yesterday afternoon. Inviting ingress. All night long. Why did he not come to me during last night's dark?

When he sees me sitting in the half-dark the head jerks back and the ladder shudders. 'My God,' he shouts. 'My God.'

'What do you think you're doing—climbing that ladder?'

'I left it here last night. I forgot it. She is put out. As it was I had to run for the train and all down Park Lane to the casino.'

'Why have you come back?'

'To get the ladder.'

'You don't take ladders away from the top. Why didn't you ring the front door-bell?'

He is silenced. For three seconds. 'I just came round the side. I saw the window was still open so I thought I'd climb up and shut it. I'm not very...' He totters.

'You'd better come in.'

He steps over the sill and sits crumpled at my feet. Thin as a fly. You never see a fat Croupier. It's the stretching and scooping, the scything and gleaning. Like the conductor of an

317

orchestra. Conductors and Croupiers live for
ever. This man looks the oldest and weirdest
little man in the world.

I stretch to the lamp beside my chaise-
longue. I light up what there is to light—the
gold looking-glass above the fireplace, the gold
and glass table with the telephone on it, and
propped by the wall the portrait of Henry the
Goat.

'Is that a Gainsborough?'

'It's his pupil.'

'I thought so. I could get you twenty
thousand pounds for that.'

'D'you know someone called Barry?'

'No, it's a man at Epsom.'

'It's a small world.'

He is dressed in black jeans and black T-
shirt, gold medallion and black shadows about
the jowl, rings on the bony fingers, clean dainty
nails. He sits at my feet. He looks me over.

He says, 'I have watched you for a long time,
Eliza Peabody.'

'Isn't it time that you were setting off for
work?'

'My night off. I have wanted you so much. I
want you now so much.'

'Isn't Miss Ingham expecting you?'

'Miss Ingham is beyond expectations.'

'Many of us are.'

'You are not.'

'How d'you know?'

'I know.'

He takes my left ankle making a white bracelet of his fingers and thumb. His lean black old, old arm. He unclasps the bracelet and moves it upwards. He moves the fingers up and up my leg. 'Beautiful,' he says. 'Long, long legs.'

'I'm over fifty.'

'Ah—you must wait for sixty. "A woman of sixty is a volcano." Wesker. Beautiful. All women should wear suspenders. So sexy—stockings. Tights are for stuffings.'

The Victoriana on the table—let it go for ever. I do not move. I have been given a mystifying command: make love with this atrocious and lascivious Croupier, Eliza Peabody, and you and Henry will be able to look each other once more in the face. You will both be saved.

Over the Croupier's shoulder I look boldly at the Goat and as the Croupier stands to switch off the light I stretch my arms up to him to pull him down.

And a voice says, 'What the hell are you doing? What is this? Eliza—why are you sitting in the dark?'

Henry stands in the door and switches on both central chandeliers, and Satan flits away.

Yes, he's here at last.

Here is Henry.

He marches across to the window and looks out, and 'Oh my God,' he says, 'Eliza you're

319

crazy. This ladder! Hullo—there's someone in the garden, for goodness sake—hullo? Who's there? Hullo—can I help you?'

There's a muffled noise below. Henry says, 'Yes? Please explain yourself. No, of course don't climb the ladder. I can't think what the ladder's doing here. If you've something to say please come to the kitchen door.'

I say—it is a moan—I am feeling very tired—'Oh Henry. No.'

'Yes. Most *certainly*,' he says. 'I'm not having people wandering about in the garden. Hold on, Eliza. I'll see to it.'

There is talk at the back door and Henry comes back with a small dark figure, hands hanging from shirt cuffs that seemed far too wide, head down.

It is Mr Deecie.

'I'm sorry. I walked through into your garden, Mrs Peabody,' he says. 'Through the weak place in the fence.'

'This is a friend, Eliza?'

'Oh yes—Mrs Peabody is a friend. She was also a friend of my...'

I ask, 'Is Mrs Deecie not with you?'

'Mrs Deecie,' he says again, 'Mrs Deecie is...'

I thought, Henry will explode now, he will lose his temper and run the man out of the door.

320

'Mrs Deecie is ...,' and Henry suddenly steps forward and lays an arm along Mr Deecie's shoulder. He says, 'All right, sir. Let me get you a drink. Sit down...' He looks for seats but there is only the chaise-longue so he goes to the hall and comes back with an upright chair. 'Take it easy, sir. Do sit down.'

'Mrs Deecie has passed away,' says Mr Deecie. 'I mustn't disturb you now. I've been meaning to make contact, but I can see that this is not an appropriate moment.'

'Of course it is,' Henry and I say together.

'No. I won't stop. I'll call perhaps again. One day.' He looks hopelessly around for a way out and drifts to the window.

'Mr Deecie is staying with his daughter. Next door,' I say, and Henry says, 'Then I shall see you home, and I hope we can get you to come back to see us tomorrow.'

'It was only last Wednesday,' says Mr Deecie. 'You know, it was all over in an hour. And the funeral so quick—Deborah's so brisk. Naturally everything took place in Leicester. Deborah and Ivan were present and I can only say that they have been towers of strength. Towers. I only wish that Mrs Deecie could have...' His face begins to shake.

Henry says, 'Come along, sir, we'll get you back to your beautiful daughter.'

'Thank you. Yes, beautiful. Thank you, Mr Peabody, you are very kind. I shall be glad to call again. Mrs Deecie took a great liking to

Mrs Peabody and talked about her all the way home in the coach. But it would be obliging if you did not mention the occasion, Mrs Peabody, I wouldn't want Deborah to know about the visit. It might have the flavour of a scored point. Yes. Thank you. Deborah is a lovely girl.'

*   *   *

Henry returns quickly and says, 'Oh dear.'

He walks to the ladder window and stands with his back to me.

'New friends?'

'Not really. They were the most exhausting people I ever met, but oh—they were all love. I can't believe it, she was like a little doll that you keep for ever.'

'You and your hangers-on,' he says. 'You still can't help gathering them, can you?'

He is standing with his back to me. I had forgotten how tall he is. What wide shoulders. What beautiful clothes. (Gieves and Hawkes? It's new.) He has his back to me, arms stretched diagonally upwards to the window's corners, head bowed. He is examining the shadowy garden like God breathing on Eden.

'The irises are poor.'

'I didn't divide them.'

He drops one hand to the ladder top, shakes it, then pushes the ladder from him and gives it a sideways shove. It disappears and thuds

322

down to the grass.

'Dangerous leaving that standing about. I hope it's not been there all day. You really ought to be careful.'

'It was yesterday. There were ladders everywhere. I expected you. I ran off. I locked myself out. You didn't come.'

'Well, I dare say Mr Deecie wouldn't have hurt you.'

He turns and smiles. He looks bleak but I remember the smile. I see all the years we had. 'It's a lovely evening,' he says. 'I think I can hear the Fair.'

'Yes.'

'Summer's here then. First of June.'

'It is the third. It's always the third. You've forgotten.'

'No.'

'We found I was pregnant the first day of the Fair.'

'Yes, I know.'

He walks away from me, takes off his glasses, pushes back his floppy hair. What could I have meant by Goat? Not ever.

'Your hair's rather long.'

He says, 'Yours is.'

'Mine's a bit grey. I ought to get something done.'

We both look at the tea-tray and he says, 'I'll get us a drink.'

'No.'

'Did you get the roses?'

323

'Yes. Thanks.'

'What colour were they?'

'Yellow.'

'Good. I told them yellow. I said not pink. Those aren't the Lancashire cups are they? Wherever did you find them? I thought they'd gone long ago.'

'I found them with some other things. Like Annie's sewing-bag. The pink one.'

*   *   *

He said, 'You knew, didn't you?' and I said, 'Yes, I always knew.'

*   *   *

The far-off music sweeps in on us like a tide and like a tide sweeps out again. He says, 'There's a bit of a breeze getting up.'

After a time he says, 'I have to tell you something else. Annie died.'

'I didn't know. *When*? I didn't know that. *When*? Why? I wasn't told!'

'Eight years ago.'

'Eight! Eight years? But she was so young. Only two years older than me—what—forty-five?'

'She'd not been well since . . . Since the child. Too old for a first child.'

'Annie? Annie a child—never! *Never!* Annie never wanted children, nor did Basil. However

324

did Basil cope?'

'Basil had died more than a year before.'

I say (in time), 'Oh yes. I see.'

'We couldn't—didn't—tell you.'

'I see.'

The wind blows again and the Fair rattles along.

He says, 'I'll shut the window.'

He says, 'Oh God.'

'And the child was...?'

'Yes. It was. She is. She's fostered. Very settled in America. Very happy. Called Joyce.'

'Called *what*? Called *Joyce*? You never called her Joyce!'

'After Annie's mother. I'm sorry. I wasn't myself.'

'You certainly weren't. Oh well, yes. I expect you were. I think I was the one that was not.'

'Oh Eliza, you don't know how jealous she was of you. How you frightened her. You were so clever. So certain of yourself. She felt you despised her. You'd always despised her. And judged her.'

And so steady and so cool am I that I can listen to my calm voice saying, 'Have you a photograph?'

He passes one across and shades his eyes with his hand as if the image of the child is dangerous, like a lazer beam. I see an easy-going large sort of girl sitting between two pleasant Americans and looking very much like them except for my fizz of red hair, and my

325

black eyebrows. Henry's face, as in a Victorian novel, is now in both his hands. I say, 'I suppose this is all true? I've been having a bit of trouble with what is and what isn't lately.'

He looks up, and I see that it's all true.

I say, 'Could you please tell me properly?' and he says, 'Oh God, Eliza.'

I say, 'Her eyes are very bright. Like bits of coal. *Joyce*! Henry, how *could* you?'

Then at last I say, 'D'you miss her?'

'Annie? No, not at all. That is worst.'

I say, 'Henry Peabody, C.B. Lay-Reader. Church-warden. All those Diocesan Prayer Meetings.'

He says, 'I love you. I never stopped. It was because you'd gone. You left when the baby left. You left me even though you never moved out of the house.'

'It was you who moved the beds.'

'That was years after. When you seemed mad.'

'I may have been a little mad. It was the best way to manage. *Joyce!*'

'Lizzie, how did you know? At first I never meant you to know. Then—I so needed you to know.'

'You must have thought me pretty frail,' I say. '*How* old is Joyce?'

'She's—well, she's eleven. I think I was mad, too. I thought you'd gone for ever. We had stopped talking.'

The phone rings and I go over to it and it is

326

Mother Ambrosine who says, 'Eliza, dear, could you come? Come now?'

* * *

At the car, Henry stands on the pavement. I sit at the wheel and he taps the glass. I let down the window and sit looking ahead.

'I've been over and over it—thinking how to tell you. For years. I've done it, and made havoc.'

I look at him not remembering a thing about him. When at last I do remember I say, 'What, falling for Annie Cartwright and giving her a baby? Oh Henry—don't look so *sad*. Grow up. I have to go.'

'But where? Why? You will come back? Lizzie—I want you back. I want to be with you. You know I always did. It was you who left me.'

I try to concentrate but the sound of the Fair keeps blowing about. I see tears in poor Henry's eyes. My hands are heavy but I haul one of them up on to the steering-wheel and drop the other down on the gears. I say, 'Promise me you'll come back tomorrow.'

'Can't I stay now? Tonight? Will you be long? Will you promise to come back?'

'I won't be long, but go. Don't come home till tomorrow. We'll talk tomorrow. Go back to the flat tonight.'

He runs along beside the car with a

miserable face and I stop again. 'I'll walk Toby,' he says. 'Save you when you come back.'

'Henry—no more!'

'Look, you know I ask you nothing. Joyce is settled. It would be cruel to move her now. You wouldn't countenance it and neither would I. I know how you hated Annie.'

'Hated Annie?'

I wonder whatever he can mean. If it is true, then I have sinned. Hatred is worse than treachery, less redeemable, especially hatred of the dead. Did I hate Annie? I was jealous from the start, but did I hate?

I can't think, because the Fair is thumping away, and as I come to the Common I see it all spangled and wheeling with lights and noise, and the people trooping in strings towards it, stumbling over the tussocks of grass. There are shouts and laughs and whistles. Children are running, not heeding their parents who are yelling at them to take care in the dark.

Up the Roman track I drive and there, standing outside The Hospice door I see something white. I park and Mother Ambrosine comes forward and takes my hands. We stand. The Fair sounds faint now. Julius Caesar's fir trees tip their points about, blowing away from The Hospice and towards the revels. Here in the precinct, all is quiet.

'You are just too late. It was very quick and peaceful at the end. What we've all prayed for so long.'

'I'm always late.'

'No. Nonsense. You were always with him. Whether you were in the room or not, you were always in his mind. Come and say some prayers. We'll go to the chapel.'

'No. Soon. I'll do that soon. Can I see him?'

'Certainly not. He's gone. You may view the body if you're feeling morbid. Or pagan. But Barry has moved off. He's far away. En route to heaven. He's maybe there already.'

'I can't believe all that.'

'Well then, you shall go and see. You'll see he's gone. Go in for one moment. Would you like me to come with you?'

'No. Could I go by myself?'

'Of course.'

*　　*　　*

Barry is sitting at the end of his bed in the chair that is usually mine, and consulting his watch. He looks so marvellously well that for a moment I can't believe it is he. He's in combat-dress and beside him on the floor is an immense pack. 'About time,' he says. 'Where were you? I was getting worried.'

'Henry turned up.'

'Thrills.'

'No. Listen. He had an affair with my awful cousin, Annie. Years ago. In Washington I think. There was a baby. He didn't

329

dare tell me.'

Barry is shining with delight, and laughing, 'And all that with the Baby Belling, Cock. Well—are we off?'

'Yes, of course.'

Neither of us pays attention to the narrow shape on the bed with the sheet over it, and the Cross above it on the wall. I open the latch of the French-windows and we step through. Barry takes a breath of summery air. 'I've not that long,' he says. 'Where's the car?'

We drive off fast down the lane, Barry balancing the pack on his knee. He doesn't speak. The traffic along the main road down Common Side is heavy and the lights coming towards us dazzle and dazzle. I say, 'You all right? Not frightened?' but looking at him see his lit young face and say, 'Sorry. I must be mad.'

He says, 'Queen of the Tambourine. The tangerine and nectarine and aubergine. Queen of the Glockenspiel and Jew's Harp, Queen of the Night—where shall we go when we get there?'

'The Big Wheel?'

'The Big Wheel.'

We park. It's quite difficult, for there are cars everywhere. When at last we're on our feet and walking towards the Fair, I keep stumbling in the boa-constrictors of the electricity supply under our feet. We pause to watch The Ultimate Whizzer—metal eggs

330

spinning horizontally out on sticks, two faces to each egg. We watch the rushing Golden Horses. Guns crack on the rifle range, there are shrieks from the Ghost Train. Dishes smash at the Coconut Shy. The Merry-Go-Rounds and the Bumpums blare, and the little pedal-cars go round and round and round. The children swing the dummy wheels and the parents smile.

I buy two tickets for the Big Wheel and strap myself in. Barry takes his place alongside. Up we go, jerkily at first, step by step as other people are strapped in below. When every compartment is full, each bell of the tambourine, we begin to move smoothly, up and up, then faster and faster, then down and down, and it's soon an exciting, windswept, regular roll. Below us is all the spilled-out electric jewellery of the Fair, beyond that the dark of the Common, beyond that the map of the lighted world. We spin in the warm wind and we shall spin for ever.

'Hey-up now,' says Barry. 'What's this then?'

There's a hitch. A hiccup. The Big Wheel judders and almost stops. It picks up again, and smoothly, smoothly we spin.

Then there's a cracking, tearing sound and the Wheel shakes and rocks. It slows and then stops and all the lights of the Fair go out.

*   *   *

We sit, and at first it's quiet, but then shouts and screams float faintly up. Our little buggy, our compartment, is balancing right at the top of the Wheel, at twelve o'clock, and the wind blows through the struts below us battering and complaining. We both look up at the stars and the enormous night.

'You had better tell it all,' says Barry.

'Must I?'

'You know you must.'

And so I say:

'There is no number thirty-four Rathbone Road. Once there was, but it went years ago when a bomb fell on it in the War and left it ruined. What was left of it remained standing for years and I remember it being pulled down and bulldozed. The land was bought by the people in the houses on either side. Dulcie's house and Dickie's house took in half each. Their gardens are bigger than the others in the road.

'There has been no family at number thirty-four since 1941, and goodness knows who they were. I made up all "Joan's" family—Charles and Sarah and Simon. It was the family I wished was mine. No Sarah ever rang to ask my help from Oxford. I did go to Oxford one day to an imaginary Sarah. She occupied my old room. I went to see it. Then I wandered round the colleges—there was no Doctor Gauntlet: I don't know where I manufactured him. I did call in on my old tutor, Mabel Pye, but I was much too difficult for her I'm afraid. I just took the train home.

'There was no Kurd. There was no Tom Hopkin, though I wish there had been. Perhaps he was the wraith of my beloved Henry of long ago. Oh, and there was no—this last one, the jogger who goes trotting about, Miss Ingham's Croupier. At least I suppose *he*'s real but he never climbed through my window to make love to me.'

'You didn't tell me about him.'

'And there was no dog. No second dog. Only my own dog, mine and Henry's. There was no Simon doing demon laughter in the Church.

'The letters I wrote to Joan I never posted after the first few and goodness knows where those went. I never put my address on the back. They're probably mystifying foreign embassies here and there. The rest of the letters are in my desk, or just tossing about the house. I think I've told you almost everything that's in them, one way and another. I'll burn them now. They're pretty sick.'

More and louder shouts are floating up now from the ground and sounds that might be fire-engines and police cars. Looking over the side of our little seat I say, 'I nearly drowned a baby today.'

'*Eliza*—be careful.'

'It's all right. It's true. That really did happen. I nearly killed a baby. In the mere. It won't ever happen again.'

333

'Why not?'

'Because Henry came back. We talked to each other aloud instead of in horrible secret. I am righted now.'

'So now, Eliza, tell me everything else that was true.'

'Well, everything else is "true". That's to say everyone in the Road is true except for at number thirty-four. Miss Ingham is true, the Gargerys, the Robins, the Baxters and Lady Gant. Deborah next door, Bernard and Lola—though I think I made up that daughter. Angela was real, all right. So was Bella and all the unmarried mother bit and The Shires and the Chaplain. And the Penumbras.'

'Nick Fish?'

'Well, of course he's true, and Vanessa and the children and the missing Granny in Bangladesh. I couldn't have made her up, there's no story in her at all. And anyway—you know Nick yourself. Oh yes, Pixie Leak and the Creative Writing Class are real.'

'I'm glad they're real. They lightened a dark day.'

'I think that's the lot.'

'So now,' he says, 'tell me the start.'

'It's getting cold up here.'

'Come on.'

'I can't. It's too cold. I can't think.'

'You must.'

'I didn't bring a coat with me. I just rushed straight out when Mother Ambrosine rang me.

334

I ran to you.'

'Don't flatter. You will be cured tonight, or never.'

I cross my arms and put my hands into my armpits. I moan and sway. I look down at the dark.

'I began to lose the baby after four months of pregnancy. It was over twenty years ago. I was thirty-one. Henry was away. Without me. He was already beginning to go away without me, though we neither of us were very happy about it then. He was far away. In India. I called in old Doctor St Thomas, the father of this one and very much like him. He said, "Well, there's really very little we can do. It's much better that these things should come away, you know. Nature's way when there's something wrong."

'"We've been trying for years."

'"Such a shame."

'"Could I go into hospital?"

'"I don't think it would make any difference you know."

'"Do I stay in bed?"

'"Well, you could stay in bed. Or you could get up. The result, I'm bound to say, will be very likely the same. But let's not be despondent. You may hold on to it. Do just as you like. Stay in bed or get up. Whatever feels right. Not alone in the house are you?"

'"Well, yes."

'"Ah well, never mind, there's always someone in the Surgery."

335

'Ten days later he called again. I was still creeping about bleeding. I hadn't written to Henry, he would have been so desolate and maybe, after all, there was nothing to worry about. I had some pain the next day and rang the Surgery. The receptionist said that she thought that the doctor had had a word with the hospital but that there was no bed at present. Dr St Thomas rang later and said, "Soldier on. Soldier on. Nil desperandum."

'Across the Road was my haunt, the garden of the ruined house, number thirty-four. For a year or so I had felt it was mine. Virginia creeper had grown up over most of its walls. It was turning blood-red that October and sending long pretty fingers over the windows. There was even still some furniture in the rooms. In a glass room to the side, a ballroom in Victorian times...'

'Not imagining this now, are you, Eliza?'

'You are young, Barry. There are still houses with ballrooms. Most of them have become granny-flats. In this ballroom there was a cobwebby stack of chairs. They were gold. Flimsy. It looked as if the house had ended after a celebration of the end of the world.

'Oh, I loved the garden. It was very wild. It had been terraced once, but now you could hardly tell. The old lawns were lumpy, like meadows, and roses had nearly strangled the fruit trees. Even so late there were some surprising flowers, very bright and brazen.

336

'Down in the end of the garden under the trees was a summerhouse with some cane furniture dropping to bits. Beyond, in the sunshine in a dell of their own was a row of broken beehives. One was surrounded by mounds of dead black bees. They looked like currants. A new swarm had taken over that hive and was clearing out old comb, purifying and singing. From the top of the garden, the half-house looked down from its one drunken eye through the strands of creeper. On its terrace, what was left of it, lavender and cat-mint flourished in huge sweet pillows. Even now, so late, there were roses and the bees busy with them.

'I had become miserable in bed with my aching back. The ache kept coming and going. The Road was still. I got up and put on my dressing-gown and went across the Road. The terrace round at the back was sunny and warm. I looked in at the deserted rooms, the ghostly ballroom. I imagined people like my parents there. I imagined them out on the terrace in the dusk, drinking cocktails. Noel Coward clothes. Laughter. I walked from the terrace down the lawn. I passed the summerhouse. I came to the apple-trees. Little crimson apples. Very hard and bitter. Very pretty. I held tight first to one tree, then another and thought, I suppose this couldn't be it? Nobody had told me that even as early as four months, you go into labour. I had thought it would be a quick thing.

'Then it was over. In the end it was a quick thing. Or at any rate, it was partly over because the thing I had voided, with its little hands was still joined on to me. I lay, wet and sweaty, and out from behind the beehive there came an old tortoise walking straight towards me. They're not slow, you know. Not at all. It came on, rather fast. Very steady on its long obscene legs, sharp claws. It lifted its snake head in the air. It had an old man's mean little mouth. Black pin-head eyes. Up on its toes it came.

'So I screamed, and tried to kick it away, but it came on and the bees buzzed in the luminous migraine dahlias.

I passed out. I'd left my front door open across the Road and in the end—in the early evening I think—somebody found me. Henry flew home. He couldn't have been kinder. I think he and the doctor had a consultation, but I didn't ask. I know there was something, but never mind.'

'You must go on.'

'I believed. I believe—that they. I'd read that foetuses are sold for research. I heard the doctor say that mine had been very perfect.'

'I'm sure it was.'

'I should have asked. I should have been asked.'

'Forget it now, Eliza.'

'They didn't tell me what sex it was. I didn't ask that either. I still don't know. I've never told anyone about the tortoise. They're harmless creatures. They're herbivores, I think—I never really dared find out. It was the claws. Yet I do know that it was nobody's fault. It was the slightest thing compared with what our ancestors ... It was just life. They were such claws. This is all true, Barry.'

'It is all true,' he says. 'And it is all over. And you are disentangled.'

'Barry—*you* are true?'

'I was always true. I was there and true from the first time we met in The Hospice. A poor specimen but of flesh and blood. For what that's worth.'

'It's worth so much. Barry, shall I ever see you any more?'

He's become not in the least faint or fuzzy but most brilliantly present. 'I'll always be with you somewhere,' he says, and is gone.

*   *   *

The seat beside me is empty. Pack and boy have vanished. I touch the cushion. It is undented and cold. I take out the awful earrings I bought in the Indian shop on Putney Bridge, where I bought the dress and the sweets. I place them on the seat. The last trace and breath of Barry registers approval. The very last whisper of him says, 'And when you get home, remember. There will be one last

thing to face. A hard thing. But only to do with
this last hour.'

* * *

The Big Wheel shakes itself. There is a
wracking shudder. The lights of the Fair come
on again and the tin-can music starts to play.
Step by step, slowly and daintily, we are all
brought down from our nests, helped out,
made much of. There's a crowd. Firemen
shout. Someone puts me down flat on my back
on the grass, and I lie there, spread.
   I hear excited voices and looking sideways I
see feet. Four of them belong to two sentinels
each holding a torch of candy-floss almost the
size of its bearer. The sentinels run off. They
return and I see between their feet, a larger
figure and a pair of dirty trainers with a broken
lace. The sentinels get down on their knees
beside me and Amanda strokes my hair. Over
Nick Fish's shoulder peeps the baby, like
arrows in their quiver.
   'Oh no,' I hear the Curate cry. 'It's Eliza
Peabody!'

Morning of mornings

They got me home, dear Joan, but I did not go
to bed. I took a bath with scented soap and I
ate some strawberries that I'd found on my

340

door-step, left by the man who has everything, with a note. My dog was kind to me, faithful bewildered dog. I shall put the rugs back for him, and the furniture and the cushions. Long-suffering, nice animal.

Through the short June night that never seemed to get quite dark I lay in the drawing room and sometimes I slept and sometimes I didn't. At some point, after I think I had probably slept, I faced Barry's last command and said, out loud, 'And finally, of course, there was no ghost.'

I dare say I wept then, but slept again and about four o'clock woke to the marvellous chorus of the summer birds, at peace.

*　　*　　*

When it was light. I looked across to see if he'd left the photograph on the mantelpiece, wondering if I could forgive him if he had. He had not. I wondered if I dare look in the hall and see if the dirty shirt bag was there. I dared not. But I laughed. Then I went to sleep again.

I woke properly at a little before six, walked stiffly across the room and looked out at the Road and its dewy gardens. I looked at where number thirty-four used to stand. Nothing. I examined my clean fingernails, thin white arcs.

The paper-boy slammed up and down the road, his feet slapping on the flights of steps, clattering the gates, fading away. One quiet early car drifted self-consciously by. Then up the Road came Old Bernard on his bike, knees out sideways like a grasshopper, off to the Common for his daily meditation on the mystery of his continuing life. He did not turn his head, but raised a hand to me in salute. I wondered if he was some sort of a sign.

Certainly not, for we need no signs. We need no extras, no tickets or labels or tags. Dulcie is wrong—it *is* sufficient just 'to be'. 'And signs only appear, it seems to me,' I said to the empty space before me, 'when the need for them is over.'

As I said it, the room behind me grew perfectly still and I turned and looked at the telephone on the gold and glass table. Presently it began to ring.

'Oh, hullo,' said a voice. 'Sorry, I'm rather early. This is Joan.'

43, Rathbone Road,
London, S.W.
1 July, 1990

My dear Joan Fish,

Do forgive me for being so long in writing. Your early morning call must now be about two weeks ago—perhaps longer—and I am ashamed of myself. I am very busy and very happy which is my only excuse, and one I think you'll understand.

It was a delightful surprise to hear you, and no, of course, you were not at all too early. Henry and I have lived abroad so much that the one thing we do understand is the time difference. I was anyway up and about.

And I was so flattered that Lucien had 'recommended' me. I am I fear rather an elderly 'au pair', but I can last, I'm sure, until Vanessa comes back to roost. I'm glad that Lucien convinced you that I would be suitable, though I believe Lucien could convince anyone of anything. I'm rather afraid, though, that he didn't tell you that I've had very little to do with children and have had none of my own.

But your grandchildren and I do get on very well, even though I'm well aware that I'm only a substitute for Vanessa, and very temporarily, for I'm sure—absolutely certain—that she'll be back. She is volatile but not irresponsible. She loves her family and they adore her. When she does get back I'm going to make Nick put her in touch with the nuns on the Common who were invaluable to me once when I was tending to get a bit low.

Now I have to tell you—but don't panic please—that before long I have to go to America with my husband where I'm to meet for the first time my sole surviving relative, and also my stepdaughter. I shall not go until the Fishes are back to normal. There's no hurry.

And you are not to make *any* plans to come over here yourself. Sorry to be bossy, but with a 'wonky leg' you should stay where you are, even if as you say you are 'not yet eighty'.

I must tell you something so nice. When you rang I happened to be standing at the window, looking out at where your old house used to be. I remember it, you know. It was very bomb-damaged but I loved its garden. I used to try and imagine what the people there had been like—I never knew that it had been Nick's family's house before he was born.

But the queer, nice thing was this. When I picked up the phone and you spoke I suddenly remembered my mother's voice, and she died when I was only six.

Now—back to the shirts. I do Lucien's and Nick's with my husband's—not Amanda's. She's all for drip-dry. I could easily send to a laundry but I'm rather good at ironing. The baby I fuss over like a fool. He is really my heart's love. I go over every day and stay till his bedtime. I'm happy in that house and there is only one thing I have been tough about—that Nick gets rid of those filthy fish-tanks and that creature they keep in a saucepan by the kitchen stove. I'm making them give the money to The Society of the Risen Christ!

My cooking improves daily. I make them eat everything. When their mother comes back they'll tell her about all my hang-ups. Butter knives, clean handkerchieves, etc. Ah well.

Some escape and some never.
Thank you for ringing. Perhaps one day
we'll meet? You don't know what you did for
me by getting in touch. God bless you for it.

Sincerely yours,
Elizabeth Peabody

We hope you have enjoyed this Large Print book. Other Chivers Press or Thorndike Press Large Print books are available at your library or directly from the publishers. For more information about current and forthcoming titles, please call or write, without obligation, to:

Chivers Press Limited
Windsor Bridge Road
Bath BA2 3AX
England
Tel. (01225) 335336

OR

Thorndike Press
P.O. Box 159
Thorndike, Maine 04986
USA
Tel. (800) 223–6121 (U.S. & Canada)
In Maine call collect: (207) 948–2962

All our Large Print titles are designed for easy reading, and all our books are made to last.